Wild Indigo

Wild Indigo

Sandi Ault

BERKLEY PRIME CRIME, NEW YORK

THE BERKLEY PUBLISHING GROUP
Published by the Penguin Group
Penguin Group (USA) Inc.
375 Hudson Street, New York, New York 10014, USA
Penguin Group (Canada), 90 Eglinton Avenue East, Suite 700, Toronto, Ontario M4P 2Y3, Canada
(a division of Pearson Penguin Canada Inc.)
Penguin Books Ltd., 80 Strand, London WC2R 0RL, England
Penguin Group Ireland, 25 St. Stephen's Green, Dublin 2, Ireland (a division of Penguin Books Ltd.)
Penguin Group (Australia), 250 Camberwell Road, Camberwell, Victoria 3124, Australia
(a division of Pearson Australia Group Pty. Ltd.)
Penguin Books India Pvt. Ltd., 11 Community Centre, Panchsheel Park, New Delhi—110 017, India
Penguin Group (NZ), Cnr. Airborne and Rosedale Roads, Albany, Auckland 1310, New Zealand
(a division of Pearson New Zealand Ltd.)
Penguin Books (South Africa) (Pty.) Ltd., 24 Sturdee Avenue, Rosebank, Johannesburg 2196,
South Africa

Penguin Books Ltd., Registered Offices: 80 Strand, London WC2R 0RL, England

This is an original publication of The Berkley Publishing Group.

This is a work of fiction. Names, characters, places, and incidents either are the product of the author's imagination or are used fictitiously, and any resemblance to actual persons, living or dead, business establishments, events, or locales is entirely coincidental. The publisher does not have any control over and does not assume any responsibility for author or third-party websites or their content.

PRINTING HISTORY
Berkley Prime Crime hardcover edition / January 2007

Library of Congress Cataloging-in-Publication Data

Ault, Sandi.
    Wild indigo / by Sandi Ault.
        p.   cm.
    ISBN 978-0-425-21369-8
    1. Indians of North America—Fiction.   I. Title.

PS3601.U45W55 2006
813'.6—dc22   2006012269

PRINTED IN THE UNITED STATES OF AMERICA

10   9   8   7   6   5   4   3   2   1

For Mountain
In Loving Memory

Nunca hay caballo ensillado que a alguno no se la ofrece viaje.

There is never a saddled horse that does not offer a journey to someone.
—Old Vaquero Saying

Author's Note

This is a work of fiction, and the characters herein are figments of the author's imagination, representing no one. Likewise, Tanoah Pueblo does not exist. Whatever similarities may exist between the imaginary Tanoah Pueblo and other pueblos are a blending of my research and experience, including travel and study concerning a variety of southwestern pueblos. I have intentionally alluded to myths, traditions, and rituals from several different Pueblo cultures, and I have mixed and changed patterns, times of year for these rituals, and cultural habits—as well as relied on imagination and invention—in a deliberate effort to keep this purely fable.

I would like to thank Sam Des Georges, Multi Resources Branch Chief, Taos Resource Area of the Bureau of Land Management, and Matt Wahlberg, United States Ranger, for their generous time and assistance with my research for this work.

Wild
Indigo

Prologue

I got there too late to save Jerome Santana.

The pueblo was closed, but I'd had a report that the buffalo herd was wandering out of its confines up on the foothills to the northwest of the reservation. And that land was in my jurisdiction—or the BLM's anyway. I work for the Bureau of Land Management as a resource protection agent. It was my job to check out the report.

Santana stood in the center of the herd, his arms outstretched and palms facing skyward. He was looking into the azure sky beyond the purple crest of Sacred Mountain. The bulls sniffed around him and pawed the ground, huffing angrily at this intruder. Santana's long black hair was tied into a rope of red cloth at the base of his neck, and his black traditional apron covered the lap of his jeans. His chest was bare, and his shoulders and back were laced with thin red welts.

The long gate on the north side of the ten-foot-high fence was open, and many of the cows and their calves had wandered into the fields of open scrub that led up to forest land and beyond. But the bulls saw the man as a threat, and they stayed—angry, circling.

I slowed my Jeep to a crawl, not wanting to provoke a stampede. I parked beside the tall hogwire fence and eased out the door, leaving it ajar so I didn't make much sound. I called to Santana, "Get out of there. Walk slowly toward me." I reached into the backseat and drew out my rifle, being careful not to make any sudden or abrupt moves.

Neither the bulls nor Santana took any notice of me, and I raised my gun and found the brave in my sights. One of the bulls closed on him and rammed him with his head. Santana fell forward, then started to get up. I sighted my gun on the bull, knowing that if I fired, they'd stampede and the man would be trampled. "Move slowly!" I screamed, but Santana made no sign that he heard. He staggered to his feet and again stretched out his arms and faced the mountain.

The bull came at him again, and butted him hard, catching the tip of his horn in Santana's thigh. I saw red blood cloud the denim of his jeans, the color swelling and growing against the faded blue. I started for the open gate, moving as quickly as I dared. "Santana! Do you hear me?" I yelled.

For just an instant, his gaze fixed on me. His face was full of a strange wonder, almost joy. Beyond his dark eyes somewhere within was a heaven all his own, and he was no longer here at all, his body just an encumbrance that kept him from being fully spirit. He smiled, a sad sweet smile. And he closed his eyes.

It seemed to happen in slow motion, the way his body flew high into the air when the bull scooped him up like a giant shovel and tossed him away. Santana's lifeless form struck the back of the bull with a dull thud, then bounced against the side of another as the bison began to run, their hooves making huge clouds of dry dust rise around their legs as they almost floated above the landscape. They surged against the gate, against the fence, mowing it down, their huge bodies moving together like one mindless fury against the confinement of their kind, as if all the years of freedoms lost had risen within their blood and caused them to rebel in concert, all of them notes within one song—one screaming chorus of anger and longing. As the bulls drove forward in the direction of Sacred Mountain, the body of Jerome Santana bounced and fell among them, and was finally trampled beneath their hooves like the once-tall white grass and the dust of red earth.

I had to run like hell to avoid being trampled myself, back along the hogwire toward my Jeep, the fence poles just behind me being snapped off at the ground one by one, making loud popping sounds like gunshots. I threw myself onto the hood of my vehicle and then scrambled for the top just in time. A section of wire flew across the hood and the fence post smashed into the windshield, causing it to shatter. One of the bulls caught the front quarter panel with his shoulder and the whole Jeep rocked and threatened to tip as I clung for life to the edge where the open door would have fit. That door was somewhere north of here now, lying on the ground in the wake of the bison, who were well on their way up the foothills, the cows running with them now, the calves crying as they struggled to keep up.

I peeled my fingers off the edge of the roof and raised myself to my hands and knees. A blue pickup was barreling along the road toward me at high speed, a fog of dust billowing behind it. I got down and began to walk toward Santana's inanimate form and the pickup squealed to a stop beside me, its worn brakes obviously metal to metal. Two men I recognized—War Chief Ruben Rael and buffalo wrangler Sonny

Warm Hands—got out of the truck's cab, each of them carrying a rifle.

"What are you doing on pueblo land, Miss Wild?" Rael said. "You know Tanoah Pueblo is closed until the end of August."

"Look, Jerome Santana is in there," I said, pointing toward the bison pasture. "He's either hurt or dead. We've got to check it out."

Rael looked at Warm Hands. They both looked at me. "Don't touch him," Rael said. "We'll take care of him." Warm Hands hurried toward the body of Santana. Rael stayed with me, his rifle barrel pointed skyward, but at the ready. I watched the wrangler turn the body over and put his ear against Santana's chest. He stood, spit, and said something in Tiwa to Rael.

"He's dead," Rael said.

"What was he doing out here?" I asked. "Why did he open the gate to let the herd out?"

"What are *you* doing out here?" Rael said, his voice sinister.

"I had a report that the buffalo were wandering loose. I have jurisdiction from the fence line." I felt my chest tightening with anger. "Why are you here?"

Rael looked in the direction of Santana. Sonny Warm Hands was standing beside the body, offering a pinch of tobacco to the mountain, muttering in Tiwa.

"I got the same report as you," Rael said. For the first time, he lowered his rifle, the stock resting in the crook of his elbow, the barrel aimed at the ground.

"Who told you?"

"Tribal police got the call. They sent someone over to the governor's office. I was in there, so I went to get Sonny. We came as soon as we heard."

As he was saying this, another vehicle approached, the sound of its tires crunching along the dirt road at high speed preceding it. It was a tribal police car. Rael and I watched in silence until it pulled alongside us and Officer Gloria Lobato got out. "Looks like we were too late to keep the herd in," she said, smiling.

"That's not all," Rael said. "There's a man trampled." It was customary not to mention the dead by name. Officer Lobato's face went slack. She did not ask, but went instead to examine the body. Rael looked at me. "We'll take care of this," he said. He moved between me and the others, blocking my view.

I gripped my back teeth together. "You can't just take care of this. I have to call the FBI, you know that."

"Yeah, the Federal Bureau of Ignorance. We'll handle them, too."

"And the buffalo?" I said, angrily.

"We'll get 'em," Rael said. "Sonny will get some helpers. They'll round 'em up."

I glared at him. He looked away. "By the time you could get everyone together, we'll have the herd back in the pen," he said. "If we need any help, Miss Wild, we'll call you." He turned away from me, a sign of dismissal. From behind him, I could see him reach into his pocket for a cigarette, take a pinch of tobacco from the end of it, and hold it toward the sky.

I walked back to my Jeep, the shell of it blown open where the door was torn off. I put my rifle in the back and slid into the driver's seat. I looked through the shattered windshield, the scene beyond it in fragments like the pieces of a jigsaw puzzle, the green of the forest land rising to the blue and purple shoulders of the Rocky Mountains, the high peaks watching like guardians over the normally peaceful, ancient village of Tanoah Pueblo. Here, kiva and religious rituals were being conducted now as they had for a thousand years in preparation for the annual pilgrimage to the summit of Sacred Mountain to the Eye of the Great Spirit, the Indigo Falls—where the spirits of their ancestors went to live.

Someone's going to have to tell his mother, I thought, *that Jerome Santana has gone ahead of them to the Wild Indigo.*

◄ 1 ►

Wild Animals

My field manager, Roy, slammed his truck door and strode toward me at a fast clip. I could tell he was angry—his forehead was a tight series of furrows beneath the brim of his hat, and his eyebrows were knitted together over his nose. "Jamaica, are you all right?" he asked.

"I'm fine, Boss." I tucked my chin and began pulling my hair into a ponytail at the nape of my neck so I wouldn't have to look into his furious face. Roy had often accused me of being able to find more trouble than anyone he'd ever known.

"You want to tell me what the hell happened here?"

"I was visiting someone. I got a report . . ."

"Yeah, I already heard that. What do you mean you got a report? You weren't in the office."

"A child. One of the pueblo children came to the house I was visiting looking for me. He said the buffalo had gotten out and were wandering onto the mountain. I drove out here to take a look." I stopped then, realizing Roy wasn't really listening, that he was too worked up to listen. I decided to wait, let him vent. Years of experience with the Boss had taught me a healthy respect for his short fuse. He would talk around a little, I guessed, gripe a little until he was ready to get down to it. He'd let me know.

Roy took off his hat and ran his fingers through his thick shock of silvery blond hair. "You didn't have that wolf of yours with you, did you?"

I shook my head no. "The pueblo dogs don't like the way Mountain smells."

"Good. Okay now, who was the guy?"

"Jerome Santana."

"Santana." He thought a moment. "I don't think I knew him. You know him?"

"Yeah, I knew him."

"Friend?"

"Kinda. I was visiting his mother when—"

"Yeah, I just had my ass chewed at the tribal council office about that," he cut in. "We'll talk about that later on. Right now, I gotta go speak with the Gs. Who's the agent in charge?"

"Diane Langstrom."

"You already talked to her?"

"Just briefly. We're going to talk again."

"So this was a suicide. You were a witness, you gave her your statement. That's pretty much it, right?—other than getting the buffalo back."

I winced.

His eyebrows lifted. "What?"

"I saw him, Roy. Yeah, it looked like a suicide, there was no one else around, he didn't even try to get out of the path of those bulls. But I still don't know."

"What do you mean you don't know?"

"He looked like he might have been drugged."

"*On* drugs, or drugged?"

"I knew the guy. He didn't do drugs."

"You tell that to Langstrom?"

"Yes."

"And?"

"She doesn't see any evidence of foul play."

"Okay, then. She's in charge."

"Yeah . . . only she's wondering about it, too."

The Boss blew out a blast of air. "Well, I don't know what we can do with that. Normally the coroner could do a drug screen but we're on Indian land—no jurisdiction for the county M.E. unless this is a suspicious death. And the tribal government won't want an autopsy, they have a religious thing about that. The only way we'd have an autopsy is . . ." Roy's head slumped to one side. "Aw shit. This could get to be a real mess."

"It would take an act of God now, and probably an exhumation, too. The tribe has already taken the body to ceremony."

"Already? How'd that happen?"

"Like I said, Langstrom had no evidence of a crime."

Roy batted the brim of his hat with one hand, knocking the dust off of it. He gripped the crown and then paused and looked out at the mountains. "And you think there was a good chance he might have been drugged?"

"I don't know, Roy. He wasn't . . ." I searched for a way to say it. ". . . right."

"Well, when the medical examiner doesn't get invited to the party, then it's up to the FBI to make the call for an autopsy. You said you told Langstrom your suspicions?"

I shook my head yes.

"And she thought it smelled funny, too?"

"She called her superiors in Albuquerque; they told her to let the tribe have the body, keep the file open, and send 'em the reports for now. She looked Santana's corpse over good, got pictures, told me to put everything in my report. There was nothing to keep the tribe from taking the body. Without evidence of foul play, it's their ball game. And it was getting late in the day—you know their thing about the sun not setting on a spirit in passage."

"Well, how bad do you want to pursue this drug thing? We could have a real mess here."

"I know."

"Up to now, the council seemed to be more worried about the fact that you were out here when the pueblo was closed than they were about losing one of their own. The war chief must have reminded me five or six times how it's Quiet Time. I got my butt dragged through a steel trap about it."

"Yeah, they were all over me when they got here. Even when I pointed to the body and told them what had happened. They tried to shoo me off like a fly until I reminded them I had to call the FBI."

Roy blew air out of his nose loudly. "Well, we'll have a big damn stink if you're going to call this thing anything but a suicide. We'll be in a cold war with the pueblo, and our asses will be strapped to the FBI's on this one like Siamese twins. If the tribe already took the body, it'll be an uphill fight. Big fight. Nobody can win, either. I don't see a happy ending on this one. This could make us both a lot of enemies."

"So, what do you want me to do? Lie in my report? Not mention that he looked like he'd been drugged?"

"I didn't say that." The Boss put his hat back on and straightened the brim. "I don't know, Jamaica. You get yourself into the weirdest predicaments. At least you weren't hurt." His eyes panned around. Then he noticed my Jeep. "Jesus Christ!"

It was dusk now and the open-sided hull of my white Cherokee stood in relief against the dark face of the mountains. Dozens of flashlights swarmed like fireflies in the foothills beyond as Indians and BLM personnel hunted for stragglers from the herd in the deep shadow of the tall peaks. The radio I had obtained for the roundup squawked and sputtered as members of the search party talked to one another. Roy had moved to the front of my vehicle and was staring at the smashed windshield and the concave front quarter panel. "Damn! You're lucky to be alive. You know that?"

I didn't say anything. I remembered Jerome Santana's eerily blissful expression just before he died—he looked as if he felt lucky.

The Boss shook his head repeatedly as he circled the vehicle, studying the damage. "I don't know what it is about you. I put you on as liaison to the pueblo so you'd have to relate with *two*-legged animals every once in a while. I thought maybe putting you closer to civilization would keep you out of trouble after that fiasco last spring. But look . . ." He pointed to my car, then put his forehead into his hand and rubbed at his temples.

Roy had been my field manager for six and a half years, the whole time I'd been with the BLM. Before this assignment, I'd been one of a handful of resource protection agents—the Range Riders—charged with riding the fence lines in open territory. Only a few months ago, Roy had transferred me from the high-terrain work I loved after I'd gotten involved in a life-threatening situation. A priest friend of mine had been murdered, and I had launched my own unofficial investigation. This culminated in a backcountry standoff that proved deadly. I'd solved the crime, but narrowly escaped suspension by the BLM for overstepping the bounds of my authority. And both the Boss and I had had to endure a lengthy internal investigation.

Roy's voice brought me back to the present: "Well, this Warm Hands guy said he doesn't need our help, says he has most of the herd rounded up. Why don't you go ahead and call your people in."

"Okay, but I'm staying."

"Suit yourself, but when your crew's done and gone, you git, too. No more visiting." He opened the door of his truck, then looked over his shoulder at me. "And before I forget, I want to see you in the office first thing on Monday morning. I'm going to get a look at that incident report before it goes anywhere else."

"Okay, Boss."

"Well, I guess I'll go say howdy to the FBI." He started to climb in the truck, but paused, turned. "You want to hear something funny?"

"What?"

"On the way here, I got a call from one of the county commissioners. He was hotter than a chile pepper because two Texans were sitting in a hot tub a few miles up the road to the ski valley, at some tourist trap, and a couple of buffalo came smashing through the privacy fence. Caught 'em with their skivvies off. Said it would hurt the tourist trade having things like this happen. Now I ask you: where else could you go and have wild animals crash your hot tub party? You just can't get that kind of action anywhere else!" He chuckled, savoring his own wry humor. Then he got in his pickup and drove toward the knot of tribal officials, FBI, and tribal police gathered in the broken pen where Jerome Santana had died.

Wild Indigo

Later, as the last traces of daylight began to burn crimson and then fuchsia against the black tips of the mountains on the west edge of Grand Mesa, I heard a faint sound from the direction of the pueblo. As I focused in on it, closing my eyes to suppress one sense and heighten another, I heard a chorus of wailing, a call like the voices of dozens of wounded souls. I pulled my field glasses from the floor of my Jeep and trained them on the ancient structure of the pueblo—the southwest edge that was four stories of adobe. Lining the multitiered rooftop, having climbed to the highest point in the village on their aspen-pole ladders, the village priests wrapped in their white blankets were stark against the lapis lazuli sky. They were ululating to the vanishing sun, a miserable song of dying, loss, and sorrow.

Long after dark, when the roundup of the buffalo had broken off for the night, I drove past the cemetery at the pueblo. Torches burned and family sat in a semicircle on the ground beside the grave of Jerome Santana, who would have been washed and buried before the sun went down on that day. Because they believed his spirit would remain near the corpse, gathering the lessons and love garnered in this lifetime, relatives would stay beside the body, keeping vigil for four days, until his spirit had made the journey to the next world. A woman, wrapped head and body in a white blanket, struggled to her feet as I drove past, her face a dark mystery within the moonlit shroud she wore, her voluminous, tall white moccasins like thick, pale trees growing beneath the dark hem of her skirt. She was facing my direction, and her body turned slightly to follow me as I drove slowly past. Because of my job, I was one of only a few non-residents allowed to drive within the reservation boundaries during this holy time preceding the Indigo Falls pilgrimage. I could not see the face of the woman, but I knew who it was.

It was my friend and mentor, my medicine teacher, my pueblo mother, and the mother of the man who died. It was Anna Santana.

◄ 2 ►

Momma Anna

Earlier that day, I had worked with Momma Anna in her kitchen. Bundles of dried wild spinach, ropes of garlic, and *ristras* of dried chiles hung from the vigas that stretched across the ceiling and supported the earthen roof. She was working over the enormous thigh of an elk, shaving the meat from the slab into thin, transparent strips. She wielded an old bone-handled knife with a wide, tarnished blade. Blood dripped into the sink, and flies buzzed around. Momma Anna shooed them off the flesh, away from her face. As she worked, she threw the meat strips into a bowl of dried chile, ground garlic, salt, and sugar. After she'd cut a bowlful, she tossed them in the spices with her hand, fished them out, and heaped them onto a Styrofoam plate. She handed the dish to me. "Take," she grunted.

I stepped out the back door into the garden, where Momma Anna worked tirelessly through the short high-desert growing season to produce a few rows of onions, garlic, chiles, corn, squash, and herbs. I walked across the caked clay soil, dried now from the heat of the summer—the plants sunburned and wilted—to a little pen where Momma Anna had strung lines of string between the fence poles. I carefully arranged the slices of elk meat so that they hung evenly in the hot sun. The flies swarmed to these new, moist strips, as the last batch had already begun to dry and harden. I draped a piece of cloth over each line to discourage the insects.

I went to the brush arbor and dipped water from the olla into a galvanized pan. I was careful to use only two dippers of the precious liquid to wash my hands. Then, as I'd been taught, I emptied my washing water into the bucket the dogs drank from. A mutt bitch and her three pups were lying under the apple tree in the backyard, gnawing on bones Momma Anna had given them when she'd first begun to carve the elk. Fresh, meaty joint knuckles distracted the dogs from trying to raid the pen for our jerky.

I wiped my face with my still-wet hands. I looked across the row of wild chokecherries along the fence line into the pasture beyond, where horses grazed in the shadow of Sacred Mountain. White cumulus clouds piled into puffy shapes in the turquoise sky, but they had failed to make much rain during this monsoon season. Momma Anna said that meant an early, hard winter.

I walked back into the kitchen. "You not cover your hair," Momma Anna said.

"I just went to the back of the house. There's no one out there."

She shook her head, pressing her lips together. "It Quiet Time. They could see you."

"I'm sorry," I said. Quiet Time: a holy time for the pueblo, when old ways and religious rituals were observed, and visitors and outsiders were not allowed on the reservation.

"You wash hands?"

"Yes."

Now the old woman wrestled with a long, tough piece of sinew, working it up the bone, shaving the meat away from it to pull it out in one piece. "In old time," she said, tugging at the stubborn strand, "we save that, use to sew. Those moccasins—sewn with deer sinew. Grandma Bird made me—my first Corn Maiden dance."

I looked at the tall, white, bootlike moccasins—footwear that all the women of Tanoah Pueblo wore for ceremony. A whole deer hide was softened and whitened for each shoe, then sewn to a sole made from buffalo leather. The long leg of the moccasin stretched to the top of the wearer's thigh, but then was rolled down into thick, soft folds that came to the knee, making the women's legs look like large, round aspen trunks beneath their long skirts.

Momma Anna had laid out many of her ceremonial items here on the kitchen table: her *jish*, or medicine pouch, which was a small, beaded deer hide bag on a thong to wear around her neck; a soft, square elk pouch to store the jerky in; a long, flat beaded belt; turquoise jewelry; a cloth bundle of loose turkey and eagle feathers; and her traditional blanket shawl. Beside these lay a neatly folded Pendleton blanket, which Momma Anna would roll behind her saddle when she rode to the Indigo Falls one week from today for the annual pilgrimage of her people—a ceremonial journey homeward to the Eye of the Great Spirit.

As I waited for the next round of jerky strips, I noticed the neglected poinsettia in the kitchen window, still lingering from Christmas when I'd given it to her as a gift. It was drooping, thirsty. I took a dipper of water to the window box and gave it to the plant.

"No water him," Momma Anna said, pointing to the small succulent in the dish next to the poinsettia. "He not like water. Only money."

A few coins rested in the dish beside the peyote plant.

Momma Anna wiped her hands on her apron. "Now. We talk about him, we have to feed him." She went to her purse, which was hanging from its strap on a peg near the door. She fished out two quarters. "Here, you feed him, too," she said, and handed me one of the coins.

I watched her press the quarter against her forehead and close her eyes, as if she were making an offering to a deity. Then she threw the coin in the dish and went back to the sink to shave more meat. I put my quarter in the dish with the plant.

"That's peyote, right?" I asked.

"That a herb. No talk about him more or we have to feed him again."

I remembered earlier in the summer when Momma Anna had told me she and the other women were going to gather herbs. I'd asked if I could go along but she'd made some excuse about my yellow hair scaring the herbs away. My attempts to learn from Momma Anna were never fed by asking questions, but rather by events like today, when we simply shared time together and I observed what she did.

This Tanoah mentor of mine had "adopted" me some time ago when we'd met at an art show. It was in the month she called Nuúpa-pana, Night Fire Moon, mid-December. I was passing by when her display threatened to collapse, and I helped her prevent this calamity. Once we'd stabilized her things, I fetched a hammer and some nails to help her remount her beautifully crafted dream-catchers, bone chokers, and silver and turquoise jewelry. We'd visited a little; I'd tried to buy a bracelet from her, but she insisted upon giving it to me. Later, in the parking lot, she'd hurried up to me breathlessly to invite me to have Christmas dinner at the pueblo with her family. She pressed a piece of paper with a phone number written on it into my hand. "That my son Frank, my daughter-in-law Lupé phone; I not have one. You call. This week. Lupé tell you how to come."

"But why? You don't even know me!" I asked.

"You no mind. I am told do this. You come."

She started to trundle away, her blanket shawl pulled around her against the winter cold. She turned back. "What your name?"

"Jamaica. Jamaica Wild."

"What kind name that? You white girl. You not from Jamaica, right?"

"No." I gave a nervous laugh. My name had always been cause for unwelcome comments and unsuccessful explanations. "My mother named me Jamaica. She . . . I guess . . . when I was born, I think she just dreamed of being anyplace besides where she was."

"Where she now?"

I drew in a breath. "I don't know." There was a long silence while we studied each other. "She left. When I was very young."

The Indian woman looked at me and pressed her lips tightly together, shaking her head. "You call me Momma Anna," she said.

◂ 3 ▸

Truth or Dare

Diane Langstrom was a stunning but deadly woman. She was almost six feet tall in her hiking boots, and I had heard that she was an expert in a variety of martial arts. Her auburn hair was cut so short it might have looked masculine except that she also had beautiful features and a lean but clearly feminine body. She had worked her way up to field inspector position in the FBI by sheer will and incredible drive. Earlier that evening, at the scene of Santana's death, she had told me that she wanted to talk with me away from the tribe. We had agreed to meet at the gas station in the tiny village of Cascada Azul, just beyond the outer boundary of the reservation. With the pueblo on Quiet Time and no tourists, the station had closed at sundown. Diane was waiting, her car idling, when I pulled in the lot.

I slid into her passenger seat. "What do you make of this one?" she asked, not hesitating to get right down to it.

I was cautious. Di and I had worked on a cattle mutilation case before, but I really didn't know her that well. "I don't know. I guess it could have been a suicide. But I think there's more to it than that. Don't you think it was strange the way they just wanted us gone, like nothing else mattered?"

"Yeah, that rang my bell, you know—that, and what you said, that he acted like he might have been drugged. Of course, he might have hopped himself up, too."

I turned away from her and looked out the window. Across the gentle slope at the foot of the mountain, I could see the flicker of several tiny bonfires where a few pueblo families gathered against the sinking chill of the evening, a tradition that was as much a part of the Tanoah Pueblo culture as the adobe their homes were built of. It was, however, generally forbidden to light fires outside during Quiet Time, unless there were ritual need of it. Perhaps these fires were to light the way for the recently departed and represented family members of the deceased. I turned back to my companion. "If I didn't know Santana, I could go with maybe he did drugs himself. But I knew the guy."

Diane shifted to face me. "Look, Jamaica, I'm going to be straight with you here—there's not much we can do on a hunch alone. Yeah, they act funny, like they could be covering something up, but then it *is* Quiet Time and there are all kinds of kiva doin's right now. They don't like whitey around when that's going on. Afraid we'll steal their culture—and they have every right to feel that way, they have a few hundred years of experience to back that up. Anyway, that could be what all the hush-hush, hurry-up-and-get-out stuff was about."

I was quiet.

"And another thing: you can know someone and still not know everything about them. Just because you never saw Santana like that before doesn't mean he never used drugs. He might have done drugs sporadically, not been a regular user. He could have been real good at keeping it hidden. Or it might have been a thing he did in the past and something triggered him to do it again after years of not using. You never really know people."

I still didn't speak.

"I didn't see any signs, no track marks, anything. Yeah, his pupils were dilated, but that could have been adrenaline, fear. Or it might have been peyote. They do that."

"I know. I thought about that. But they don't do it just to get high. They do it as a religious ritual, in ceremony. They don't take it and go wandering out in a herd of buffalo."

"Maybe he was vision questing or something."

"In the buffalo pasture?"

We were both quiet after that. Then Langstrom spoke again: "You know, you look great. What do you do to stay in such good shape?"

"I run. Sometimes I press a few weights."

"Ever try hapkido?" she asked. "I'm looking for someone to spar with."

"I never tried it."

"Well, maybe we'll work out together sometime. Did you see how they acted, coupla babes like us in charge of the investigation?" She chuckled. "They didn't know whether to have a hard-on or be afraid."

"Yeah." I grinned. "I get that a lot."

"Me, too. Anyway, Jamaica, all I got is what you said, that he might have been drugged. I mean, I didn't personally see anything to support that. There was nothing on his person, there were no needle marks or anything, no smell, no signs of any kind. There's just no evidence of a *crime*, no hard data. Even peyote, I have to have something, a reason to bring that up. I mean, it was clear he was killed by stampeding buffalo, whatever his state of mind."

"What about those welts on his back?"

"They do that sometimes, I guess, in the kiva. Whip themselves, or have others whip them."

"True, but we don't know that he got those in the kiva. Or that they came from a whip."

"You're right, but I'm not interested in even trying to find that out. Because let me tell you, it would be a political nightmare. We're getting into their religious rituals, that's a major taboo. I'd have to have a note from God to go there. The war chief, Rael, he said those marks were from religious rituals, and then he clammed right up."

She looked out through the windshield now, watching the flickering bonfires, too, and moments passed. Then suddenly she dropped her forehead into her hand. "Aw, I'm full of shit. I'm trying to talk myself out of this because I can see looking for the truth's a losing cause, and even if I did find the truth, there's no way to prove it. I mean, why was he in the damn buffalo pen if he wasn't either high as a kite or just plain trying to die? But if that was a suicide, it's the strangest way to do it that I ever saw. I mean, most people, they want to do themselves in, they'll make sure it gets done. There's a lot better ways than a buffalo stampede. Jump off the gorge bridge. Take some sleeping pills. Drive over a cliff. He could have just been gored or trampled and still survived. Which leads back to he had to be blottoed. It stinks somehow."

I let her talk, didn't say anything.

"I got a buzz on this one. It's weak, but it's there."

"What are you going to do?" I asked.

"What can I do? There's no evidence. I'd have to have evidence to get an autopsy order, some way to justify my suspicions. The Albuquerque office was real clear on that. I better do everything by the numbers. I could get my butt stationed in the northernmost tip of Alaska investigating baby seal kills, I shake too many trees. I guess I'll mention 'possible drug related/no evidence of foul play' and file the damn thing. It will get shuffled upstairs and stuffed in some black hole. All I can do after that is keep my eyes and ears open. What are you going to do?" She looked at me again.

"Same thing, I guess."

We were both quiet after that. Then she shook her head. "God, Jamaica, I would not like to have your job after this. They acted like you had the plague and they couldn't get rid of you soon enough. That's got to make it hard to do what you gotta do every day."

"Well, normally it's not like that, but I sure wasn't winning any popularity contests today. They were pretty mad that I was out at the pueblo when this came down. I couldn't help but notice that it seemed more important to them than a man's death."

"Looked like it to me, too."

"Okay, so we're playing it down then?"

"What?"

"You know, the buzz."

"What buzz?" Not looking at me.

I grabbed the door handle. "Right, well, we're done here, then, yes?"

"Yeah, we're done here. For now, anyway. But I just wanted to say . . . I guess I just wanted to suggest that you watch your back."

"What do you mean?" I turned toward her.

She met my gaze. "I don't know. Just be careful."

"You do the same," I said and got out.

Diane backed the Crown Victoria past me, and then turned out onto the narrow county road.

Wild Indigo

I stood there alone in the dark for a few minutes, looked again at the tiny fire lights on the foothills. *This time,* I told myself, *I'm going to play it straight. For once in my life, I'm going to make it easy on myself, and stay out of trouble.*

Walking back to my car, I said out loud, "Buzz? What buzz?"

◀ 4 ▶

The Wolf

When I got home that night, my place had been ransacked and many of my personal effects destroyed. The culprit in this event was my wolf cub, Mountain. Unaccustomed to being left alone so much, and—as all wolves do—suffering from separation anxiety anytime he felt divided from his "pack," the wolf had seen my leaving as permanent abandonment. He attacked me the moment I came in the door, raising up on his hind legs like a bear and throwing his upper body into my chest, knocking me down. His breath was quick, hard, and shallow, and he whined. As he wagged his tail and pawed at me, he urinated submissively on the floor, his ears down with a combination of fear and anger. When I managed to get back to my feet, he pressed his haunches into me, his tail beating against my legs, and he continued to huff as if he couldn't get enough air. He whimpered and cried and vocalized angrily.

"I'm so sorry, Mountain," I said, pressing my hand at the junction between his abdomen and his hip, which seemed to have a calming effect sometimes, though he was clearly too upset now for it to matter.

He yelped in response. More puffing, his tail battering my legs, pounding against the open door, knocking over the jackets on the coatrack, and the rack itself, which crashed to the floor. Surprised by the loud sound and the sudden animation of something he'd never seen move before, the wolf yelped and circled, burying his tail deep between his legs. He scooted over toward the table in the center of the room, hoping to hide beneath it, but he was too large.

I went to him, put a hand on his hip, and held it in place. "I had no idea I would be gone more than a few hours. Something happened. I didn't mean to leave you for so long."

Another yelp. The wolf raced in tight hoops around me, panting. In his extreme agitation, he was shedding—and hair was flying everywhere, adhering to my jeans and even my hands when I touched him. He was so upset, nothing seemed to console him.

"I'm so sorry," I kept saying, over and over, as I maintained constant touch, never breaking contact between my hand and some part of his body.

He continued to circle around me, breathing hard, rubbing his haunches against me, and whining, nuzzling his neck into my thighs.

"Poor baby," I cooed.

He whimpered time and again, made occasional eye contact, and panted, unable to calm himself.

Finally, I coaxed him outside, and he moved only slightly away from me to pee, then raced back to rub against my legs. We went back into the cabin, and I surveyed the damage.

He had ripped open my pillow and its case, so a white snow of down covered my bed and most of the cabin floor. He'd pulled four pairs of shoes and a pair of cowboy boots out of the closet, and he'd managed to dismantle and devour the better part of one of the boots and all of the shoes. He'd overturned a big potted plant, pulled the vegetation out by the roots, and dug to the bottom of the pot, spreading soil in a wide wake, then tracking brown prints everywhere, including across the top of the small kitchen table. The two chairs that normally sat tucked beneath the table were both turned on their sides, and the backrest of one of them had a good dent where the corner had been chewed off. There were deep grooves where he'd scratched the inside of the door and the wood on the windowsills, probably trying to get out.

There was a horrible smell, which I tracked to a puddle of urine and a huge pile of shit on the bathroom floor, and there were paw prints in the bathtub where he'd tracked some of it.

Gagging from the stink, I used a dustpan and paper towels to gather up the moist pile and dump it into the toilet. All the while, the wolf watched me and whined, still breathing fast and heavy from fear. I used more paper towels to mop up the urine and then bagged those up and took them out to the trash behind the cabin.

Mountain followed my every step, never more than a yard from me. It took me almost two hours to clean up the place, the wolf shadowing me the whole time. Although he seemed concerned that I'd be angry, he was also clearly proud of his handiwork and had no shame.

Six months ago he'd been rescued by one of our wildlife rangers outside Yellowstone—his mother had been killed by a rancher, and Mountain was the only cub who had survived. He and I had been almost inseparable ever since. The ranger who had worked with me on the adoption process had warned me about wolves' separation anxiety and urged me to keep Mountain with me as much as I possibly could. "To wolves, abandonment is death. They're pack animals, they never spend any time alone unless they're put out of the pack. When that happens, unless they find another family that will accept them, they die. Wolves hunt together, raise their young in community, and are very social. They mate for life, and they're fiercely loyal to their pack. Don't leave him unconfined if you have to leave him for *any* length of time. These animals are tremendously destructive, and he'll take his anger out on the things around him for what he perceives as your abandonment. Get as good and strong a crate as you can, and lock it down tight if you can't supervise him directly. Best thing, though, is to try to take him with you everywhere for the first year or so, until he settles into the idea that you're not going to leave him."

I found the biggest dog crate that I could. In the first few months, Mountain managed to bend and distort the slim metal bars, so I used baling wire to reinforce the joints where the top panel met the sides. But soon, the wolf discovered that he could hurl himself at the door, and eventually, the springs and latches would bend enough to permit him an exit. I bought stainless steel S-hooks and began latching him in with those and a pair of pliers. By the time Mountain reached his six-month birthday, he weighed well over a hundred pounds, and his strength was much greater than any dog of that size. The last time he stayed in that crate while I ran an errand, Mountain broke the metal bars across the top and along one side, and bent the whole apparatus into a new geodesic configuration. After that, I found that it was easier just to take the wolf with me almost all the time, even if it meant leaving him in the car for an hour or two sometimes, which he typically didn't mind.

And I began working on the separation anxiety problem from a new perspective. I started by choosing a time when Mountain was tired from a walk or a run with me: I'd let him settle down and fall asleep, and then walk out of the cabin for a few minutes. I would watch through the window, and when he became agitated—usually in a minute or two—I would come back in. I did this time and again, gradually increasing the time he was inside the cabin alone. Finally, I added a new element—getting in my

Jeep and driving down to the end of my road and back, then coming back in the front door. I worked on it steadily, stretching the interval by one or two minutes each time, until I could safely leave the wolf for an hour or two without any adverse effect to either him or my cabin and its contents.

But in the end, no matter what, if I left the wolf for more than an hour or two, the consequences were disastrous. This was the longest we'd ever been apart, and the damage he did meant little to me compared to the trauma my best friend had suffered. I never wanted to upset or worry him like that again. I would need to get my Jeep fixed so that I could take him with me. Those few times when I left Mountain at home usually resulted in an episode like tonight's. I'd lost a lot of my personal effects to that wolf.

With the cleanup complete, I did what I always did to comfort Mountain—and me. I got down on the floor beside him and stroked him and cooed to him. I caressed his face, his ears, and ran my hands along his strong back, the beautiful long ruff at his neck. He began to calm, to breathe a little more easily. He let out a long sigh, then another whimper, still huffing from time to time as he quieted down.

Then I moved around behind him on the floor and lay down on my side. I pushed the front of my body into his back, spooning him, and I put my arm around him and rubbed the top of his chest, between his front legs. I could feel his big heart beating in his breast, still rapid. His eyes remained wide with fear, but he was starting to settle a little. I kissed the back of his head and sang to him, as I always did, from the first night when I put him in his crate as a tiny pup. It was a silly little song I'd made up then, and sung to him hundreds of times since:

Stars shine on us,
Wind sings to us,

Wild Indigo

Moon smiles on us,
You and me.
No more lonely,
We are family.

I opened my heart
And in you came
You gave me wild,
I gave you tame.
No more lonely,
You and me.
No more lonely,
We are family.

◄ 5 ►

Talking with the Stars

My body was stiff from lying on the cold ground. I sat upright, pulled the edges of my Pendleton around me, and continued to watch the stars twinkle and fall across the night sky. I could smell the mountain sage and the spicy incense of *trementina*, the sap of the favored piñon wood the locals loved to burn in their fireplaces and woodstoves. Here in the mountains of northern New Mexico, the late summer nights were already growing cold in contrast to the hot days created by the intense, high-altitude sunlight. Momma Anna had taught me that this was the time called Paw'epana, Lake Moon time. Mountain lay beside me on the ground, his long legs trembling as he dreamed of the chase. He whimpered a little and I reached out a hand to soothe him, stroking his thick ruff.

An owl hooted softly in a grove of junipers on the slope above my cabin. The local tribes believed the owl represented either death or witches.

Wild Indigo

It seemed a fitting tribute to have one singing to me tonight. The meteor shower I had been witnessing all evening had seemed like a heavenly send-off with fireworks—but the owl's persistent voice haunted me like the images of Santana's death.

A rustling sound on the ground to my left forced my attention from the sky, and I watched as a lone coyote emerged from some scrub and padded across the flats toward the rocks and higher ground above my cabin. Mountain woke instantly and rolled onto his stomach, ready. He raised his head and then lowered it, ears back, watching. "Shhhhh . . . ," I told him, my hand on his neck. "Let coyote go."

And then we heard the sound of a car approaching in the darkness. The wolf's ears rotated, alert. The vehicle came from far away, its engine growing louder as it turned and barreled down my long, ungraded dirt and rock road. Lights flooded over me as the automobile pulled in front of the house. The engine stopped, the lights died, and a car door opened and closed. Steps came toward me, and the figure of a man emerged from the shadow of the cabin walls. Mountain got up and ran to greet him, tail wagging. The man came toward me and stood above me, looking down. We were both silent. Finally, he spoke. "I saw you in my headlights when I was coming down the road."

I opened my blanket to him. Kerry Reed, the forest ranger who had been gracing my life lately, sat down beside me and pulled the edges of the blanket around him. He smelled like the woods, campfire smoke, and *man*. I felt us both softening—like two dancers taking position—before beginning the ritual of greeting. First, he engaged my eyes: a slow, sensual drinking-in. Then, that little, half-crooked smile of his: loaded, sexy, full of mischief. He leaned forward and brushed his lips over my nose, my cheeks—so soft, so delicate, like butterfly wings, only the suggestion of touch, making me long for more. His mouth found mine, pulled at my lower lip as his fingers touched mine.

"Babe, you're freezing," he said, clutching my hands. "Are you okay?"

Something about his voice, his concern for me, made me want to cry. I didn't speak.

He put a warm arm around me and pulled me close, my forehead against his chin. I could smell his neck; that wonderful fragrance of soap and warm flesh. He stroked my hair. "I heard about the stampede at the pueblo." He rubbed my shoulder softly, looking up at the sky.

After a few minutes, I said, "I watched someone die today. I couldn't help him."

Stroking my arm, my back. "Talk to me."

"I've seen a lot of death."

"I know."

"This one was different."

"Tell me."

"I don't know. It's not over."

"What do you mean?"

"I don't know."

We were both quiet again.

"So, you're okay, though, right?" He looked at me.

"Sure. But wait till you see my Jeep."

"I don't give a damn about your Jeep, as long as you're okay."

I couldn't help it, I smiled at him. He was a beautiful man: brown hair cut short and neat, eyebrows that yearned to merge across his prominent brow, eyes full of light and tenderness; a narrow face with a tiny scar beside one eye, another to one side of his mouth, two larger ones on the underside of his chin—each one with a story.

"So what are you doing out here?" he asked, looking around.

"Sometimes I just feel like I have to get outside. You know? I used to spend all my time outside before, when I was riding range. I feel closed in after a while. I have to get out and talk with the stars."

Kerry rubbed his face, his heavy growth of daily stubble making a sandpaper sound against his hand. "So, you've been talking to the stars, huh? What are they saying to you?"

"You really want to know?"

He nodded, putting a warm arm around my back and pulling me toward him.

"Oh, they're lying. They're telling me what they always do—that everything's right with the world. That everything is beautiful and in its place. That there is magic all around us, all the time, and there's nothing else to life than that."

"And you think they're lying?"

"Yeah. And I've been listening to an owl over there, too. The owl agrees with me. Something's not right."

"Maybe it's the owl who's lying." He gave me a squeeze.

We were both quiet awhile, listening.

Then I said, "I'm the one who's a liar."

He pulled away so he could look in my face. "What do you mean?"

"I filled out a report that was politically correct, playing down a gut instinct, something I saw, something I can't prove. But I can't stop thinking about what happened today, going over and over it in my mind. Something was wrong with Jerome Santana, the man who was killed in the stampede. He acted like he was high on something. There were welts on his back, like he'd been whipped—or clawed by some large animal. He looked like he was out of his mind."

"Crazy?"

"No, that was the weird part. He looked clear, like he was experiencing some strange ecstasy."

"Why? What was he doing?"

"It was like he was going toward something wonderful—something he loved—instead of going to his death. Like he'd already left his body in pursuit of it. All that was left was . . ." I searched for an explanation, but before I could find one a loud whooshing sound rushed toward me, the sky darkening as the swooping dive of massive wings blocked out the light of the stars. An abrupt thwack of hard talons scudded against my scalp, pulling at my hair as the owl soared past and climbed into the night sky behind us.

Both Mountain and I shot upright, the blanket falling back to the ground and over Kerry's head. "Did you see that?"

He found his way out of the drape of the Pendleton. "Wow! Maybe you better go talk to Tecolote," he said.

"Tecolote? The old *bruja*?"

"Doesn't her name mean 'owl' in Spanish?"

I rubbed my scalp. "Yes, it does."

"I think you're right. There's something strange going on."

◄ 6 ►

The Elders

The next morning I drove to a market in Taos and ordered four large fruit baskets. I hated to leave Mountain alone again after last night, but the doorless Jeep wouldn't hold him and this was a task that could not be postponed. While the baskets were being made up, I shopped. I bought four of everything: cans of coffee, canned peaches, packets of Kool-Aid, plus four large bags of roasted Hatch green chiles—the smell of these permeated the air throughout August, as vendors roasted the vegetables in dirt drives and parking lots, selling them by the sackful.

I stopped by the butcher counter. "Hey there, Jesse," I said to the man with the red-stained apron and the big knife in his hand.

"Señorita Wild. ¿Cómo está?"

"I'm good, Jesse, I'm good. How 'bout you?"

"I can't complain. My wife is mad at me. I didn't go to mass today, but I told her I had a lot of work to do. You have to make a living, so what are you going to do?"

I smiled.

"Hey, I kept back some juicy trimmings for Mountain. Is he in the car?"

"Not today. But I hoped you had some for him. And I'll need to buy some meat to mix with his food."

"We got some good ground lamb over there in that cooler," he said. He went in the back and came out with a jumbo bagful of meaty bones, beef parts and pieces, and trimmings from the roasts and steaks he cut to order for his clientele.

"Mountain will love you for this," I said.

"Too bad he's not here. I was going to hand him this leg joint personally." He held up a large, gristly cow fibula, then wrapped it in some waxed butcher paper and taped it up.

"Oh, man, you're going to be that wolf's hero."

"You tell El Lobo this is from Jesse," he said as he handed the plastic bag and the paper parcel over the counter.

"He knows you're the man," I said.

When the fruit baskets were ready, I loaded everything in the backseat of my Jeep and drove five miles north of town across Grand Mesa in the direction of the Colorado border, then turned off the highway just before the parking lot of Tanoah Falls Casino, busy even at this hour on a Sunday. I drove toward the mountains and took the winding road through the village of Cascada Azul, a tiny town that catered largely to winter skiers and the few summer tourists visiting Tanoah Pueblo, a back-roads, less-well-preserved sister to the larger, more popular Taos Pueblo. The village was all but deserted now—late summer, the pueblo closed to visitors, and the imminent beginning of the school year urging tourist families back home. I turned off the main street onto an unmarked dirt lane, Rattlesnake Road—the back way into Tanoah Pueblo. From there, I drove behind the wall at the western side of the old village. I parked near a corral and separated out a fourth of the packaged goods into one sack. I took this, one of the large bags of chiles, and one of the fruit baskets and climbed the steps leading over the wall.

I knocked at a door washed with turquoise paint, stark against the pinkish tan adobe walls it was set within. When the door opened, Momma Anna's sister, Serena, peered out at me. "Oh, Jamaica." Then she turned and spoke to someone in Tiwa, the door still only slightly ajar. I heard her say my name.

The door opened wide now, and a tiny old woman wrapped in a thin blanket came toward me exuding a long wail, an emotional greeting that contained gratitude and suffering all at the same time. "Oh-h-h-h-h-h," she said. "Jamaica. Come in. Sit. Sit. You must eat."

"Grandma Bird," I said, taking her hand with the tips of my fingers, as Serena slipped the bags out of my arms to help me unload them.

Grandma embraced me, her eyes full of tears. "Did you come, our grandson?" she asked.

Serena spoke again in Tiwa. Grandma inhaled a gasp, her eyes growing large and round beneath her shawl. Then she looked at me again—obviously Serena had told her about my presence at Jerome's death. "You need ceremony," Grandma said, and she scurried away to the mudroom, where personal belongings and food stores were kept. Serena took the things I had brought into the small kitchen.

In this old part of the pueblo, there was no running water or electricity, and it was mostly elders that kept life in the old ways. Serena came every day to care for her mother and father, Bird Woman and Nazario Lujan, to bring water for them from the pump over the wall, and to keep the wood fires going against the cold that clung to the adobe walls from the cool mountain nights. The cooking was shared by Serena and her sister, Anna Santana, and Grandma Bird still cooked a little, too. The men in the family—Serena and Anna's brothers and their sons and grandsons—cut firewood and kept a large supply of it piled against the wall. It took a lot of firewood to keep the kiva fireplace in the corner of the main room going all the time, and more still for the cooking. The men also hunted rabbit, deer, pheasant, grouse, elk, and even bear to provide meat for all the family.

Grandpa Nazario sat on one of the two twin beds in the corner of the room, the gas lamp hanging from the ceiling making shadows against his face. He was rocking and humming to himself. I went to him and took his hand, squatting down to put my eyes lower than his. I looked up at him and he smiled at me. He patted the bed beside him and I sat down. He gripped my hand tightly, and with his free hand, he beat against his thigh in a steady rhythm. Grandpa Nazario was once the head drummer at Tanoah Pueblo. He knew only a few words in English. He turned to look at me. "Burn cedar," he said. "You pray."

Just then Grandma Bird came back from the mudroom and handed me a deerskin pouch tied with a piece of leather thong. "This," she said. Then she bent down and whispered into my ear, "You—no clothes tonight; bathe in spring, water move, you know? Rub"—she made a gesture to demonstrate rubbing the skin, then pointed to the pouch—"this." I nodded my head. Then she handed me a turkey feather. "After, throw in water for one we lost. Come back, four days, ceremony."

I stood and started for the door. "No!" Grandpa Nazario barked. "You eat!"

I let out a long breath. I really wanted to get back for Mountain, but there was no escaping it. I would have to eat, and eat well. The feast at the elders' home was a tradition for all family rites and rituals. There was nothing more insulting than refusing the nourishment these generous

people provided. Serena brought me a Styrofoam plate full of rich venison stew in red chili sauce, posole made with buffalo meat, a spoonful
of spicy beans, and two thick slices of the beautiful rose-scented bread
baked in the *hornos*, the beehive-shaped adobe ovens outside every
home in the pueblo. I pulled back one of the rickety wooden benches
that had been set around the plywood and sawhorse table erected for
the family feasts normally taking place at this time of the year—now
being used to feed the mourners who came to pay their respects. A red-
and-white-checkered plastic tablecloth was spread over half of the
large sheet of plywood, a white vinyl shower curtain over the other
half. In the center, where they met, stacks of Styrofoam cups, paper
napkins, and plastic tableware formed a high-tech, white, disposable
centerpiece. Serena brought me a cup of orange Kool-Aid. "Eat! Eat!"
she said. I ate.

While I was dining, the door opened and Hunter Contreras, Serena's
boyfriend, came in with Serena's two small grandchildren in his arms.
Dressed in a traditional apron over his jeans, and with his hair bound at
the nape of the neck, he gave me a beaming smile and set the children
down in order to greet me further with a hug. After we exchanged greet-
ings, Hunter sat beside me, and the children went to the other side of the
plywood table. Serena brought steaming plates of food for each of them.

"We've been at ceremony," Hunter said, "and the children were getting too restless. They needed to come home, take a nap."

"It's good of you to care for them while Serena's handling the
feast," I said.

He spoke to the five-year-old girl in Tiwa and she smiled, but obedi-
ently returned the meat she had been eating with her fingers to the plate
and took up a fork. The younger child, a boy not quite two, ate no more
than a few bites, then came to Hunter and wanted to be held again.
Contreras put the toddler in his lap and held him, stroking him with one

hand as he ate with the other, smiling affectionately and offering small bites of his food to the boy, who laughed and pushed his hand away. It was good to see these children treated so tenderly, as were most of the children in the pueblo. Although they were technically no relation to Hunter, Serena's grandchildren were clearly accustomed to his care and attention.

"Are you still teaching Tiwa to the children?" I asked.

"Yes, they gave me a spot at the Indian Center, in the new lab."

"So you're in the same space where they have the Computer Project for Tribal Youth?" I didn't mention Jerome Santana, who had been in charge of that program, and had written the grant—which paid for the portable metal building used as a lab, and also the computers—so the young people of Tanoah Pueblo might have a fighting chance in today's world of technology.

"Yes, we use the same space. The children from Head Start come in the morning, the elementary school children come in the early after-noon, and we're all out of there by three o'clock, when the older kids get out of school and come to the computer lab." He mopped up red chili with a wedge of bread.

"It's good you're doing that," I said.

"We don't want our young people to grow up without their native ways and their language, and many of the parents are not teaching these things to the children. This way, we keep our culture alive through the future generations." Contreras continued to eat and to talk in between bites while he mopped up meat gravy with the slices of freshly baked Pueblo bread. "You can usually tell the age of a person from Tanoah Pueblo by how much English and how little Tiwa he speaks. Like Grandma and Grandpa: they struggle with English and can barely get by. But they can talk up a blue streak in Tiwa. That's the elders. Now you take Serena—she's quite a bit younger than her sister, Anna. Serena speaks fluent English so she doesn't bother to talk to her kids or her grandkids in Tiwa. Those young ones wouldn't even know their native language if it weren't for this program. But on the other hand, Anna—because she is older—grew up with mostly Tiwa and so taught her children Tiwa first." He pushed his foam plate away.

Serena's granddaughter was finished with her meal, too, and she came to stand beside Contreras, clutching his massive arm as if she were hugging a tree. He smiled at her. "Did you get enough to eat, little one?"

She grinned shyly and nodded her head yes. She ducked under his arm and climbed into his lap. At this, her brother got down and went to lie on the bed beside Grandpa Nazario.

"I'm so happy that Tanoah Pueblo has kept its culture intact," I said. "It makes it a magical place to me."

"Well, one reason we have held on to what we have is just a matter of luck. We have never been relocated to another place, had to march hundreds of miles and be confined like other tribes. But we have suffered other things. When the Spanish tried to take our children and make them into slaves, we hid them—up in the mountains. If we couldn't take them, we trained them to run, told them where to go, where to hide and wait until it was safe to come back. We stayed together as much as we could. We have always been here." He tapped the table with the end of his index finger. "Right here."

"I guess that's what makes Tanoah Pueblo so special."

He nodded his head in agreement. "But even so, we see more and more of our traditions dying, eroding, being stolen. That's why we've become so protective of our culture. We guard it carefully. When you come to the pueblo on a feast day and the dancers are drumming and chanting and singing, you can see that much of our culture is contained and transmitted in sound, in vibration. As a people, we are but a vibration, a breath of the Great Spirit—and we came into being on that breath, that resonance.

"Our pueblo—this old part inside the walls right here where Grandpa and Grandma live—it is designed to resonate with the earth around it, and to give the people who live within it the experience of vibrating with Grandmother Earth. Our language is an extension of that. Our chants and songs, the drums we make here at the pueblo—all these are sacred. Our language is sacred. It is a life-or-death matter for our culture. To lose it would be to lose our very souls. It is our means of existing, our way of weaving in and out of the world of nothingness and the world of Creator's breath. This is why we made a decision a long time ago to keep the Tiwa language an oral tradition."

I was so moved by Contreras's words that I could not speak. I wanted to thank him for his eloquence in sharing with me what I had never fully understood, yet now—due to his careful teaching—knew to be true about my medicine teacher and the family that had welcomed me in their midst. Their language, their culture, and the sacredness of these—this was what drew me to be right where I was at that very moment.

Serena poked her head out of the kitchen and said something in Tiwa, her voice soft, submissive, a kind of sustained cry so typical of the flat, extended tones of the language.

The big man lifted the child to the floor and patted her bottom as she scampered toward the bed to join her brother in a nap. Then Contreras rose from the wooden bench and extended a large brown palm to me. "It was good to see you again, Jamaica," he said.

I took his hand. "Good to see you, too, Hunter. You going back?"

"Yes," he said. "We'll be taking turns for the next few days."

He went through the open doorway to the kitchen, and I could hear him speaking softly in Tiwa to Serena. I heard her crying as he spoke. When she answered, it was in the long nasal vowels of her native tongue. Then I heard the kitchen door squeak on its hinges and thud shut.

I rose from my seat, ready to leave, and Grandma Bird Woman again stood and went to the mudroom, calling behind her for me to wait. She came out with a thin white blanket. "This," she said, making a gesture as if to cover her hair. "People the village, they talk. Pueblo closed, you know, no white people. You, yellow hair. You put this."

"I'm sorry," I said, wrapping the blanket around my head and shoulders. Because of my height, it only came to my hips. Serena, who had come in wiping her eyes to say good-bye, laughed at this. She said something to her mother in Tiwa. Then to me, she said, "I told my mom to give you one of Daddy's blankets. You're too big to wear one of hers."

Grandma Bird went again to the mudroom. The blanket she brought this time had a series of pale mauve stripes at each end. "Go back way," she told me, adjusting the blanket so it covered more of my face. "Over wall. Keep head . . ." She made a gesture as if to pull a blanket over her own head.

As I was crossing over the wall and down the steps, I heard a screen door slam. Serena caught up to me, a little out of breath. She pulled a blanket over her own hair and said, "I'll walk with you to the corral."

We made our way down the thin plank steps and across the narrow dirt road that ran along the back wall of the pueblo. When we got to my car, Serena said, "I wanted to tell you that my sister Anna's heart is broken."

"I can imagine," I said.

"It's not just the loss of her son. His wife, Madonna . . . they were . . . having a hard time."

I wasn't sure where this was headed, but I had a hunch. Gossip was a mainstay of the relationships between the women at the pueblo. It was used as a sort of Tanoah version of our Supreme Court—each party arguing the merits of moral issues arising from the questionable behaviors of the subject. The ladies, in the course of their daily activities, would intone the name of someone whose behavior was considered suspect, then debate one viewpoint against the other until the group arrived at some sort of consensus. This accord was a kind of binding decision about the rightness or wrongness of a certain type of behavior—and the one they were gossiping about was then let know that she had been *talked about.* One of the worst things one could do at Tanoah Pueblo was to set the talking tongues loose over something done or not done. Hence, it was very important to avoid bringing any unwanted attention to Grandma Bird because I came to her house. I was more than happy to wear a blanket over my head to avoid bringing the scrutiny and stricture of gossip upon her.

Serena continued, "It's sad when your kids are not getting along, especially when there's a little grandchild involved."

"Yes, of course. I'm sorry to hear that."

"Madonna works at the casino, you know."

"Yeah, I think I heard that."

"She wanted a lot of things from him all the time. 'Build me a house. Buy me a leather coat. I want a new car.' And the one who passed: he was always working in that computer lab. All the time, never at home. It was breaking Anna's heart to see that."

We stood in silence for a moment.

"I know you will be there for Anna," Serena said. "She's going to need us all a lot right now."

I took the gifts of food to two other family households—the home of Jerome's surviving brother, Frank, and his family, and of course to the home of Momma Anna Santana. In each case, though, I left the groceries with a cousin or uncle, because the immediate family was at the graveside of their loved one. The last house on my delivery list was that of the late Jerome and his wife, Madonna, and their small son, Angel, behind Momma Anna's adobe home.

Wild Indigo

I drove into a bare dirt yard and parked beside a pair of abandoned cars, then walked across the board bridge that spanned the narrow *acequia*, my boots making loud proclamations of my visit on the dry, hollow wood. The house was large, especially by pueblo standards—two stories, with elaborate second-story *portales* and big arched windows—but it was largely unfinished. The scratch coat of adobe plaster had been applied to some walls, leaving the hulking structure a dull gray with tar paper showing on some of the unplastered exterior walls. Sheets of plywood covered openings where more windows and doors would one day be, and through the grand arched front window, I could see more plywood dividing rooms where stub walls would be added. Only one side of the ground floor looked inhabitable. I knocked loudly on the door and waited, but no one came.

I was prepared to leave my parcels on the front *portal* when I noticed a small face at the front window. I waved at the boy. Recognizing me, he hurried to open the door.

"Angel? Are you here by yourself?" I asked.

The child nodded, his long dark hair swishing around his face. He pulled the earphones off his head and shut off the portable CD player that was stuffed into the chest pocket of his overalls.

"No one is here with you?" I was alarmed that such a small child, perhaps five years old, would be left alone.

"I stay here by myself every day," he said indignantly, "after Head Start."

"You do?" I asked, shaking my head in disbelief. The custom of the tribe was to lavish care and attention on their children. I was having trouble believing Angel didn't have a grandmother or auntie with him now, much less on a regular basis.

"I'm not big enough to play on the computer all day. So I have to come home. Then Momma has to go to work. I stay here. I like it here,"

47

he said. "I don't want to go to Grandma Anna's. I like it here! I'm a good boy. I don't tell when it's a secret."

"You don't tell when it's a secret?" I asked, perplexed.

"I'm a good boy. Daddy can trust me. Momma can trust me. I'm good."

"Of course you are, Angel," I said, reaching down and stroking his waist-length black hair. "Do you want a hug?"

He looked up into my face and I thought for a moment he was going to cry. Instead, he lowered his eyes. Then he suddenly reached out his arms and jumped into mine.

I straightened, lifting him into my chest, and he wrapped his legs around my waist. "When are you getting your first haircut?" he asked, fingering my long strands of blonde hair. "I'm getting my first haircut when I finish my training and I get nishyated. Only my daddy can't train with me now because my daddy . . ." He stopped, horrified. "I'm not supposed to talk about that!" He buried his face in my shoulder.

"Shhhhh," I said, stroking his back. "It's okay. I know what you mean. It's okay."

As I was pulling out of the dirt drive that led to the late Jerome Santana's house, a tribal police car pulled up beside me. The driver lowered his window and Chief Epifanio Moon Eagle looked at me. He studied me in the blanket Grandma Bird Woman had given me. Then he gave me a wry grin. "That blanket's not gonna git it for you. And it's gonna get cold if you don't put a door on that car," he said, "some way to close it up. People could steal what you keep inside."

"I know," I said. "The buffalo . . ."

"Yeah, I know," he said. "You on business here?" He nodded his head in the direction of the unfinished adobe.

"No, I was just bringing some groceries."

"Good," he said. "That's nice of you. But you know the pueblo's closed until the end of August, right?"

"Yes, but . . ." I started to tell him these people were my family. That Momma Anna was my medicine teacher, and that her son was therefore something like an adopted brother to me. That I had been welcomed into the homes and ceremonies of the Lujan/Santana family, and needed to be here to provide comfort and solace in their time of loss.

Before I could find a way to say any of this, Chief Moon Eagle interrupted. "You're only supposed to be out here if you're on official business," he said. "Why don't you just head on out the main gate up by the casino, and I'll have the officer up there radio and let me know when you've left the reservation." And then he pulled away before I could answer.

I proceeded down the narrow, winding dirt road, the *latilla* fences coming right up to the Jeep's side mirrors in some places, the ruts in the road forcing me to drive slowly. As I came upon Yellow Hawk Lujan's house, I felt a wave of shame. He was Jerome's uncle and Momma Anna's brother. I should have brought a basket for him, too. I applied the brake and looked into the backseat, hoping to find something I could give as a gift. Two apples nestled in my jacket, probably fallen from one of the baskets. It wasn't much, but I decided to go and at least pay my respects. I pulled in the drive and proceeded back past a horse corral to the low adobe house under some old cottonwoods. Beside the house stood a saddled gelding, and behind him an old green pickup with a sizable dent in the driver's-side door. It was obvious the horse had grown restless or bored and had kicked the truck. The animal raised his nose and sniffed at me when I got out of the Jeep. He whinnied urgently. I thought it was awfully hot to leave him standing in the sun—saddled, with no water. As dry as the ground beyond him was, it was obvious from the damp soil under the horse that he had urinated in that same place several times and then pounded the earth beneath him into a muddy mess.

I went to the door of Yellow Hawk's house and knocked, but there was no answer. I walked around the pickup and looked into the pole barn in back. No one was home. The horse neighed at me repeatedly and began to stir and stomp as if he were about to kick the truck again. I found an old pail beside the barn and set the apples on a stump near an old outdoor pump. I pumped water into the bucket. The gelding began to stamp eagerly as I approached with the container, the water sloshing over the edge. He drank voraciously, as if he hadn't had water in days. I pulled the bucket away, fearing I would cause him to bloat from drinking too fast. He raised his muzzle and looked at me, his big eyes imploring me to offer the bucket again.

"I don't know what to say, big guy," I said to him, reaching out to stroke his withers. He pawed at the ground. "I'm already in trouble with the police and I shouldn't be here at all." I examined his saddle. There was a bedroll tied behind it, a traditional one—a tanned hide and a trade blanket. From the leathers hung several handmade deerskin pouches, probably containing jerky and tobacco. There was a large sack made of soft elk hide hanging from the rear of the saddle. I looked around cautiously, then groped the worn leather to see if I could discern by shape and feel what was inside. I felt the hard, round globe of what was probably a gourd rattle and another long, narrow, cylindrical shape, which might have been a short lance or a ceremonial pipe. Several small bundles.

I looked around again. The horse had eaten all the grass near him and there was nothing but dust and mud within range of his tether. I looked back at the barn. Beside it was a pole fence, a grassy place, and the shade from the cottonwoods. I loosed the gelding's reins from their tie and led the horse to the kinder ground. He began to pull at the grass immediately. I tied him securely to the pole fence and patted his rump. "You'll be a little better off there till Yellow Hawk returns," I said to him. I went and got the two apples and offered one to him, which he took eagerly. I tossed the other on the ground in front of him and walked back to my Jeep.

On the way back to Taos, I stopped at the gas station in Cascada Azul to fill up. I was watching the numbers fly by in the pump's window when I heard a voice call my name. I looked behind me, over the top of my Jeep. Gilbert Valdez came toward me, a big grin across his handsome brown face. "Hey, good-lookin'. How you doing?"

"Hi, Gilbert."

"What happened to your car?" he asked.

"Buffalo," I said. Valdez was the manager of the Tanoah Falls Casino, an enterprise that stole from the poor and gave to the rich in the name of progress. I often derided him for this in a friendly, joking way, but underneath my teasing I was disappointed that this attractive, intelligent, college-educated Indian was employing his talents in what I judged to be such a disservice to his tribe.

"I heard about the stampede. I didn't know they got your car, too. What are you up to?"

"I was just taking some food baskets to the Santana/Lujan family."

"It's too bad about the one who passed, right? Maybe the family can finally heal now."

"What do you mean?" I finished pumping and put the nozzle back on the hook.

He looked away. "I mean, you know . . . there were some problems."

I studied him. He was clearly nervous. Either he'd said more than he meant to or he thought I was privy to some information I wasn't. "I'm not sure I understand you, Gilbert. Can you clear it up for me?"

His eyes darted briefly to my face, then away again. He looked alarmed. "You know, things have just been hard for some people," he said, and he turned abruptly and walked to a slick red Mustang convertible parked beside the station. He got in and looked at me in the rearview mirror. Then he fumbled in his shirt and drew out a small pouch. He appeared to be rummaging through it for something, then withdrew pinched-together fingers. He made a little gesture, circling his head with one hand, and then he threw something over the side of the driver's door. I saw tiny particles sprinkle toward the asphalt. Gilbert started the engine, backed out of his parking place, and drove away.

I went to the place where he'd been parked and studied the ground. Tiny specks of something white and granular clung to what appeared to be crushed chile seeds, little clumps of which were embedded in the pits of the asphalt. I wet my finger and pressed against a pocket of the stuff, and then I examined the tip of my finger. I sniffed, then I tested it with my tongue. *Salt. Chile. And something bitter, acrid. But what?*

Momma Anna would know. I'd seen her make that same gesture before, with a similar concoction. It was at the bake.

◄ 7 ►

The Bake

Earlier in the summer, I had been privileged to be a part of what Momma Anna called a "bake." Her grandson was to marry. For several weeks, ceremonies and rituals prepared the couple for the sacred vows they were about to take. Elders gathered at the family homes and shared their experience and wisdom with them. The two lovers were kept apart during this time while their families questioned them about the seriousness of their intentions, the extent of their commitment, and the possibilities of both failure and success in the lifelong journey of marriage. Finally, they were gathered together, along with their clans, at the end of these arduous few weeks, and there was much feasting and gift giving.

Throughout the long period of instruction, there had been feasting every night. But for this last night before the wedding, when the two clans came together, the responsibility for the largest repast of all fell on the family of the groom.

In preparation for this final banquet, the night before it was to take place, a dozen women gathered at the home of my medicine teacher—just an hour after all the food had been put away and the dishes washed from the large meal for the Santana clan that evening. It was late by then, and we were just beginning. Anna's son Frank, father of the groom, brought in three large plastic trash cans with lids. Lupé, his wife, carried huge galvanized washtubs, the kind you might set out in the yard to shampoo a big dog. A pair of young men set up two long wooden benches in Momma Anna's living room. Others carried in twenty-five-pound bags of flour, and one of these was emptied into each of the twelve washtubs, which sat in a row, six on each bench.

"You! White Girl!" One of the pueblo women pointed to me. "Pull back hair."

I gathered my tresses into an elastic band and pulled them back at the nape of my neck. I rolled up my sleeves, ready to do anything that was required of me.

The women giggled and spoke to one another in Tiwa. One of them said in English: "Let White Girl do it."

Lupé pointed at a washtub. "Get ready," she said. I went to stand beside the vessel she had indicated.

Serena mixed yeast with warm water in a large camp-style coffeepot, stirring the slurry with a wooden spoon. She poured some into the first few tubs, then went to make more. An auntie I knew, Momma Anna's sister-in-law Yohe, went about with a ten-pound sack of salt and a measuring cup, doling some of the seasoning into each tub. Lupé came with a bucket of rose water to each woman's starting mixture. She peered in and determined how much was needed, then tipped the bucket and poured what she judged to be the right amount of the liquid into each vat, often adding as much as a gallon or more of the rose-scented water. Another woman took large cans of shortening, one to each tub, and paddled the goop out and into the flour. Then the work began.

The women bent over from the hips and plunged their large, round upper bodies into the tubs, working deep inside with their hands and arms, muscling around the mixture within until they had huge balls of dough. I followed suit, but found the quantity of flour, shortening, water, and salt made for tremendous resistance to my every attempt to shape and form it. I felt like I was wrestling a giant jellyfish. I couldn't lift the enormous ball of dough because it was too heavy, and I could barely manipulate it to incorporate in the pan. This fact was not missed by the Tanoah women—all of them laughed at me. Finally a woman everyone called Auntie, who was easily three times my age and looked soft and dumpy for all I could see, shoved me aside. "Let me do, White Girl," she said.

And into the vat her arms and elbows went. She pounded and pressed, lifted and plopped, and thwacked and smacked the great dough ball until it looked like a living thing, massive and elastic. The kneading went on all around me.

"Come here," Momma Anna said. "Do mine. I need rest." I reached into the vat and pounded on her beautifully formed globe of dough. I punched as fiercely as I could, and then worked hard to try to turn and press and knead the stuff, but it resisted me. Eventually another elder pushed me aside. "White Girl weak," she said, and everyone laughed.

At last another auntie found a job for me that I could do. She showed me how to grease the trash cans completely with a thick coating of the shortening. To do this, I had to lay the cans on their sides and crawl in, glopping the stuff on the bottom first, and then working my way back up to the rim in a circular pattern. When I emerged, I had shortening on my forehead, shoulders, and upper arms. The ladies laughed at me. "Silly White Girl," one said.

The dough was dumped into the trash cans and covered to rise overnight. It was time to wash up the tubs and put them away. "Let White Girl do," Yohe said.

While the bread makers sipped coffee at the kitchen table, and giggled and talked with one another, I worked at the sink to clean the large tubs. Auntie brought in a big basket of gifts she'd prepared for the couple. She showed them to Lupé, holding up bolts of fabric, pot holders, a skillet, and—saving the best for last—a beautiful Pendleton blanket. All the women made enthusiastic oohs and aahs for every item. Lupé started to cry, and Serena got up from the kitchen table to fetch a box of tissues. The others patted Lupé and made little comforting whimpers along with her.

Momma Anna got up from the table and came to see how I was doing at the sink. I whispered, "Why is Lupé crying?"

"She lose son. He got new parent now, not her son no more. These two children, when marry, choose sponsors, new parent. Lupé not mother to her boy now." She shook her head with concern, pressing her lips together and making a little sharp sound with her tongue. She filled her coffee cup and went back to the table.

When I finished washing and drying all the big tubs and the other implements from the dough making, the women jumped up with amazing vigor and started carrying the tubs outside. They took the benches out, too, and the remaining flour and other supplies, all moving as spryly as if they'd not done a thing all day.

While the rest of the women busied themselves with loading their trucks and cars, Momma Anna headed behind the house to the edge of the field with a determined look on her face. I followed her and watched her reach into her pocket and unfold a cotton hankie. Her fingers drew up a pinch of the mixture inside—it looked like chile seeds, salt, and something yellow. She circled her head with her clamped fingers, then sprinkled the offering onto the slight nighttime breeze. She looked at me with her lips pinched together tightly. "That for Lupé," she said. "That kind sadness, she cry over lose her son, that need healing, or we all get sick, wedding go bad."

She was quiet a moment, then barked at me, "You come three in morning. Don't be late. You be fire bringer," she said.

I asked her what this meant but she pressed her lips together tightly.

"Anything I need to bring?" I tried.

"Pull back hair," she said.

I barely slept that night, and when I arrived at three a.m., I could see fires already burning in the back of the two large hornos that had been built especially to handle the tremendous volume of baking needed for this three-week event. I found Momma Anna among the women, all of them busy chopping off hunks of dough from the full mounds swelling out the tops of the trash cans.

"You're so la-ate!" Momma Anna whined. She handed me a can of shortening, a giant stack of aluminum pie plates, and a piece of cotton. She made a little circular motion with the cotton, demonstrating how to grease the pans. "Get pan ready," she said.

"Yah," another elder joked. "White Girl maybe can do that!" All the women laughed.

As fast as I could grease the pie plates, the women slapped and punched and formed the dough into perfect rounds to put into them. When we had well over two hundred of them lined up on two outdoor picnic tables, Yohe deemed it time to start baking.

She dipped an old, blackened deerskin in a big bucket of water, then fetched a long aspen pole and tied the wet hide onto one end with some sinew that had already been soaked. Yohe used this implement to swab out the ashes and pull live embers left in the hornos out and onto the packed dirt in front of the ovens, removing all the live fire and ash. Then she reached in her pocket and removed a stem of straw. She held this in one horno, and I watched it burst into flame after only a few seconds. Yohe nodded—the temperature was perfect.

Serena fetched a long paddle and headed for the door of one of the hornos. She laid the peel flat and the women began bringing the pans of bread dough, lining them up six at a time on the blade of it, and while Serena shoved these into the hornos, the dough brigade shuffled back and forth from the picnic table to the paddle with more pans. They loaded the peel again and again. We managed to fit over 125 pans in each oven.

Frank lifted large, flat chunks of sandstone into place, using them as doors to close up the hornos. There was a tiny glimmer of green light along the edge of the horizon, against a deep indigo sky full of stars. It would be dawn within the next hour or so.

The women hurried back inside to take the bits of remaining dough and shape them into cookies, making intricate ropes and forming them into flat panels that looked like Celtic knot-work, each cookie as large as a man's hand. They sprinkled these with colored sugar, taking great care to create as beautiful a masterpiece each time as they could.

Momma Anna had me fry sausage and scramble two dozen eggs while the artisans prepared their work. When the women had designed several hundred cookies, they came in the kitchen and got breakfast and ate it hurriedly from foam plates, slurping more coffee as they ate.

They rose from the table at some unheard signal and filed outside. It was time to remove the loaves of bread.

After the stones were rolled back from the openings, Yohe manned the paddle and started removing the loaves from the hornos. The women put padded oven mitts on their hands and began scuttling back and forth from the ovens to the picnic tables. Golden brown domes of bread, their smell warm and yeasty and delicious, lined up like soldiers in long, even rows. I noticed that there was none of the usual chatter, that the women were working in silence. I used a dish towel to maneuver the hot pie plates and keep the rows straight. When all the bread was out of the ovens, the cookies were put in just as the loaves had been. A few women also brought out loaves of store-bought sliced white bread and threw the pieces randomly onto the hot stones on the floor of the hornos. The doors were left slightly ajar for this last round of baking. Lupé went into the house and came back with a small cast-iron skillet. Inside, I saw the green tips of cedar. She struck a wooden kitchen match against the bottom of the pan and when the flame was ready, she put it to the cedar and held it there until the smudge began to make smoke. The women lined up along either side of the two tables, and Lupé passed by each one of them fanning the smoke onto them and onto the loaves of bread. The aunties and grandmas gathered the smoke into the palms of their hands and used it to wash their hair, their faces, their upper bodies. They turned their eyes skyward. Then they helped to fan the smoke across the rose-scented bread.

When my turn came, I inhaled the sharp, clean smell of the burning cedar and washed myself in it. I saw the sun peek over the shoulder of Sacred Mountain and make a starburst of shooting rays into the gray dawn sky.

While the other women carried the cooling loaves into the house, I saw Momma Anna walk behind the hornos, into the shadows. I followed her, and as before, she removed her hankie, circled her head with pinched fingers, and sprinkled her potion into the air.

"Is that for Lupé again?" I asked.

She said nothing.

"Is she still sad?" I tried.

She turned to me and gave a rare, tender smile. She blinked both eyes. "That for you. You got no family. Only that wolf."

Later, as I washed the pie pans from the bake and the women shoved the cooled loaves by the dozens into plastic bags and then into the trash cans to transport to that evening's feast and giveaway, I said to Momma Anna, "Boy, this baking is a lot of work!"

She looked at me and snorted. "This one easy. We not make prune pies this time. Most time, we do prune pies right after cookies."

◄ 8 ►

Bone Man

After my encounter with Gilbert Valdez at the gas station in Cascada Azul, I headed toward Taos. On the way back to the highway, I saw a hitchhiker waiting with his dog beside the road, a common sight. The BLM encouraged a Good Samaritan practice. I pulled over on the shoulder, leaving plenty of room between me and the hitcher so I'd have time to prepare. I unlocked my glove box and took out my Browning high-power automatic. I unsnapped the holster, but left the gun in it, then reached across my body and clipped it onto my belt over my left hip, away from the passenger seat, but making sure I could get to it if I needed it. I reached into the backseat and skewed my rifle on the floor, wedging the butt end under my seat so it would be hard to dislodge quickly.

It was then that I noticed a regrettably familiar face approaching in the rearview mirror on the passenger side. "Oh, Jesus," I whispered harshly to myself, "it's Bone Man!"

Under an enormous knit cap and a swirling tangle of greasy dread-locks, a cheesy smile lit up a leathery face smeared with dirt. "Wow, Jamaica, I thought that was you. Dude, what happened to your Jeep?" He folded down the seat back in order to throw his duffel bag behind it, then started when he saw my rifle. He threw up his hands in a mock gesture of being held up. "Whoa! Peace, man! Don't you know it's dangerous to live by all that hardware? I'm almost afraid to get next to it, dude. Bad karma."

"Okay by me," I said, and put my Jeep back in gear. "Get your stuff out, then."

"No, wait, okay, I was just kidding," he said. "Is it all right if Bob Marley sits in the backseat?" He urged his golden retriever in the back without waiting for me to answer.

Once inside, he fastened himself in with the seat belt, and I noticed a terrible stench. "God, Bone Man, don't you ever wash?" I waved my hand in front of my face, then leaned toward the opening where my door once was to breathe air that wasn't fouled.

He grinned at me, his teeth edged with detritus around the gums. His army-surplus fatigues were stained and torn. "They charge six bucks for a shower at the Northtown gym. Maybe if you could help me out with a little change?"

I blew out a breath, hoping not to have to take one in again soon. "Where you headed?" I asked, eager to drop him off anywhere I could.

"Bob Marley and I were up visiting friends at the pueblo," he said, reaching behind him to fondle the panting retriever. "We don't have to be anywhere in particular now. We're just hangin'. Where are you going?"

"You were at the pueblo? It's closed now; it's Quiet Time. Besides, they don't allow you to bring your dog in. They don't even allow pedestrians."

He shrugged uncomfortably and started picking at his front teeth with a grit-packed thumbnail. "I got a buddy who meets me down at the gas station by the casino. We go in the back way, in his truck." Then, looking at his dog in the backseat, he said, "Hey, is it all right if Bob Marley chews on that Kong toy?"

"No! That's Mountain's. He'll know if someone else has been gnawing on it. Wolves are very territorial about their stuff. It's going to be bad enough when he smells your dog in my Jeep."

"Okay, okay. Give me that, Marley." Bone Man reached in back and grabbed the big black rubber cone. "What do you want me to do with it?"

"Give it to me." I snatched it out of his hand and laid the toy in my lap.

"Sorry, dude."

I pulled onto the highway and headed back toward Taos. "Why don't I let you and Bob Marley off at the gym and you grab a shower, okay?"

"Cool," he said. "And if you could spare us some—"

"I'll see what I've got," I said, cutting him off.

And then he began to perform the ritual that had earned him his name. He reached under his shirt and pulled out a long necklace made of chicken thigh bones strung tightly against one another—there were literally hundreds of them on one long strand. He closed his eyes and began running his fingers up and down the bones, playing them like piano keys. "I feel a vibration of danger here, Jamaica. I feel an animal coming for you. A big animal . . ."

I pulled into the gravel lot in front of the Northtown gym. "Save it!" I snapped, as my tires slid against the crushed stone and the Jeep jerked to a rocking halt. "I'm not interested, Bone Man."

He looked offended, but he hurried out of his seat belt. "But you said you'd help me with some spare change . . ."

I reached in my pocket and found a wad of several dollar bills. "I'm not giving you a ride again if you don't do something about that smell," I warned as I tendered the cash.

He nodded his head in gratitude. "Okay, Jamaica. Thanks." He opened the door of the Jeep and began extracting his dog, his things. Then he leaned down and looked in at me. "I really did see a big animal," he said. "It was coming after you. Maybe it was trying to get you but it got your Jeep."

"Yeah," I said. "Brilliant deduction there, Bone Man. You really hit it right on this time."

"No, I mean, there's something coming for you, Jamaica. It's out there."

"Okay, Bone Man," I said. "I gotta go."

He pressed the flats of his palms together and held them to his greasy forehead in a prayerful salute.

I shifted into reverse, dug into the gravel, and spun my Jeep around, then pointed the nose toward the highway again and paused, waiting for oncoming traffic to pass.

But Bone Man wasn't done with me. While I sat watching for an opening in the traffic, he suddenly appeared beside my face, his breath like a feedlot on a warm day. "I guess it's probably a good thing you have those firearms after all, Jamaica," he said. "The bones tell me you're going to need all the protection you can get." He held up the chicken-bone necklace and rattled it at me, as if to verify the fact.

◄ **9** ►

Tecolote

In the hills above the tiny village of Agua Azuela lived an old bruja named Esperanza. The villagers, mostly Hispanos, called her Tecolote, which meant Owl. They half-feared her, half-revered her, and most of them sought her out as a *curandera*, or healer, in spite of the fact that they also thought she was a sorceress or witch of some sort.

The bruja and I had a short but intense history together. The previous spring, Tecolote had approached me in a churchyard—a complete stranger, without benefit of introduction—and demanded I visit her at home. A week later, following the directions she had given me, I climbed the mountain to find her waiting for me, even though I'd never let her know I would come. That first visit, she made me a potion that gave me an unforgettable hallucinatory experience. We had several subsequent and equally peculiar meetings. I'd been writing then about *Los Penitentes,* an ancient and secretive brotherhood that still practiced ritual flagellation and—some said—crucifixion in the remote high mountain villages of northern New Mexico. A priest I'd consulted in my research had been found dead, his lifeless body roped to a cross. Esperanza seemed tied somehow to the enigma through her associations and her clairvoyant visions, which were shrouded in mystic symbolism. She offered me cryptic clues, then appeared—and disappeared—in public places as I followed those clues. She tendered disconcerting advice that seemed irrelevant, but—when followed—ultimately led me to solve the mystery involving the murder of my friend the priest. That episode left me with an inestimable respect for the mysterious powers of Esperanza de Tecolote.

As I approached her remote casita now, again without notice, she was waiting expectantly on the *portal* as she had been the first time. "Mirasol," she called, waving me forward, "come in. I made tea." *Mirasol* was the word for sunflower, a nickname she had given me. This time, I didn't even bother to ask her how she knew I was coming. "Montaña." She waved to the wolf. He ran to her. "*¿Cómo está? Ven aquí,*" she continued as she ambled inside, the wolf right behind her.

I stooped down to pass through the low doorway of the tiny adobe home and entered her spartan living space. As always, candles were lit in the *nicho* before the carved santos, and the low adobe hearth was covered with pottery jars and iron pots. The teakettle hissed over the fire, above which was the slab of adobe that was Tecolote's bed—what the locals called a shepherd's bed. The only furniture in the one-room house was the cottonwood plank and stick table and two chairs.

Tecolote held a meaty bone up before Mountain, whispering to him in Spanish as he watched her and drooled. She raised one hand and pointed with two fingers at her eyes. The wolf followed this gesture and looked at her submissively. The wildlife ranger who'd placed Mountain with me for adoption had instructed me never to stare directly at the pup because wolves saw this as a threat. But Mountain never seemed threatened by Tecolote. Rather, he seemed to sense that she was in charge. The bruja handed the bone to the wolf and he took it delicately from her and curled up on the adobe floor.

Then Tecolote turned to the hearth and busied herself with teacups. The large hump at the base of her neck caused her frame to twist to one side and the shoulders to slope downward at an angle from one side to the other so that she seemed always about to tip over. She was short and lean and brown, and her thick calves were knotted with hard muscle. She always wore a plain sackcloth dress, a shawl, and unlaced, brown, curled-up-at-the-toes men's wingtip shoes. Her thin white hair was pulled tightly back at the nape of the neck.

She toddled toward the table with my cup and set it down, giving me a mostly toothless smile. Her few teeth, like her long, gnarled fingernails, were stained brown. "I'm glad that good boy recognized me," she said. "You better hold on to that one, Mirasol."

At first I thought she was referring to the wolf. Then I wasn't sure. I frowned, confused. "What are you talking about?"

"That beautiful boy. The one you spend time with. He's good to look at. And smart, too. He's good for you. I'll bet he's good in the sack, too." She cackled loudly at this, her eyes squeezing into tight squints of delight.

"Kerry? How do you know about Kerry?"

She slapped the tabletop and twisted her head, laughing hoarsely. "Maybe I saw you with him. Maybe I was flying by and looked in your window. Or maybe I heard some people talking. How did you get that bump on your head?" She turned back to the hearth to fill her own cup.

While her back was turned, I quickly sniffed my tea to make sure it wasn't the same thing I'd had the first time I'd come here.

"It's not a *cura*, Mirasol. It's just some Indian tea. It grows on the mountain. Do not be afraid." She turned then to face me, smiling again.

I shook my head. There was no fooling Esperanza. She could see out of the back of her skull. "What bump on my head?" I instinctively placed my hand on my scalp and found a knot beneath my thick mane of hair where the owl struck me. She couldn't have seen that small knob through my tresses. "How did you know I had a bump on my head?"

"I'm a bruja, Mirasol. That's why people come to me, because they need healing. I can see what ails them and I give them a *cura*." She seemed irritated with me that I would question her talents. "You know, that beautiful boy of yours has more brains than you do, Mirasol. Maybe I should work with him instead of you. At least he knew what to do when you got that smack on your *cabeza*."

I clamped my lips shut, trying to control my face. It was only feeding Esperanza's ego for me to show my incredulity. She had a diverse bag of mysterious tricks. On previous occasions, she'd disappeared, practically in front of my eyes, and I now knew that she did this partly to impress me. I took a drink of my tea.

"I see you've taken up with my good friend Mrs. Santana," she said. "This is good. She is a good teacher for you."

My mind was reeling. *How did she know about Momma Anna? What else did she know about me?*

"It's too bad about her son. I felt very sorry about that. I don't know much about that, of course; you know I can't see into everyone's secrets. But I can tell you this: it's not what it seems. And I think there's another one dead, but maybe he doesn't know it yet. One of their brujos. I think he was the first one of them that died over this."

"Over what? What are you talking about, Esperanza?"

"I'm talking about what you think was done by *los búfalos*."

"You mean the stampede? I saw it happen."

"You only think you saw it."

"I saw the man die, Esperanza. He was gored and then trampled by a herd of bison. I couldn't do anything to save him. I nearly got killed myself."

"You are the only one who was in any danger from those beasts. That other one? He was already dead. Now you have a different kind of beast to worry about."

I had enough experience with Tecolote to take this last thing seriously. In our previous situation, she had warned me about what she called "the black thing" that was stalking me. And she had turned out to be right: a person with a dark purpose had indeed been looking for an opportunity to silence me and end my search for my friend's killer. Though her visions were hard to read literally, hindsight had taught me that they were true enough to be trusted.

I felt my pulse escalate. "Am I in danger?"

She raised a bony finger and pointed it at me, its knobbly knuckle causing it to hook and curve before it settled on a path generally in my direction. "You were trying to decide that yourself just last night, no? Whether to follow your own nature or leave things alone?"

I remembered my conversation with Kerry about the messages of the stars versus the owl. I looked hard at Esperanza, whose black eyes were fixed on me like two tiny headlights. "What are you saying?"

She lowered the finger and twisted her chin up and her ear down, looking sideways at me, as if to study me from a different perspective. "It is your nature I am talking about, Mirasol. You're always going to be seeking the truth. That is usually dangerous, wouldn't you agree?"

I didn't answer. I was considering now what Roy had said about me always finding trouble.

"This is why you came here," Esperanza said, pushing her cup aside as if she needed more space. She placed both her palms on the table and leaned forward over it. "You are in the dark. They want you in the dark.

And we need to let in the light so you don't get swallowed up. You know, they go into the ground, in the dark down there. Then they eat the peyote so they can fly out the little hole at the top and be free of their bodies, of the darkness. But you, you must go another way to find the light. What about your writing? Are you writing?" Esperanza had a way of raising the pitch of her voice to a shrill batlike squeak when she was getting ready to show power.

Instinctively, I drew back from her, as if to brace myself. I felt defensive and fearful. "I'm working on a book about the pueblo's life and ways. That's what I'm doing with Anna Santana."

Esperanza leaned even farther forward, rising a little out of her chair so that her upper body was completely over the table. "You are not an Indian! That's not who you are. What about Santa Lucia? Do you still carry her with you?"

I fingered the silver St. Lucy medallion inside my shirt. Esperanza had given it to me last spring and told me she was a white saint, a yellow-haired saint, the patron saint of writers.

Just then, the bruja's hand flew out and seized the medallion, pulling me forward by the neck so that the chain bit into my flesh in back and I was forced to throw my hands out on the table to keep from falling face-first into the scarred wood plane between us.

The light in the room vanished and I was underground, in the dark. A small red glow came from some fiery embers in a pit in the center of the room, and when my eyes adjusted to the blackness, I could see the naked man lying prone in the dirt, his back bloody with a pattern of claw marks. Three peyote buttons nested in the center of a tiny micaceous clay bowl on the ground beside him, along with an olla, a pottery water jar.

I heard a snakelike rattle and spun around just in time to see the bear coming toward me, his face a man's face—painted white on one side and black on the other—a red strip of cloth tied across his fore-head. The bear's huge arm suddenly swiped at me and clawed me across the face. I fell backward and hit my head on something hard, something so hard it caused my ears to ring and ring and ring.

I felt the cool wetness of the cloth on my burning cheek. I opened my eyes and found Tecolote's face inches from mine, her eyes black moons in a sea of flesh arroyos. "Mirasol," she said tenderly. "You have been marked by *el oso.*"

◄ 10 ►

The Scar

As Mountain and I came in the door of the BLM, Rosa, the receptionist, looked at me, jumped to her feet, moved to the edge of the counter she was stationed behind, and gasped with horror. "Eeee! Jamaica! What happened to your face?" Her eyes were wide, her mouth gaping.

That morning I had woken numb and angry, although I had no clarity about why. I laced my smoke-jumper boots, tucked my tan BLM shirt into my brown uniform pants, put on my RPA belt with the pistol holster, extra ammunition clips, collapsible nightstick, knife, and handcuffs. I pulled on my multipocket khaki vest with the shield pinned on it. I looked in the mirror and felt disconnected, as if I weren't in my own body, almost as if I were looking at someone else. My wavy blonde hair streamed around my face, over my shoulders, and down my back. I squared my hat up even with my eyebrows, then tipped it a little to the left—just the way I liked it, as if I saw nothing out of the ordinary. The four claw marks on my face looked like war paint, bright scarlet, crossing the right cheek on the diagonal from the corner of my eye and ear to the edge of my mouth and the jawline. I had a strange feeling of detachment about my disfigurement.

Now Rosa's face was a very different kind of mirror, reflecting a heady mix of revulsion and dismay. She couldn't stop staring at me.

For some reason, I felt irritated by her interest—or more likely, by having to explain something I couldn't. "It was wild animals," I said, and I continued down the hall toward Roy's office, leaving Rosa staring after me, her mouth still agape.

Roy was behind his desk, which was littered with papers. He had his head down studying the incident report I'd filed late Saturday night. I tapped on the door frame, and he looked up over the little cheater glasses he'd been using to read. He ripped them off and stared at me. His mouth fell open, too. Mountain ran around Roy's desk and wagged his tail. Roy reached out absentmindedly and patted the wolf on the back, but he never took his eyes off my face. Mountain was obviously frustrated by the lack of attention. Normally he was the object of intense adoration when we visited the BLM—or anyplace else, for that matter.

"Mind if we come in?"

"What the hell happened to your face?" Roy stood up from his desk and came around to study me up close, the pup following him, hoping for more rubs. Roy went to the door and pushed it shut. "Looks like you been in a damn fight with a big cat."

"Close," I said, moving in front of the desk and lowering myself into one of the two chrome and leather chairs—the one farther from the entry since I don't like to sit with my back to a door. Mountain took his place beside me and sat down, too.

The Boss sunk into the chair next to me, a gaze of disbelief on his face as he studied my cheek. "How'd you get that?"

"Well, it's hard to explain." I felt uncomfortable in his unbridled stare.

"Not the wolf."

I snorted. "No."

"Was it that thing with the buffalo? I didn't notice anything the other night."

"No."

"You're not getting into it with that forest ranger of yours, are you? I thought he was a—"

I cut in. "You know better than that. It was . . . You know what? You wouldn't believe me if I told you."

Roy twisted his mouth to one side, impatient. "Try me."

I shook my head no.

"You gonna need shots or anything?"

I raised my eyebrows.

"You'll need to see a doctor anyway or that thing could be a permanent fixture on your mug."

"Yeah, maybe."

"Don't mess around with it, Jamaica. Better safe than sorry. There's a dermatologist in Santa Fe who took care of my wife when she got a spot of skin cancer on her nose. You can't hardly tell where he cut it out." He picked up his pencil. "I'll get you his number." Before he could say more, there was a sharp rap at the door. The Boss vented loudly at it. "Go 'way. I'm in a meeting." He thumbed his Rolodex.

But the doorknob twisted and Rosa stuck her head in the narrow opening she made. "It's kind of important."

"What?" Roy barked, still holding the pencil, ready to write.

"It's the governor of Tanoah Pueblo, Eliseo Contreras. And War

Chief Ruben Rael." She looked at me then. "They asked to see Jamaica's supervisor."

Roy snapped the pencil in two. "Oh, hell. What now?" Then he looked at me. "You stay right here." He started toward the door, pointing at Rosa. "Go put them in the conference room. And don't say a word about Jamaica being here."

I sat in Roy's office and counted to twenty, then to fifty. I could feel the claw marks on my face burning as if hot coals were being held against my skin. My breathing was shallow and my teeth were clamped together. I gripped the arms of the chair so tightly my wrists ached. I tried to imagine why they had asked to see my supervisor, why the governor of the pueblo would come here, especially during a holy time.

Finally my anxiety gave way to anger and I rose from the chair. I opened the door of Roy's office. I put the flat of my hand against Mountain's nose where he lay on the floor. "Stay!" I barked. Then I started for the conference room. In the blind-covered window of the office next to Roy's, I could see my reflection as I walked past. I looked like a fierce warrior.

When I opened the door, all three men were standing and the air was charged with anger. I hesitated. They hadn't seen me. I stepped into the room. Rael was dressed in a black apron over jeans and a black shirt, his hair pulled back at the nape of the neck and tied with cloth. But Eliseo Contreras was observing a much older tradition in his dress. He wore a white burnoose, rarely seen anymore but once a mainstay of Pueblo men's traditional costume. The wrapped cloth headpiece sat high on his wide, smooth forehead, light against his deep amber skin. Beneath it, his eyes had a dark severity. He was cloaked in a blanket that draped over his shoulders but was open in front. Inside the neck of his shirt, he wore a necklace of bear claws and chunk turquoise. The door slammed behind me and they all turned. Rael's expression registered first as he drew back when he saw my cheek. Governor Contreras's reaction was similar.

I met Roy's alarmed gaze. "Is this about me?" I asked.

The Boss answered, "Governor Contreras and War Chief Rael are concerned about the incident with the buffalo. We just need a few minutes to talk, Jamaica. Why don't you wait in my office?" He narrowed his eyes at me.

"If I can be of any help . . . ," I said.

"No, we got this under control," Roy said. "You go on and wait in my office. I'll be there directly." He flagged the back of his hand at the door to shoo me away. I hesitated, but couldn't see a good alternative, so I left.

It was almost a half hour later when Roy walked in. Mountain had fallen asleep on the floor, and he raised his head just enough to see who it was and then returned to his nap. Roy looked at me and shook his head in frustration.

"What'd I do?" I said.

He didn't say anything, but went instead to his desk, where he slumped into his chair as if he could no longer resist the immense pull of gravity. His face bore a pained expression.

"Is this about Jerome Santana?"

He shook his head no.

"What then?"

He leaned forward and touched the intercom button on his phone, then picked up the receiver. "Rosa, get me the guy at the BIA, what's his name? Yeah. And get the area super in Albuquerque, too. Find out if we have an attorney in this part of the state. We're gonna need one." He hung up the phone and looked across the desk at me.

"I'll get someone to look at your Jeep as soon as I can. I'm pretty sure the BLM will either fix it or replace it, since you were trying to do your job when the damage happened—even if you weren't supposed to be out at the pueblo right then. You better get what you need and go home, Jamaica. Looks like you're going to be off the clock for a while."

"What the hell is going on, Roy?"

He set his elbow on the desk, chin on his fist, and looked right in my eyes. "The tribal council is claiming it was you who started the stampede. That you're responsible for Santana's death."

I leaped from my chair. "What?"

"Calm down. There's no way they can make that stick. If they were serious about this claim, they'd have gone to the sheriff or the FBI, not come here to me. My guess is they're trying to punish you for being out there when you shouldn't have. Just the same, a charge like this is serious, no matter who they bring it to. I'm going to suspend you with pay pending an investigation, Jamaica. It's for your own protection."

I couldn't believe what I was hearing. "But how can they say that? The buffalo were already wandering out of the fence. Someone had opened the gate. It was inevitable the bulls would run."

"They say the gate was shut. They're claiming Santana was just out there praying near the buffalo pen and that you drove up too fast and too close along the fence and incited the stampede."

I started pacing. Mountain, who had noticed my distress, fell on a close heel and began panting nervously, watching my every move as he shadowed me.

Finally I stopped and faced the Boss. "This is bullshit, Roy. This is fucking bullshit."

He shook his head. "Yeah, I know. I know. But it's some serious bullshit, Jamaica. It's some real serious bullshit."

"I want to change that report," I said, gesturing toward his desk.

Roy grabbed the paper protectively. "Now, try not to go off half-cocked, Jamaica . . ."

"Give it to me!" I said, holding my hand out. "I'm going to say what

I really saw instead of playing it down, putting it between the lines!"

The Boss held the report to his chest. "Let's just calm down for a little bit. Let me think about it. We may want to amend this, but let's talk to a lawyer first, find out what's best for everybody."

"What's best for everybody? They're accusing me of causing a man's death! I think it's best that I tell the truth."

He looked at me and set his jaw. "I'm not going to have you rushing me on this, Jamaica. Now, I told you, go home. I'm going to get right on top of this, get some advice. I think we need to keep our heads cool so we can do the right thing. I wish to hell it hadn't happened while you were off duty. And while the pueblo was closed."

I glared at him. Then I went for the door.

Roy stood. "Jamaica, stay away from the pueblo."

"But the family . . ."

"They'll just have to understand."

"They'll see it as a slight."

"And the tribal council will see it as an offense on the part of the federal government against the sovereign nation of Tanoah Pueblo if you don't do what I say. You'll just have to make it up to your friends later."

"But, Boss—"

He interrupted with a stern tone. "I'm not asking you a favor, Jamaica. I'm telling you what's going to happen. You're suspended with pay pending an investigation. Now, the sooner we start working together instead of fighting each other on this, the better it will be. You got the tribe on the warpath for you; do you really want to fight me, too?"

I didn't say anything.

"Now go home."

I looked up at the ceiling and drew in a breath. "What am I supposed to do? Can't you at least transfer me back to Range? I could do my old job."

"Why don't you go see that doctor?" He looked down at his desk, ripped the card right out of the Rolodex, and offered it to me.

I didn't take it. Mountain moved in beside me, eager to go. "I'm not going to take this lying down."

Roy lowered his hand to the desk, the card still in it. "Listen, this is a delicate situation. We need to be as careful as mice or it could go real bad. We've got to get someone in here who can mediate."

I snorted, then swung the door open and made to leave.

He called to me. "Jamaica?"

I turned and looked at him.

"Are you going to tell me what happened to your face?"

"No," I said. And I went out the door.

◄ 11 ►

The Nachi

When I came out of the BLM office, a package waited on the front seat of my Jeep. The slim brown parcel was a flattened cylinder perhaps sixteen inches long. It was neither taped nor tied, but the paper, cut from a grocery bag, had been folded carefully and tucked at each end. I unfolded these tips and began to unroll the wrapper. Whoever had made the bundle had turned the printed side of the bag inward so that only brown kraft paper showed on the outside. I thought of Kerry—*perhaps a rose? Or a print of one of his photographs?* Maybe he'd had a reason to leave the ranger station in Tres Piedras and come to the Forest Service offices next door to the BLM. I felt a twinge of eagerness. *Maybe this day is taking a turn for the better.*

But once I had removed the wrapping I couldn't be sure of that. The object within was a peeled willow branch, perhaps an inch in diameter, which had been painted blue on one side and yellow on the other. The thicker end of the branch had a series of carved grooves and notches. The other end of the stick had a crown of feathers tied to it with a wrap of white leather thong. The feathers—seven of them—were the stiff wing feathers of the nighthawk, slim and pointed, dark gray with a wide bar of white about midway up the length. As I lifted the wand from its packet, I saw grains of blue and yellow cornmeal in the paper beneath it.

I looked around the parking lot. Two BLM vehicles, Roy's truck, Rosa's old Dodge Charger. And next door at the Forest Service, just a few of their trucks and a station wagon. Nothing extraordinary.

I looked at the feathered object again, turning it over, examining it from all sides. A thin strip of thong slipped from among the feathers and dangled from the stick. On the end of the leather thong was a tiny bear fetish. *Momma Anna! She's from the Bear Clan! This must be from her.* I looked around again to see who might have brought the cryptic gift. No one in sight.

I loaded Mountain into the back of the Jeep. As I was standing beside the driver's seat, tucking the mysterious feathered wand back into its wrapping, a car pulled into the space next to me. Noah Sherman, reporter for the *Taos Times,* got out of his vehicle and came around the back of mine. I leaned into my Jeep to toss the package on the passenger seat. The parcel was lighter than I estimated, and sailed across the seat and onto the floor.

"Ms. Wild? Can I talk to you a minute?" Sherman asked, pulling a steno pad from the bag dangling off his shoulder, juggling a camera to one side as it hung by its strap from his neck.

"What about?" I frowned, leaning farther into my jeep to retrieve the misplaced item. Mountain stuck his head out the opening where the door had been and eyed the stranger.

Sherman took out a pen, balanced his steno pad on his thigh as he thumbed to a fresh page, and then asked, "I understand you witnessed the death of Jerome Santana?"

"My boss already gave a statement on Saturday," I said.

"Yes, but he wasn't there when Santana died, was he?"

"I don't have anything to add to what he said." I rubbed Mountain's head to calm him. And me.

"The BLM statement said it was an apparent suicide."

"That's what the statement said, all right," I said, pulling my keys out of my pocket, indicating I was ready to leave.

"A tribal spokesman has told the press that Jerome Santana was involved in prayer rituals near the bison confine when he was killed by a sudden stampede."

I kept my eyes toward my Jeep. "They said *near* the bison confine? Is that how they put it?"

"In so many words," Sherman said. "There was some indication that they believe the stampede might have started when you drove up."

"Did they say why Santana was performing the rituals at the bison pasture?"

The reporter laughed. "Hey, correct me if I'm wrong, but in an interview, it's the reporter who's supposed to ask the questions. Is there going to be an investigation at the BLM?"

I turned then to look at Sherman. "Why would you ask about an investigation?"

He winced at the marks on my face. "How did that happen?" was all he could manage.

"Wild animals," I said. I hopped into my Jeep, started it up, and began backing carefully alongside Sherman, who appeared shell-shocked and unable to move.

"They got your Jeep, too, huh?" he said, fumbling again with his camera as I pulled past him, then turned and headed out of the BLM parking lot.

◄ 12 ►

Diane

I called Diane Langstrom from a pay phone near the plaza, asked her if she had a few minutes. "I'm glad you called," she said. "I have to do something to get out of my stinking little cubicle. I'm going stir crazy looking at all this paperwork. I'm on the way to the gym; meet me there in fifteen."

I took the back way through town and parked my Jeep in the shade. I improvised and hooked Mountain up with his leash to the hitch on the back, where he could lie under the rear of the vehicle.

"Sorry, buddy, you'll have to stay back here," I told him as I poured water from an insulated bottle into the collapsible dish I kept in the back.

He wagged his tail and nosed at the dish, slopping a little of the liquid onto my shirt. I laughed.

"Here ya go, baby wolf," I said, and as he lapped, I nuzzled my nose in the thick cape of fur just below his neck.

He tossed his head and dropped to his front elbows, a position I'd learned meant, *Let's play!*

I took a wide stance, spread my arms, like a goalie at the soccer game. But before I could brace myself, the wolf lunged into me, knocking me down. He collapsed on top of me and began licking furiously at the red welts on my face, which sent pain shooting through my skin.

"No, no, sorry, buddy," I said, shoving him off me, getting up to avoid more tongue contact. "I guess I'm no match for you today."

My four-legged companion looked worried.

"No, it's all right, it's okay," I said, reassuring him with some long strokes. "You didn't do anything wrong. Here's a little yummy for you." I reached into his pack in the back of my Jeep and gave him a rawhide bone to worry on.

When I came in the locker room Diane was sitting on the long bench, removing her shoes. She rose to her feet, looking at me. "What happened to you?"

"It's hard to explain."

She moved in closer, tipped her head, and winced at the sight. "Crap. That's got to hurt."

"Not too bad," I said.

"You gotta tell me."

This was getting old. I thought for a moment, then decided to make up a story, spare myself some trouble. "My wolf," I said. "We were just playing, he didn't mean to hurt me."

"No way." She continued to gape.

"I'm afraid so."

"I hope he's had all his shots."

"Don't worry," I said. "He's current. I'll be fine, too."

"I hope so. Looks like it might scar. But you know what? It kinda looks good, in an odd sort of way."

I tried to smile, but it hurt. "You know, I thought that, too. It kind of looks like war paint, something like that."

She went back to her gym bag and continued changing. "So what's up that couldn't wait?"

"The tribal council is accusing me of causing the stampede, being responsible for Santana's death. The fact that I was out there off duty when it happened, not on business, it makes it bad for me. I'm suspended."

"You're kidding, right?" Stopping to look at me again.

"Do I look like I'm kidding?"

She closed her eyes. "Aw hell. What are you going to do?"

I sat down on the bench. "I don't know. I thought maybe you . . . I don't know."

We were both quiet a minute. Then Diane stepped into her spandex shorts, tugged them up to her waist. "Come work out with me. We'll brainstorm."

I thought a minute. "Okay, let me get some clothes out of the Jeep." I went out to my car and found Mountain still diligently gnawing away on the big rawhide bone I'd given him. Although he wagged his tail when he saw me, he soon went back to his treat as if I didn't exist. I delved into the cargo area among my gear in the back: a CamelBak that I faithfully drained and refilled after every use, hiking boots, running shoes, Mountain's pack of food, treats, and supplies, a fully outfitted pack of my own, all manner of clothes, blankets, even survival food. When you lived and worked in the kind of terrain I did, you learned to be prepared. I found a T-shirt, some shorts, and my running shoes and took them back inside.

Diane was working out on the heavy bag when I came in, big padded gloves on her hands, a film of perspiration on her bare abdomen and upper body. The bag was swaying pretty good, showing the power in her punch. I got behind it, held it for her. Right away, I had to work hard to hold it still.

"Roy actually suspended you?" she panted, still punching. Right. Right. Right. Left. Right, left. She was forcing the bag back with every jab, hitting hard.

I tried to anticipate her strikes, keep from letting the bag swing. I was starting to sweat. "He said it was for my own good."

"But that's bullshit about you causing the stampede. He didn't go for that, right? He's just doing what he has to?" She started working uppercuts: right, left, right, left. Heavy now in the left. Her feet dancing.

I had to dance around, too, to keep the bag between us. I was starting to heat up, working pretty good to hold against her forceful blows. "He said he was going to get some legal advice, that he had to open an investigation. Meanwhile, I'm hung out to dry. I'm trying to figure out what to do. But one thing this tells me: I was right about Santana's death being suspicious. They wouldn't be pointing their fingers at me if they weren't afraid I knew something. Otherwise, they'd be busy mourning, comforting the family, getting it behind them, whatever. They think I know something. Trouble is, I don't know whatever it is they think I know." I was sweating pretty good now.

Langstrom stopped punching the bag, stood stock-still. I peeked around the side of it just in time to see her foot suddenly fly like a speeding projectile up from the floor and straight toward me at eye level, striking the bag next to my face with such force that it sent me reeling backward, sprawling onto my behind on the floor.

Diane came to stand above me, pulled off a glove, and offered me her hand. "Sorry, I should have warned you."

I took the hand up and dusted off my shorts. "Man, that kick was like a bullet coming at me. That's some serious power you got in that leg."

She pulled off her other glove, threw them both to the side. "I told you. You should try hapkido. It's good stuff. I know how to break a man's hand five different ways."

I smirked. "I'm a resource protection agent. I don't have to break hands for a living."

She smiled. "You never know. C'mere." She raised her palm and waved for me to move closer.

I stepped forward. Her left hand shot out and grabbed my wrist, pulling me off balance as she caught me by the throat, gripping me with the thumb and forefinger of her right hand. She held me there by the neck, pulling hard down and forward on my wrist, keeping me off center and ready to tip. She was looking right into my eyes. "I could have killed you right then," she said.

I tried to straighten, but she held my wrist painfully tight, still pressing with the other palm against my throat. "Okay, Diane," I said, "you can let go now. I'm impressed."

"Where's the weak point?" she asked, still holding me hostage.

I thought a second. Then I twisted my forearm away and down and broke her hold. As soon as I freed my wrist, I brought my other arm up and struck her forearm from underneath, driving her palm away from my neck.

She smiled. "Right. Good."

"It was a lucky guess."

"No, it was instinct. You've got good instincts. You'd be good at this. We ought to spar."

"I think we just did."

"Yeah, a little bit." She walked to the corner of the room, where she picked up a towel and wiped at her neck, her chest. "That's what you do when you're faced with a threat, Jamaica. Look for the weak point. There's always a weak point." She threw me the towel.

I mopped my chest and neck, too.

She walked back to me and stood inches from my face, looked into my eyes, daring me. "I'll help you on one condition."

"What's that?"

"You gotta spar with me. I've been looking for a worthy opponent, and you look to be the one."

"Look, I gotta get my job back. Maybe after that."

"Shit. You've got time now. You can spare a couple hours a week. You want me to help or not?"

"Yes."

"Okay. Let's get started."

◄ 13 ►

Good Hunting

Diane let me drive her personal vehicle—a Suburban—while she drove the FBI's Crown Vic to the tribal offices. She had called ahead to say that she needed to meet with tribal officials to "clarify some things." Her job was to run interference so that I could find the child who had come to tell me about the buffalo wandering out on the mountain.

"C'mon, buddy." I gestured to the wolf to climb in the back of Diane's car as I loaded in his pack. He balked. Strange things, unusual surfaces, anything out of the ordinary often frightened him and made him skittish and unpredictable. Mountain lowered his ears and wagged his tail, clearly a little afraid.

"No, c'mon, big guy. It's all right. I'm going to drive it, see? It's just for an hour or so. I'll get in front and you'll be in back, just like my Jeep."

He lay down on the ground, pleading with me not to force him into this big metal box he didn't recognize.

I bent down and comforted him, scratching behind his ears. "You trust me, baby wolf?"

He wagged his tail.

"It will be all right, I promise." I took hold of his collar, but Mountain started backing up, straining against me. He weighed more than a hundred pounds and had a lot of strength in that chest of his. It was getting to be a real tug-of-war.

I stopped pulling and looked around. How could I get the wolf to cooperate? I didn't see anything to use as a bribe. Then it occurred to me to get in the back of the Burb myself. I climbed in, patted the floor in back. Mountain balked a little but sniffed at the open door. I spoke calmly to him, reassuring him, holding my open palm out to invite him in. "It's okay, buddy. It's nice in here, see? Come on in and be with me." I patted the floor in back.

He put one paw up on the floor of the car, as if to feel it with his pads. His tail continued to wag. His ears were up; some of the fear was gone.

I unzipped one side of his pack and started rummaging among his toys, pretending to be looking for one to play with. "Oh, look! Here's a rope toy! And you can't have it." I put the toy in my mouth and began shaking my head, making a growling noise.

That did it. Mountain leaped into the Suburban and aimed right for my face. I pulled the rope out of my mouth just in time, threw it toward the back of the car, and exited the side door just as the wolf lunged into the far back to retrieve the object. I closed the door.

Mountain looked at me with hurt and surprise. I'd tricked him!

"Sorry, buddy," I said, and walked around to the driver's side. I climbed in. "I had to do it."

Before I took the back entrance into the pueblo, I wrapped my head and upper torso in the blanket Grandma Bird had given me. I drove slowly down the dirt lane toward Momma Anna's house, figuring the child had to live somewhere nearby, since he had come there on foot. I examined children at play in fields, standing on bare dirt lots, and riding bareback on horses in corrals, looking among them for the face that matched my memory. I got to Momma Anna's, which was at the end of the road. I looked around in frustration, then spied a seldom-used course through some brush leading off to a diagonal after the graded area played out. I pulled to the edge of the road, raised my binoculars, and looked farther down the track. One house stood far back in a field, a place so run-down it might not have been inhabited. I decided to check it out.

Weeds had grown up in the yard, and on one side of the house there was an old Camaro on cement blocks with high clumps of white rice-grass waving around its concrete footings. Plywood covered the only window on the facade of the house, but there were dogs napping in a patch of bare dirt in front, their tails occasionally whipping about to ward off flies. I pulled up beside the dry-docked Chevy and cut the engine on the Suburban. I examined the yard and the face of the old adobe. Other than the dogs, who showed no more interest in me than to raise their heads slightly and then drop them to the dirt again, there was no sign of life. I lowered the driver's window to listen for sounds, and a gust of hot wind blew. A flag of colored fabric flew up at the rear corner of the house, giving away the unseen clothesline behind it, obviously hung with wash.

Two children raced around the side of the tumbledown dwelling and stopped short when they saw the car. One of them was the boy I'd been looking for. I called to him. "Hi there, son. Remember me?"

Both boys looked at me suspiciously. But the younger child, the one I'd spoken to before, stepped tentatively forward.

"Remember?" I coaxed. "You came to get me the other day?"

The older boy reached for his playmate but too late. The youngster started toward the automobile, dropping the stick he'd been carrying in their play. "I know who you are," he said, smiling nervously.

I pulled the blanket away from my hair, realizing this was probably not helping. "I guess I must look a little strange, don't I?"

He nodded his head. I got out of the vehicle, struggled out of the blanket, closed the car door behind me, and stood looking down at the little man.

He looked at Mountain, who was hanging his head out the window, having moved up to sit in the driver's seat of Diane's car.

"That dog looks like a wolf."

"Yes, that's a wolf cub. He's still just a puppy, about nine months old."

"No way. A *real* wolf?"

"Yes, a real wolf. You want to pet him?"

"No!"

"Okay. That's okay. What's your name?" I asked.

"Don't tell her, Sam!" the older child called, still staying back near the house.

I held up my hands, as if to show I meant no harm. "It's okay, I don't blame you," I said, looking right into the older boy's eyes. "I don't blame you for being cautious." I held his gaze until I felt his resolve melt a little.

Finally he spoke directly to me: "How did you get that?" He raised his hand in the general direction of my face.

"Wild animals!" I grinned.

"Wow," he responded, but he stayed his ground.

"Wow," Sam echoed. Their black pupils shone as large as quarters, and they stared at me with naive fascination, uninhibited by shame or propriety.

I lowered my hands slowly, and then I squatted down. I looked at little Sam, then back at the older boy again. "Let's take this slow, okay?"

Sam nodded at me and began to squeeze at his fingers, not sure what to do next.

"My name's Jamaica," I said. "I work for the BLM. We talked before when you came to tell me about the buffalo on Saturday."

"I know who you are," Sam said.

His friend stepped a little nearer. "Don't tell her anything, Sam," he warned. "Remember, you're not supposed to talk to anyone."

I looked again at the elder boy. "You're right," I said to him. "It's good not to talk to strangers. But Sam and I are not strangers. He's talked with me before. And he knows who I am, that I work for the BLM. He came to get me at Momma Anna's—"

Sam interrupted, "Did that wolf do that?"

"No, no, he's my friend. He would never hurt me. He's very gentle, he loves me. No, this was . . . an accident."

"I don't remember your face like that," he said and reached out and traced one of the raised red lines with small brown fingers. I tried not to wince.

"It just happened yesterday," I said, "but it will heal."

He pulled his hand away. "I don't know. My friend Anthony got cut by his brother with a knife. It goes like this"—he made a long diagonal line across his own face—"and it didn't never heal."

"Well, I'm hoping this will. So you do remember talking to me before. And you remember what we talked about?"

"I'm not supposed to talk to anyone."

"Wait! It's okay. You don't have to say anything."

Then the older boy came to stand beside Sam. He placed a protective arm around him. "All my brother and me were doing on Saturday was practicing for the footraces," he said.

"And what's your name?" I asked him.

"Rolando."

"I'm Jamaica."

Rolando extended a cautious hand and shook mine. "You still look kinda good, even with that," he said.

I smiled. "Thanks." I turned to the smaller boy. "So your name is Sam?"

"Sam Dreams Eagle. I think you look pretty, too. I don't mind that." He gestured at my face.

I smiled again. "So how did you know you could find me at Momma Anna's?"

"I see you there a lot. I have a friend who lives behind there. He always talks about you, says you are pretty." Both boys giggled.

"And why did you come to me about the buffalo? Why not go to someone in the tribe?"

"We were just practicing for the footraces. That's all we were doing." He edged backward.

"Listen, I'm glad you came to get me. It was a good thing you did, Sam Dreams Eagle." Mountain, tired of being confined, and lacking his usual center-of-attention status, yipped at us and pawed at the window, now covered with drool and nose prints. I stood up. Both boys looked nervous. Rolando began to hop back and forth on his feet. He started backing up. Sam stepped back, too.

I held up my hands. "It's okay, I'm just going to walk over here by the car and give Mountain a little pat so he'll calm down." I moved back to the Suburban and reached through the opening and rubbed the wolf's head. I kept my eyes on the boys. "Is this where you live?" I pointed to the run-down abode.

Rolando was already pulling at his brother. He whispered something in his ear.

Sam turned and they started running and giggling, then Sam let out a shriek of laughter as Rolando raced away ahead. "Bye!" they both called back to me, and disappeared behind the house and into the field beyond.

When I got back in the car, I saw drool and smears all over both the driver's- and passenger's-side windows. Hair and paw prints decorated the bucket seats on both sides of the Suburban.

"Diane's gonna kill me!" I told Mountain.

He wagged his tail.

"Okay, buddy, I'm sorry to have to do this, but . . ." I got out and went around to the side door of the car. I lashed Mountain's leash to the back of the bench seat in the middle of the vehicle, then hooked the leash to his collar, forcing him to remain in the rear of the car.

Mountain yipped at me and strained against his confinement.

"Sorry, big guy," I said, and closed the side door.

I had to stop at the crossroads where Rattlesnake Road led off the main paved thoroughfare leading to the pueblo, to let a small herd of sheep pass. They were being led by two young boys carrying long aspen sticks. As I waited, I looked around and saw Hunter Contreras loading a bale of hay into the bed of a pickup from a pile of bales in the pasture beside the road. He looked at the Suburban. I no longer wore the blanket around my head and shoulders but hoped that the tinted windows were enough to disguise me. Hunter's face broke into a broad smile and he started toward the car.

I sighed. *Busted.* I rolled down the window. "How ya doin'?" I asked him, forcing a smile.

"Get you a new ride?" Contreras asked, extending a large, warm hand right into the vehicle. Then he saw my face and sobered. His hand hung in front of my chest.

I took the big palm and squeezed it. "No, this is my friend's car. I borrowed it."

"What happened there?" He nodded at my face.

"I got hurt," I said. "It's not that bad really, just fresh. It'll heal."

"Looks bad," he said. "Something claw you?"

"Just an accident," I said. "It's nothing."

He shook his head in quiet disagreement, looking disturbed. Then he collected himself somewhat. "Come to see the family?" he managed. "Most of 'em are still at ceremony."

"No," I said. Then I wished I hadn't been so truthful. I tried to think of an explanation for being there.

He waited, my silence not concerning him so much as the matter of my face, which obviously still bothered him gravely.

I waited, too. I didn't know what to say, how much to trust this man, whether to admit that I'd been there at the pueblo that day looking for the child who told me about the buffalo escaping their confines.

Hunter seemed to read my mind and managed to shift gears. "You know, I heard what they are saying about you—about the stampede and all that. I couldn't believe it."

I shrugged. "It's not true. The pen was open when I got there. I was trying to get Santana out."

Contreras winced at my mention of the dead man's name.

"I'm sorry," I hurried to say. "I'm so sorry, I forgot I'm not supposed to . . ."

"It's all right," he said. "You're not from here. I might break some of your cultural traditions, too," he went on forcing a small smile onto his broad face. "We are the ones who have to keep our own traditions. We don't expect others to do it for us."

"I really am so sorry."

"Don't say any more about it," Contreras said, patting my shoulder. "I really do understand. Listen, maybe I can help you. You know, my brother is the governor of the pueblo. I'll talk to him. Tell me what happened, and I'll take the story to him. Sometimes it helps if someone who knows our ways does the talking."

Mountain yipped from the back of the car, complaining of being left out of all the activity up front. Contreras tipped his head, trying to see into the rear of the Suburban, but my position in the driver's seat prevented that.

I took the wolf's interruption as a cue to leave. I felt uncomfortable sitting there, not knowing how much I should say, who I could really trust. I wasn't even supposed to be at the pueblo, and I didn't want to make the situation worse than it already was. "Thanks, Hunter," I said. "I'd really appreciate that. But I'm late to meet my friend. Can I talk to you another time?"

He looked disappointed. "I guess. But this thing is really heating up."

"Right," I said. "But this is my friend's car, and I borrowed it from her. I've got to get it back. She'll be waiting."

"Okay," Contreras said. "Just let me know when you're ready. You know, you shouldn't be here until this thing is settled. Better head on out the gate before somebody sees you. And take care of that," he added, gesturing toward my face. He turned then and hurried away, shaking his head. I saw him draw a tobacco pouch from the pocket of his shirt as he walked quickly past the hay bales he'd been loading. He made a beeline for the cab of his pickup, hoisted his massive frame onto the seat with amazing speed and dexterity, and then he started the engine and drove away, the tailgate still down, the unsecured hay bales bouncing in the back of the bed as the truck jostled over the ruts in the field.

◄ 14 ►

The Apparition

Mountain and I struck out on the west rim trail of the Rio Grande Gorge on our usual run. Even though it was nearing the end of the day, the intense sun burned my bare back around the edges of my running bra. I paced myself due to the heat, stopping frequently to give the wolf water from the tube of my CamelBak, and varying my speed when I felt myself overheating. We had a fairly set route that went out about a mile and a half on open ground, at which point we always cut across the high rim of the gorge, and went back along the narrow rim trail another mile to the starting point. As I ran the open part of the path, sweat streamed down my forehead and stung the lacerations on my face.

From the rim of the gorge, which carved through a high mesa above the Taos Valley, I could see a beautiful panorama of mountain ranges as I ran, the high desert floor beneath the mountains, and the small town of Taos nestled against the Sangre de Cristos in a low basin nearly fifteen miles away. Deep below me, in a slender canyon lined with sheer rock, was the Rio Grande. The turquoise sky held only a few puffy white clouds, and the bright sun cast an elongated twenty-foot shadow of my figure before me as I went. I reached my turnaround, where the rim trail narrowed and clung to the edge, occasionally curving through outcroppings of rock and dipping into the gorge a few feet against slick basalt walls, always rising again to the very rim. I stopped to lean against a large boulder for some shade, jacking one foot back against it and breathing hard. I mopped at my forehead with one arm.

The harsh contrast of deep, dark shadow and brilliant, sunlit patches of scorched earth strained my eyes. Here in the long eclipse of this boulder, it was cool and very dark, the air around me almost gray. Beyond the silhouette it cast, there was a fiery, white glare of sun on desert grass and stones in the open ground I'd just crossed. Winded and tired, I began to feel a little disoriented looking from one to the other. I forced myself back onto the loop, moving into the narrow rim trail that would lead me back to my Jeep, ready to complete the course, thinking it would be dark soon if I didn't keep a good pace. Just as I rolled into a jog again, Mountain darted out ahead of me and then pulled up abruptly right in my path, as if someone had yanked on his brake. I nearly tripped over him. The hair on the back of his neck rose in a ridge, and he pulled his lips back from his teeth and uttered a low growl as he stared at an outcropping of boulders near the canyon rim ahead and slightly above us.

I followed his gaze, but saw nothing in particular. Mountain growled again.

"What's up, buddy?" I asked.

He quickly darted around behind me and pulled into a tight heel beside me, his neck touching my left thigh. His hair continued to stand all along his back, and he mouthed again, pulling his lips back and baring his teeth. I had never seen him show any aggression before and I didn't know quite what to do. I reached down and patted him, stroking his neck, but he nudged my hand away.

I shook my head in confusion. "C'mon, Mountain," I urged, and began jogging in place. "Let's go. Gonna be dark soon."

But he didn't hear me. He postured aggressively in the direction of the outcrop and refused to move from his turf.

I looked once more, still not seeing what had upset him. I decided to walk ahead and show the wolf there was nothing to fear. I took a few steps and felt the hair on my forearms tingle. A faint, cool breeze suddenly wafted over the rim of the gorge, where there was nothing but shadow now, the sun too low to illuminate that deep crevice. I shivered, the sweat still standing on my upper back and shoulders. I stopped and looked back at Mountain. He whimpered at me.

"Look, I don't see whatever it is you're afraid of," I said. "I'm gonna go check it out." I wagged my arm at him. "C'mon. Go with me."

He lowered his head, his hair still standing on end. He remained planted.

I turned then to walk ahead and saw a glimpse of movement, as if something large had just darted from one of the boulders across the open narrow section of trail to behind the stone on the opposite side. I caught only a trace of shadow, no image, but my impression was that of something weightless, dark, like a bat or a gigantic moth, some creature of flight.

"It's probably nothing," I said aloud, but not so much to reassure Mountain as myself. "Anybody there?" I called. I took a few steps forward. "Who's up there?"

As if on cue, another breeze stirred, this one making a low wailing sound in the sage scrub along the rim of the gorge. I smelled rocks cooling, exuding the day's heat. I tasted metal in my mouth from overexertion. Again, I shivered.

Mountain growled, this time viciously, a serious warning. I froze, now trusting his instincts as my senses opened wider.

The sun's rays, low against the western horizon, made a penumbra around the giant boulders ahead, and the ground between them and me lay in darkness. I looked around, noticing the pink glow of the high mountains north of Taos. Pink time. Sunset. It would be dark in minutes and this rim trail would become a dangerous precipice to walk or run without light.

I retreated a few steps to stand beside Mountain and take his collar in my left hand. He stood, unmoving, in the same low crouch he had held for what seemed like an eternity now. I considered whether to go back—or skirt the rim and head for open, high ground. In my mind, I searched the contents of my CamelBak pack for a weapon, and remembered I had a good-sized pocketknife in there. I reached to unhook the waist strap.

And then I saw him.

He stepped onto the trail for only a moment, the sun behind him, illuminating the fine hairs of his fur robe. His face was encased in the mouth of an enormous brown bear, the teeth bared and the large black nose extending out beyond the man's forehead as if the bear had swallowed the man and they had become one. The immense arms and claws of the pelt hung against the man's bare chest. His face was in shadow, but I saw brilliant red claw marks on both cheeks and two black eyes peering angrily at me. Around his neck, he wore a long necklace of giant bear claws, at least a dozen of them. In his left hand, he held a lance, and he wore nothing else but a loincloth with sprigs of cedar tucked in the waist.

In the next instant, I saw only a shadow where he had stood, and the deepening gray cast of cool, retreating light filtering between the boulders.

Mountain lunged from beside me and pulled out of my grasp. He bolted for the space where the Indian had stood, but found nothing. He sniffed persistently around the large stones, looking for a sign, his back still a ridge of punklike spikes of hair. I realized as I watched him that I had been standing for some time with my mouth open. I closed it and walked toward the gap, joining Mountain in his search. There was no evidence that anyone had been there, no footprints in the dusty trail, nothing.

Just as I was about to give up, I spotted red markings on one of the boulders. I stepped back and to one side to take in the full image. An ancient-looking red pictograph appeared to have been painted into the stone with blood. It depicted an anthropomorphic figure, nearly life-size. Part man and part bear, the figure wore a necklace of claws and held a raised staff.

I've seen this same image before, I thought. *Where was it?*

Then I remembered: *It was in the ruins.*

While I pondered this, the red painting faded like moisture evaporating from a hot surface. The rock's veneer became a blank, gray slab.

I shook with a deep, involuntary shudder.

"Time to get back," I told Mountain, and we broke into a fast-paced run, neither of us tired now.

◀ 15 ▶

The Ruins

In my first year with the BLM, I'd been assigned to a sector of land on the northern aspect of Sacred Mountain. Just off a two-lane road headed for the Colorado border, an unassuming stretch of sage and chamisa pasture was cordoned off with barbed wire. Some of the locals knew what lay beyond. They needed a good four-wheel drive vehicle, preferably one they didn't mind risking to scratches, dents, and maybe even a damaged oil pan. The heartiest among them would open an inconspicuous cattle gate and drive through, closing it carefully behind them lest their secret be discovered. Then they would grind their way up a gradual ascent, wind and turn and twist as they climbed, dip through ruts and ease over rocks in the red dirt track, scrape through stands of juniper and piñon and hear the paint scratching, claw their way across red dirt washes that ran like rivers in the monsoon season but were dry gulches the rest of the year, bang and jolt and jostle and dip and tip and list and yaw over the roughest terrain around, rising toward the top. And if they survived this two-hour ordeal without getting stuck, breaking down, bottoming out, giving up, or going back, they would be rewarded with a beautiful, remote, and largely unspoiled treasure—a camp high on a canyon rim among ancient ruins.

They say the Indigo River used to run through here, forming this deep gorge. The cliffs on the south-facing slope of the canyon were dotted with ruins and ceremonial caves. The People who once lived here hunted the high mesas above, planted corn in the mountain valleys, and drew water from the river. Thus, they had everything they needed. But one day, the river turned away, cutting through rocks and boulders in the other direction, twisting through arroyos and bubbling down slopes until a little brook flowing down into the valley land below was formed. The People followed the water, and it showed them a new place to live. They no longer needed to dwell in caves or behind piled stone walls under overhangs of rock. The hallowed water from the falls led them to a beautiful valley nestled at the base of Sacred Mountain. And so Tanoah Pueblo was built, and the People came to live there.

Now the canyon above was dry and desolate. High on each side of the ravine were ruins of round houses made from stacked rocks— lookout stations to protect from attacking tribes. A courageous modern-day traveler who made it this far could make camp next to one of these ruins and watch the moon rise over the peaks on one edge of this wide split in the earth, then see it set over the summit of Sacred Mountain on the other side. And an even more brave, hale, and athletic adventurer could cross the narrow wash atop the mouth of the chasm and then skirt the rim on the other side and find ways to navigate the ledges and stretches of sheer rock face to get to the many aboriginal sites. It was difficult and dangerous climbing, but the mystery—the lure of the silent, empty ruins—was irresistible.

Wild Indigo

And so, one day when I was just doing my job, I rode a paint mare named Redhead up to the canyon rim ruins. I had packed in gear and provisions for a quiet night among the ancient spirits. I arrived close to dusk and worked fast to settle my horse and roll out my sleeping bag. I built a campfire on a flat of stone overlooking the seven-hundred-foot drop down into the gorge. It was midsummer, hot days and cold nights up here close to the stars. I could hear water running below me, a spring or mountain seep falling on rock. I ate jerky and drank from my canteen while an enormous pink-gold moon floated up over the rim and bathed the canyon with rosy light. A demoiselle rose like a church spire above the lip of the cliff wall, a stem of stone-colored purple and terra-cotta, indigo and gray, with a perfect red-clay turban for a hat. Coyotes howled a call to prayer.

That night, I lay on flat rock and looked at the sky. Even with a full moon, I saw dozens of shooting stars. There was no sound except that of wind and water, the crackle of piñon wood as it burned inside a ring of stones nearby. I smelled *trementina,* cooling rock, juniper sap, the wonderful charred scent of my campfire.

In the stillness of that night, I could imagine the People doing ceremony in one of the caves, building a fire as I had, and singing and dancing to celebrate life and its wondrous mystery. I envisioned them making simple offerings to gods that inspired both devotion and fear.

In the morning, I broke camp early, scattered the ashes of my fire, and rode down the rim a ways to look through my binoculars at the dozens of ruins on the opposite side. One place in particular interested me—a narrow ledge perhaps four feet wide with part of a stacked rock wall still intact. Above it, on a sheer slab of cliff face, a prodigious petroglyph loomed like the face of the moon. It was a large circle with eyes and a smile and a headdress. I decided to follow the lip of the canyon back to my campsite, then cross the wash and head along the opposite rim. Perhaps I could see a way to get down to that ruin.

I tied Redhead in the shade of a twisted old juniper near the only suitable place I could find to drop down into the gorge. Wearing my backpack and good leather gloves, I lowered myself between two giant boulders and started climbing, hand and foot, down the cliff wall. I worked at this for more than two hours, climbing deep into the ravine, across ledges, back up a rock-slide area, then over a huge, precariously placed round of stone to a spot where I could get a handhold up to the narrow ledge that led to the ruin I sought.

I passed several other ruins as I worked my way along the face of the canyon wall. On some, brass markers indicated their registration as archaeological sites. Small corncobs spilled out of round, stacked rock storage silos built into cliff overhangs. Pot shards littered the sites.

In one place, a shattered ledge led to a pond that had formed deep in the mouth of a high stone overhang, a basin that reached back into the belly of rock that made up the wall. The lagoon was no doubt fed by the seep that I'd heard running in the night. Reeds and grasses grew out of the edges of the pool. I could almost see the People wading there, the women washing pots, the children splashing in the water that collected in this stone depression hundreds of feet above the floor of the gorge.

The ledge had given way in places, and I took a detour downslope to go around some giant stones. On the other side, I found that I needed to pull myself up by my upper body alone to regain the ledge. My boots perched on a narrow mantle of basalt. I saw no way to use my feet or legs. I found myself fearful and off balance. There was no other route up, and the only alternative was to go down. I wasn't even sure I could go back the way I came, since I couldn't see to place my feet. I clung to the outcropping and studied my possibilities. I knew that if I lost my grip before I got my boots on that shelf, I would not be able to keep from falling to my death. I had gotten myself into a real predicament.

Wild Indigo

Finally it seemed there was nothing to do but to take the risk and try to hoist my body up to the overhang. Perhaps because no one was around, I found myself whimpering under my breath. My hands and arms were trembling. I sucked in my gut, rose up on my toes, gave a little jump, and pulled my weight up to where my chest mashed into the rim of the ledge. I swung my right leg and got the tip of my boot to lodge, shoulder height, on the rock, then pressed and pulled and hauled my body over the edge and onto the foot-wide outcrop of stone, flat on my face, lying down. I lay there for a moment quietly celebrating, sniffing back tears, until I realized that I was facing the wrong direction. I would have to stand up on the thin shelf, cling to the rock face, and change directions. I waited for courage, but it never came. Eventually, I resigned myself to the task. Carefully gauging my balance as I went, I cautiously maneuvered my body into an about-face. I edged forward on the ledge to the place I had spied through my binoculars.

There was another body-lift ahead of me, this one easier than the last. I pressed my hands into the flat floor of the narrow ruin and pushed up until I could get a knee on the ground. When I finally stood on firm base, I saw the great glyph above me like a smiley face. There were hundreds more petroglyphs on the walls: bear tracks, mountain goats, deer, badger, snakes, spirals, alien-looking people with large hands and fancy headdresses, a mountain lion, and even what appeared to be the story of a man falling off the very ledge I'd just traversed.

A magnificent and solitary glyph was etched into the cliff wall where the rock face jutted out to create the end of the room. It was a large figure, nearly life-size—and though carved, he was also stained with red tint. He stood alone: part man, part bear, wearing a necklace of what might have been bear claws. He held a raised staff to challenge all comers. He was the only figure adorned with the blood red color, or with any color, for that matter. He was partly covered with adobe plaster, and slabs of dried stucco had fallen away and mounded in a heap beneath him, as if he were emerging from a tomb where he'd been sealed in the wall.

The space was narrow, no more than four or five feet wide, and perhaps twelve feet in length. The rubble of a rock and plaster wall still held on the outer edge of this room. There was evidence of a firepit against the cliff face. There were no corn bins here, or anywhere nearby, no other dwelling-type ruins, not even any caves. There were no pot shards either. Suddenly I realized that this must have been a place of ceremony, a sort of kivalike space, with the legends recorded on the walls of the room, the venerated images of bear and deer—their sustenance and their strength—carved and pecked with loving reverence into the sanctuary itself. The one large, facelike image above all the others must certainly have represented the sun.

What rituals had been held, what sacrifices offered in this ancient and sacred place? I closed my eyes and felt the presence of the People, who lived in the shoulders of the Earth Mother, revered the Sun Father, and took energy from the deer, fortitude from the bear, and warrior spirit from the badger. The remnants of their life here were immersed in mystery and enchantment, like the crypts beneath ancient cathedrals— dark and full of wonder, hidden, forbidden, steeped in secrecy and soul. I looked again at the Sun Father image and felt transformed by its radiance. Somehow, I knew I had seen something, felt something, sensed something that was an uncommon privilege. I turned to leave and said aloud, "Thank you." My voice echoed in the ravine, and a chorus of thank-you's added to mine.

In those days, I didn't know to leave an offering, but my expression of gratitude was given with the same spirit.

When I made my way out of there and back to the canyon rim, I felt a new strength. The climb out was not as difficult as it had been coming in, yet still dangerous. But I felt a quiet calm. I had been somehow altered by what I had seen and where I had been.

◄ 16 ►

Learning Pueblo Ways

I should have been tired, but after the startling vision I'd seen on my run that evening, I returned to my cabin and moved and restacked the better part of a cord of firewood in the dark, trying to burn off some of my nervous energy. Mountain, too, remained disturbed—and rather than fall into a pleasant slumber as he normally did after a run—he paced back and forth with me as I carried the logs from one place to the other.

Later that night, I tried to write. My collection of notes from my many visits with Momma Anna lay heaped on the table before me, and I sifted through them to avoid looking at the blank page awaiting proof of inspiration. Each time I had visited, Momma Anna told me a story or demonstrated a tradition, teaching me—in the course of performing her daily routines—about what she called "Indun Way." She had warned me that writing these things down would surely bring the disapproval of the tribe, as they guarded their cultural traditions fiercely. Another author had written a book about the more beautiful and better-known Taos Pueblo, and its sister pueblo, Picuris—and those tribes had banned him from their reservations. Tanoah Pueblo joined together with Taos and Picuris and the other northern Indian pueblos and raised funds to buy all the copies of the book they could find, and then burned them in a colossal ceremonial bonfire while they circled the blaze, screeching war hoops and firing off rifle rounds. The book was now out of print. The publisher refused to reissue it, for fear of reprisal. The author never returned to Taos after his house was destroyed in a fire of suspicious origin.

I promised Momma Anna that I would not write anything personal about anyone related to the tribe, nor would I include photographs, as the banned author had done. I told her I would not mention any names, and I would not reveal anything about the religion, the dances, or any other sensitive rituals, should I succeed in getting the book published.

Momma Anna warned, "I not tell you religion. We not talk religion, we *do*. Religion not think, talk—religion doing. So you not hear me talk any religion. But they knew I tell you even this—stories, way to cook, all that—they stone me, maybe burn my house down. They take revenge my relatives. My grandchildren, even *their* children be made suffer. That man write that next other book, 'bout Taos and Picuris? Those ones he take picture, those ones talk to him—they make them leave, go live Utes. They not welcome among Tiwa, not here, not Picuris, not Taos Pueblo—not them, or any they family. It sad day when they leave the People, they can never come back."

"Why do you risk it?" I asked her.

"No one teach old ways now. They say we tell—give away power. But Tanoah children not speak Indun language. My grandma's stories, *her* grandma's stories—these dying. Our ways dying, too—feasts, baking, what we cook, thing we do." She paused for a moment, then looked me right in the eye. "I am told do this. You want learn. This way you learn, this writing. There something here you need."

And she was right about that. I needed what Momma Anna gave me— both with her teaching and by including me in her family. I was a child of a broken home, abandoned by my mother and neglected by my alcoholic father, who never recovered from my mother's leaving, and later from a farm accident that left him minus one arm. Since I was raised alone by a man absorbed in his own misery on a solitary plot of land in Kansas, I felt drawn to the strong sense of custom, tradition, and especially family that I saw in the Pueblo Indians. I looked on in wonder at the joyful gatherings of extended relatives that gave every Tanoah child a host of aunties and uncles, cousins, grandparents, godparents, and even extra parents when he came of age and could choose them as teachers and protectors. In contrast my childhood was lonely, isolated—even during the school year when I would take a bus nineteen miles to a small, one-room schoolhouse for my education and then ride the same, near-empty bus home to the end of its route. A still, vacant house awaited me when I returned each day, my father out in the fields working, an endless list of chores inscribed in my mind beckoning me. In the late evenings, I cared for my father after he came in from the fields to commence his long nights of drinking. When the supper dishes were done, I escaped upstairs to my room to read and write and dream, always lonely, always alone.

In writing a book, I was trying to capture—both for myself and for anyone who might read it—the guidance and teaching, the care, the presence, the love of a large family, the privilege of gathering with them for baking, cooking, feasting, even for burying the dead, which proved to be another forlorn chore for me when my father finally died.

I sifted through recipes for red chili and greasy bread and cookies and prune pies, all of which were coupled with stories. I had notes and drawings from the day I'd watched the plastering of the old part of the pueblo, where Grandpa and Grandma lived—how all the females, from young girls to old women, hauled water in buckets from the river to mix with mud and straw in wheelbarrows, and then applied it bare-handed to the walls of their ancient structure. I'd drawn the brush arbors the tribe erected in a circle for the summer ceremonies, told of the day I went gathering piñon nuts with the women in the family. There were more notes from the day of the bake. I had made drawings of Yohe swabbing the ashes out, and sketched the long paddle that Serena used as a peel to place and extract the loaves from the hot caves. Then I had jotted down how the women threw in day-old sliced white bread to toast on the hot stones after the handmade loaves were done baking, and later made *supa*, or bread pudding, with the toast—a delicacy rich with raisins and caramel sauce.

I sorted through these stacks of myths and stories that my pueblo mother had shared with me. I pulled out one sheet of paper and studied what I had written there. Two words caught my attention, and I read through my notes:

It is late afternoon, and Momma Anna is making posole, a rich venison stew made of plump dried kernels of hominy, elk meat, and green chiles. As she pokes at the iron skillet full of frying meat, she tells me that the men in the family are away gathering feathers for the making of prayer sticks and will be hungry when they return. I am sitting at her kitchen table writing as she browns the elk meat while the hominy bubbles in a pot with the animal's bones. "Those men. Their hands gonna be red, red, red," she mutters, shaking her head and pressing her lips together with disgust. "They get red on everything, no matter I tell them hundred times, wash hands."

"Why will their hands be red?" I ask.

She grabs a long stick and stirs at the cauldron of posole. "They make eagle feathers, give to Red Bear."

I jumped up from my own table in my cabin and dropped the paper on the pile before me. I hurried to the door and grabbed my jean jacket. Mountain, who had been dreaming restlessly on the floor beneath my feet, rose to join me. I reached down to pet him, then went to the refrigerator and removed the big bone Jesse had given me. The wolf leaped up and sat before me as I unwrapped it, a long strand of drool growing from his lip. I handed it to him, and though he was clearly excited by the juicy treat, he took it almost reluctantly. He knew the drill; this meant I was leaving.

"I know, I know," I said. "I'm sorry—this isn't fair, is it? But my Jeep still doesn't have a door on it, and there's no way I can tie you to the back this time. I hate to leave you, buddy, but I promise I'll make it up to you as soon as I get my car fixed." I felt a horrible pang of guilt as I went out the door.

There were still two torches burning at the cemetery as I approached. I pulled over and parked under a tree more than a hundred yards before it, cut my lights, and got out and walked the rest of the way. Two egg-shaped mounds covered in blankets were perched near the torches. When I came toward them, one of them unfolded and rose to full height. It was Momma Anna. The other figure stirred, but Momma Anna reached down and signaled, saying, "Shhhhh."

I drew near my medicine teacher and looked down into her face, unable to make out her expression in the darkness, even with the torches just yards away. "Momma Anna, I'm so sorry—"

But she interrupted me harshly. "You should not come, that yellow hair! Why you come? You know you should not be here."

"I have to talk to you."

Just then, the other figure stirred again, and I saw Grandma Bird peer out of her blanket wrap. "You bathe spring?" she asked.

I had forgotten about her instructions to bathe and rub myself with the herbs she'd given me. So much had happened! "No, I—"

Then Momma Anna barked at me again, "Why you come, you not do what Grandma said? You maybe bring us all trouble."

"I'm sorry," I stammered. There was nothing more I could say. I rocked back and forth on my two feet, trying to decide whether to press my luck and stay or simply go away.

"Sit down!" Momma Anna ordered. She fumbled around on the ground and found a bag, from which she pulled a piece of cloth. "Cover hair."

I did as she told me, then looked around in the black night. "Are you the only ones here?" I asked.

She sat down between me and Grandma Bird. "Others at feast. They come back soon. We have only short time, then I take Grandma, put her bed. Someone else stay tonight, I rest. Two days, my son make journey. He will go to the ridge and wait."

Suddenly I realized the selfishness of my mission. Without regard for Momma Anna's suffering, I had come to ply her for information. I felt foolish. "I'm so sorry for your loss," I said.

"Three days, ancestors come sundown for feast. After, they take him with them to other side of ridge." She raised an arm draped with blanket and pointed in the direction of Sacred Mountain. "Then you, me, we talk again."

"Okay," I said, and I rose to go.

She stood, too. She took my arm and steered me away from Grandma Bird, who remained wrapped in an upright bundle on the ground. Momma Anna's grip was tight and her fingers—even through her blanket and my jacket—dug deeply into my flesh. "I talk you. I need help something."

I turned to look at her.

She was facing me, but I could not make out her expression. We had walked away from the only light, and the moon had not yet risen. The night was as dark as the inside of Jerome Santana's coffin. "My son spirit almost gone," she said, "but there still mystery."

"I know."

"You find out."

"Find out?"

"You find out."

"You mean what happened?"

"Yes, you find out."

I swallowed. "Okay, I'll do my best."

She threw off her grip. "Why you say that? *I do my best . . .*," she mimicked me in a high, whiny voice. "You find out!"

"Okay."

"Why you come? You know they not happy you. They talk bad about you."

I was embarrassed, but I dared not lie to my medicine teacher. "It was selfish," I said, looking down at the ground. "I wanted to ask you a question. No, two questions."

"You know we don't like question over here."

"I know, I'm sorry."

"What you want?"

"Well, first—did you leave something in my car?"

She shook her head no.

"A stick, a carved willow stick, painted, with feathers on it?"

"You got a *nachi*?" she gasped.

"A nachi? Is that what it's called?"

"What color paint?"

"Blue with yellow."

She drew in a sharp breath. "Eeeeee."

"What?"

"What kind feathers?"

"Nighthawk, I think."

"Eeeeee."

"What?"

"Don't speak this again. Don't show nachi anyone—could hurt them. You bathe herbs. I tell you few days what do with nachi."

"What is it, exactly?"

"What next other you want ask?"

Typical. Questions never worked with Momma Anna. I felt reluctant even to tell her what else I had come for. "I wanted to ask you who Red Bear is."

Just then a car drove by on the road to the pueblo gates, its headlamps sweeping us briefly with light.

Momma Anna drew in a sharp breath. "Your face! Why you don't tell me that?" She raised a hand to point at the claw marks on my cheek, then fixed her lips together hard, clearly angry at me. "You got mark of bear!" She reached up and jerked the cloth off my head, then turned to go back to the graveside. "Red Bear war god," she muttered softly under her breath, without turning around.

◄ 17 ►

Saving Face

When I got back to my cabin, Mountain had taken his revenge. He'd scratched more grooves into the inside of the door and raided the kitchen counters, turning over my coffeemaker and canisters of sugar and coffee and breaking a glass that had been left beside the sink. He'd tugged my leather jacket off the coatrack and chewed through the cuff of one sleeve, then peed on the lining. And he'd raided my laundry basket, pulling out all the dirty clothes, focusing especially on a pair of recently worn panties, which he had ripped to shreds. In the bathroom, he'd torn down the blind from the window next to the shower and chomped holes in a bottle of body lotion, my bath pillow, and a plastic tube of shower gel. He'd gathered all his objects of devastation into the center of the one main room and heaped them in a pile.

He sat enthroned in the middle of this creation when I opened the door, and he wagged his tail at me without an ounce of shame.

"Aw, Mountain! Two times in one week? You're a bad wolf!" I began to chastise him, but he paid no attention. Instead, he nervously licked and nuzzled me, his tail beating wildly and his breathing heavy, obviously only wanting reassurance that I would never, ever leave him again. I tried to make my voice harsh and rebuking, but the more I tried, the more that wolf clung to me, as if the sounds I was making were music to his ears. Frustrated, I pushed him out the door and hooked his collar to the carabiner and length of airplane wire I'd secured to the porch for times when we needed a break from one another. "You stay outside!" I commanded. But no sooner had I slammed the cabin door shut than he began scratching at it, demanding to be let back in.

I ignored him and started cleaning up the mess.

The wolf continued to pound and scrape at the door.

At least the scratches on the outside will match the ones on the inside, I thought. *I'm going to have to buy my landlord a new door before it's all over with.*

When I had hauled the broken blinds out back to the trash container and cleaned up all the mess, I let Mountain back into the cabin. I sat at the table and drank a cup of tea and ate a bowl of cereal while he nuzzled his head against my feet, just wanting the contact with me. He was panting heavily, still afraid of being abandoned again.

I moved to the floor and sat beside him. He buried his head in my lap, his tail beating on the floor. "Is that the best you can do for an apology?"

He raised his head and looked at me, lowered his ears.

"Okay, that's better." I kissed him on the nose and then held his face against my chest. Mountain rolled onto his side and let out a big sigh. "I'm never going to abandon you, buddy. I just had to run an errand. I'm always going to come right back if I have to leave you here—I'll never leave you for long, I promise."

He pushed his head against me, then pressed his muzzle into my hand, demanding more pets and rubs. Finally, I stretched out on the floor beside him, pressing my body against his back. He calmed with this and lay still, his eyes open, his breathing quick but heavy.

"You're worthless," I said as I rubbed my hand along his side.

He wagged his tail with delight. To Mountain, my voice was like an angel singing, no matter what I said. All he wanted was to be near me, to smell me and feel me and hear me.

It wasn't bad being loved so dearly, even if it meant a lot of my stuff got shredded.

The sound of the car motor woke me but I didn't move from under the covers. Mountain rose and ran to the door.

A few soft knocks.

"It's open," I called. Mountain gave a little whimper of glee and I heard his tail whacking loudly against the cabin door as it swung open. Kerry's lean silhouette was framed in the moonlit portal as he reached down, patting the wolf and speaking softly: "Hey there, Mountain. How's my pal? How are you doing?" Then Kerry called to me through the dark: "I saw your lights were out, but I just wanted to make sure you're okay."

"I'm okay," I called back.

"So, I'll let you get back to sleep then," he said, hesitantly.

"Okay."

"Unless you want company . . . or anything."

I considered.

"Or I could just come in and kiss you good night, and then go."

"Okay," I said.

I heard the door shut and his boots thud across the floor. "Man, it's pitch-black in here, where are you?"

"You're getting warm," I teased, and then I felt him groping along the bed. He found my arm, then my shoulder. His hands were cold.

"You're all toasty. It's kind of chilly out there."

"Yeah, I know, it will be fall before we know it."

He brushed the side of my neck with the backs of his fingers. "Turn on your lamp there and let me see your beautiful face," he said.

"No."

"Aw, c'mon."

"What's this—*you* want the light on? You spend every spare moment in a dark room developing photos."

"I want to see who I'm kissing. I don't just kiss any stranger in the dark."

"You know it's me. Take it or leave it."

He sat on the side of the bed and was quiet a moment. "What is it you don't want me to see?"

"I don't know what you're talking about."

"You do, too." He got up and walked to the door, where he flipped on the switch that powered the ceiling fan and light.

I raised an arm and winced at the sudden shock to my eyes. "Hey, cut that out!" I clutched at the covers, but too late.

"Oh, babe." He whispered it.

I didn't reply.

We stared at each other, measuring with our silence. Finally he came to the bed again and sat down beside me.

"Don't ask me," I warned.

He blew out air in frustration. "Okay," he said, and waved his arms in disgust as he got up. He walked over to the table, pulled out a chair, and straddled it from behind, facing the bed. He shook his head.

I felt vulnerable, lying supine. I pulled myself up to a sitting position and leaned against the aspen logs that framed the headboard. I kept the covers drawn up to my neck as if my secret were beneath them.

"Have you been to a doctor?" he finally managed.

"No."

He shook his head again. Then his face softened, and he cocked his head slightly to one side and raised those thick eyebrows. "Babe, I'm going to ask."

"No, don't ask. Please, don't ask. Everybody asks. I'm sick of it."

He twisted his head the other way, and then he gave me that crooked little half grin of his. "Then I won't ask."

"Good."

"But you have to tell me, babe. Otherwise, I'll have to ask."

A pot of coffee later, we sat at the table, our hands twisting together in a kind of passionate petting that seemed to be the trademark of our relationship. He held my fingers and stroked them, then rubbed the back of my hand with his fingers while I tickled his palm with mine. "You need to see a doctor," he said.

"How'm I going to explain it?"

"It doesn't matter. You just make something up. You don't want it to scar for life, do you?"

I pulled my hand away, got up, and went to the little tin-framed mirror beside the door. I twisted my chin and examined my visage. "Sometimes I think I kind of like it," I said. "Except I get tired of everyone asking about it."

"What about Tecolote? Can she give you something for it?"

I returned to my seat at the table. "I hadn't thought about that. I'm almost afraid to go see her again."

"No doubt. I would be."

He stood up then and leaned over the table to kiss me, brushing his lips first across my forehead, and then on the bridge of my nose. Suddenly, he was softly brushing the wounds on my face with his lips. And then he kissed my mouth. "We wasted a lot of time talking. We could have been doing other things." His hand moved to my breast. I could feel the warmth through my nightie.

"Want to start over?" I said, reaching for his jeans, pulling at his belt.

After our lovemaking, Kerry sat on the side of the bed. "I better go. I have some developing to do. I'm taking some of my landscapes down to that gallery in Santa Fe in the morning."

I rubbed his back. His skin smelled warm, like clean sweat. "You never sleep."

"I sleep."

"Not much."

He stood up. "I sleep enough. Sleep's overrated."

I stood, too, and followed him to the door.

He turned before he opened it, but he didn't speak.

"I'll be all right," I said.

His hand cupped my neck and he pulled me toward him, kissing me sweetly on the nose. "You're better than all right," he said, with that grin of his. Then, his hand on the doorknob, he hesitated once more. "Hey, do you know some reporter named Noah Sherman?"

"Why?"

"He called and left a message for me at the ranger station."

"He called you?"

"Yeah, left a message—just his name and number. I was in the field."

I shook my head with disgust. "Yeah, I know him. He was at the BLM when I got suspended."

"I thought it might have been about that whole deal. Don't worry. I got nothin' to say to him. Go back to bed, now, okay, babe?" He went out the door, pulling it softly shut behind him.

Later, unable to sleep, I rose and wrapped myself in a flannel sheet. I took the bag of herbs and the turkey feather Grandma Bird had given me and went out the door. Mountain loped ahead of me as I headed for the little stream that crossed forest land adjacent to the property on which my cabin was situated. Locals called this stream La Petaca, which technically meant cigar or tobacco pouch, because of the little pockets or basins along its course that filled up with brownish water. It was a small spring-fed brook that frequently went dry in early summer and then was usually revived again by the late summer monsoons. The late-rising quarter moon lit my path and made the water glimmer silver. I threw off my clothes and waded into the narrow rivulet, which was icy cold. I splashed myself with the water and shivered with the shock of it. Mountain drank a little from the flow and then stood on the bank watching me as if he thought I was insane. When I had wet myself down from head to toe, I stood on a rock on the bank, shaking with cold, and rubbed the rough herbs over my skin, barely touching the wounds on my face, but rubbing more vigorously on my torso. I felt a sudden glow of warmth, as if a fire had been lit within me. My scars, in particular, began to radiate and when I put my fingers to them, they felt as if they were burning. I held up the turkey feather and closed my eyes, wishing Jerome Santana a happy journey beyond the ridge. Then I threw it into the current and watched it float away. I wrapped up in the flannel sheet and Mountain and I made our way back to the cabin.

◄ 18 ►

The Hole in the Top of Everything

Before I went back inside, I stopped by my Jeep and pulled out the paper parcel I'd tucked beneath the passenger seat. I opened it carefully and re-examined the nachi. I wondered what meaning it held for the giver—and for me. Momma Anna had seemed alarmed when I told her about it, but I felt a sense of comfort when I handled the object, even looked at it. I fingered the small bear fetish and thought about the tiny pottery bears my medicine teacher made to sell to tourists and at art shows.

One day early in the spring, she had asked me to take her to go get clay for her pottery making. It was Naxöpana, Ash Moon, the middle of March. We'd driven far up in the mountains near the pueblo of Picuris—another Tiwa village—to a place in the side of a slope where snowmelt had eroded the ground. A small, seasonal stream, fed by the dissipating snowpack, gushed through a wide swath of red mud. There, using large coffee cans, we harvested micaceous clay from the banks of the brook, filling five-gallon plastic paint buckets. When we had three of them packed full, we used a hammer to tamp down the fitted lids, so the contents would not ooze out while being transported back to Tanoah Pueblo. Momma Anna tied a sturdy rope to the handle of one of the buckets, and then, holding the other end, clambered up the incline to the road. "You stay," she ordered.

Still holding the end of the rope, she went to the car and took a bag of cookies she'd been munching from out of the passenger seat. She fished one hand into the sack and brought out a few of the treats, then threw them down the hill toward me. "Put on bank, where we dig clay. We take something, we give something back." I watched her bend the rope around a ponderosa pine trunk and use it as a come-along to topple and then begin to drag the heavy bucket up the sluice of mud toward the top. Her slow, labored progress was painful to watch.

"Here," I said, making my way up to the road and grabbing the rope ahead of where she gripped it. "Let me do that. We'll trade places."

She tipped her head a little, as if she were uncertain whether I could actually manage the job. Then she shrugged and headed back down to the streambed. I began to draw the bucket upward, hand over hand. I felt enormous resistance from the weight of the pail and the wet mud I was pulling it through. I stopped for a moment, looping the rope around the tree and tying a clove hitch. "Hang on a second," I called to Momma Anna, who was looking at me quizzically. "I'm going to get some gloves." I went to my Jeep and pulled out a pair and put them on.

I looked down and saw my medicine teacher smirking at me.

"Okay, I'm ready now. I got it." Again, I worked to draw the bucket upward, and it felt like I was trying to bring the *Queen Mary* into port through a sea of gelatin. I breathed hard, exhaling sharply with every tug. Soon, I broke a sweat. When the container was up high enough for me to reach the handle, once again I looped the rope around the tree and tied it to secure it. Then I tried to lift the bucket. It must have weighed seventy or eighty pounds. I ended up dropping into a deep squat and then dragging it onto the road. I untied my knot and threw the standing end of the rope back down to Momma Anna. "Whew!" I said, unbuttoning my flannel shirt and then lifting the neck of the T-shirt I wore underneath over my face to mop the sweat off my brow. "Those things are heavy!"

Momma Anna gave me a wry smile. "That why I ask you come." She chuckled a little to herself, then went to tie the rope on another bucket handle.

A few days later, I visited Momma Anna and found her out working on the *portal* in back of her house. It was a cold day, and she had a warm fire in her woodstove inside. She was using the tip of a knife to carve eyes in one of a host of small clay bears she had formed. I smiled at the natural, childlike wonder expressed in these little, unrefined bears. They were so unpretentious, and yet so full of reverence for this animal and its spirit. After she'd finished the eyes, Momma Anna took a straight pin and made a tiny puncture in the top of the bear's head. I noticed that each of them had the same mark. "Why do you do that?" I asked.

She gave no answer, but lifted a seed pot that she'd prepared for firing. It featured a lizard circling the tiny opening in the top of the pot. "Old day, we all have door to house in roof," she said. She set the seed pot down, then picked up a small orb with a tiny, perfect perforation in its crown, holding it out in the palm of her hand, looking it over. "Time before time, the People come out of hole in Indigo Falls. We find bear here. Deer. Elk. Rabbit. Blossom of medicine plant. Indun tea. Bird. Water. Everything we need. We stay until we die. Then, go back beyond ridge, inside Earth, deep inside. Baby start life with hole in top of head, only soft skin there. This how Creator blow in breath of life. That how life come out and into all things. We need hole in top of everything to re-mind where we came, where we next go." She picked up a pinch of cornmeal from a little dish on the table and offered it to the five direc-tions, beginning and ending with the east. She took another pinch and made a circle above her head, tossing the meal into the air. She offered me the dish, and I did the same.

We carried the prepared pottery pieces into the house on cookie sheets. Momma Anna opened the door to her woodstove and used a blunt-ended ash shovel to distribute the coals evenly. She motioned for me to hand her a newspaper-wrapped bundle on a nearby table. I did as she requested. She unwrapped the package. Inside was a variety of dried ani-mal dung: what looked to be a cow pie, some kind of bird droppings, and possibly dog or coyote turds. Momma Anna plucked a long black and sil-ver hair from the top of her head with one hand while she balanced the open parcel with the other. She gestured for me to take the latter, so I opened my palms and she set the paper and its contents in them. She snatched up one of the dog turds and quickly knotted the hair around it, then threw it into the fire. Then, using her bare hands, she fed the other excreta in. She went to the table and picked up some branches of local desert sage. She rubbed her hands with these, then closed her eyes and tilted her head toward the roof. After a moment, she threw the sage in the fire, too, and I smelled the pungent incense of its smudge. Then she care-fully set the pottery, one item at a time, in the blade of the small ash shovel and loaded the items into the woodstove, as if it were a kiln. When all were safely nestled inside, she closed and clamped down the woodstove door and turned to me.

"Wash hands!" she barked.

◄ 19 ►

See No Evil

After my midnight dip in La Petaca, and my rubdown with Grandma's herbs, I slept like I'd been drugged. The next morning, as I was pulling down to the end of the dirt drive leading from my cabin, a motorist on the connecting gravel road flagged me over, waving his arm out the driver's-side window. I pulled alongside his sedan. He opened an I.D. wallet—he was an attorney for the Department of the Interior. "You don't have a phone," he said.

"Nope. There are no lines out this way. No line-of-sight to a cellular tower. No towers anywhere in this part of the state tall enough to go over the mountains."

"How can you live in this day and age without a phone?"

Probably a rhetorical question, but I couldn't resist. "Well, when I moved out here, the phone company told me that as soon as I had the thirty-five grand it would take to lay phone lines all the way from Tres

Piedras, they'd get me hooked up. I figured right then I could learn how to live without a phone."

He didn't seem amused. "Well, I'd like to talk to you about the stampede incident. Can we arrange a time when we could meet at the BLM office, perhaps? How about tomorrow?"

When I got to Diane's office, she was pacing the floor. "I've been trying to reach you. You don't have a phone!"

I sighed.

"There's an investigation into the stampede incident. It includes me. The Albuquerque office has instructed me to write a narrative, supporting the determination that it was a suicide. There's a shit-storm coming."

"Why does it involve you? They're saying I caused the stampede, not you."

"I don't know, but I'll guarantee you if my agency thinks someone has to take a fall to appease the tribe, it'll be me."

"We'll get that Sam Dreams Eagle kid to make a statement. He's the one that saw the buffalo out of the confine and told me about them. He can prove that I didn't cause the stampede, and that ought to put this thing right all the way around."

We took Diane's fed car to the pueblo, and Mountain rode in the backseat like a dignitary being chauffeured. I'd promised to use a lint roller to clean up all the hair from the upholstery after we were done. I rode hunched down in the passenger seat, only poking my head up occasionally to give Diane directions. We took the back roads, and wound from the end of Momma Anna's dirt lane onto the two-lane, rutted track through the meadow to where Sam Dreams Eagle lived.

Wild Indigo

We waited a long time before an old woman answered the door, and when she did, her apparent loss of hearing and limited English made communication a trial. I let Diane do the talking, as we had agreed.

"Does a boy named Sam Dreams Eagle live here?" Di said.

The plump little grandmother wrung her hands in her apron and looked at the dirt floor. "No English."

I nudged Diane and whispered, "Ask about Rolando, his brother."

Diane raised her voice to address the elder: "Where is Rolando?"

"Not here," she muttered.

"Sam's not here? Or Rolando's not here?" Diane persisted.

The old woman raised her hand to her ear and turned a strained face to the side to hear better.

"Sam? Rolando?" Diane nearly shouted.

"Nobody home," the old woman said, obviously nervous.

"Do you know where we can find them?"

"School," the elder said, then held up a finger for us to wait. She shuffled away from the door, back into the dark hovel of her old adobe. She came back with a battered calendar from the First State Bank. She pointed at a date nearly ten days ago. The only notation on the calendar was in the block for that day. Someone a good deal more literate than this crone seemed to have written *St. Catherine Indian School, Santa Fe* in neat blue hand printing. "Indun School. Santa Fe." She grinned, showing bare gums. She nodded her head up and down.

Diane looked at me, puzzled. I took over: "But they come home sometimes, right? I saw them here yesterday. I talked to both of them."

"Nobody home," she said again. She pointed again to the box on the calendar. "Indun School. Santa Fe." Then she grinned meekly and began to slowly close the door, bobbing her head up and down—as if to smile and do it slowly would not be taken as rude.

Diane and I looked at each other in bafflement as the door shut.

135

"Look, I can prove that Sam Dreams Eagle wasn't in school since then. Let's go to Momma Anna's house. It's right up at the end of the road, where we got off the graded surface. I hate to bother her while she's grieving, but she saw Sam when he came to the house for me. She heard him say the buffalo were getting out. She'll tell you."

On the dirt porch in front of Momma Anna's house, the pack of pueblo dogs yapped and pawed at us while we waited for an answer to our knock. Mountain hung his head out of the back window of Diane's car and yipped in jealousy. I tried to ignore him. The heat of the afternoon was abated by the cool shade of the brush arbor and the limbs of a nearby apple tree. Momma Anna peered through the window next to the door and gave me a stern look. She opened the door just a few inches. "I'm so ti-ired," she moaned in a high-pitched voice, making the word *tired* into two, painfully long syllables. This was a common tone used by the women of the tribe when they were giving notice of suffering or complaint.

"I know, Momma Anna," I apologized. "I'm so sorry to bother you. I just need to take a minute or two of your time." I expected her to invite us in as she always did—this was a custom even for strangers that came to her door. The Tanoah way was to be generous and welcoming with all and to give abundantly to everyone, especially strangers.

"I not feel good," she said. "Maybe next time." She wore the same sheepish grin that signified the gentle, passive resistance often practiced by her people.

"Just tell my friend here about Sam Dreams Eagle coming to the door on Saturday. Just tell her real quickly what you saw and what he said, and we'll be on our way."

"I not know," Momma Anna said, clasping a hand to her head

while she kept the other one firmly on the door to keep it from opening any farther. "Lot been happening, me. I not remember good. My mind tired."

My mouth dropped open in surprise. For a minute I couldn't speak. Then I drew in a big breath. "You know Sam Dreams Eagle, right, Momma Anna? The little boy who came here? The one who interrupted us when we were making jerky, and I had to leave because he said the buffalo were getting out?"

Momma Anna shook her head and pressed her lips together in a frown. She kept shaking her head as she looked down and said, "No more. I am old. I need take nap." She quietly but firmly pressed the door closed.

Diane cocked her head at me and frowned. "Strike two."

We turned to leave, but a flash of shiny red behind Momma Anna's house caught my eye. I looked to the back lot, to Jerome Santana's place. A familiar red Mustang convertible was parked in front of the house, the same one I'd seen Gilbert Valdez driving on Sunday morning.

As we were turning onto Rattlesnake Road to leave the pueblo, I raised myself from the low crouch I'd been folded in and sat upright in the car. "Wait! Stop!" I told Diane, and she braked, raising a cloud of dust. "Back up a little, to the edge of that *latilla* fence back there."

On the side of the road at the corner of the fence was a small brown boy with his head buried in his knees as he squatted in the dirt. I opened the car door and got out. The child raised his head to look at me. I saw tears streaking his dusty face. "Angel, what's wrong?"

He looked at me but didn't speak. Instead, he folded his face into his arms as if he were ashamed of his tears.

I squatted down beside him and stroked the crown of his head gently.

"My friend is hiding from me. I can't find him."

"You were playing with a friend, playing hide-and-seek?"

"I always play with him. He's hiding. I can't find him."

I patted his shoulder and stood up. "Don't give up, Angel. You'll find him."

He stood and shuffled off without speaking.

When we got back to the FBI office, Diane stopped at the front desk to pick up her messages while I went in her cubicle to use the phone.

I called Roy. "Don't come in to the office, Jamaica," he warned.

"I have an interview tomorrow with that attorney."

"Well, okay, but don't come in today. That Sherman guy—that reporter from the *Taos Times?* He's lurking around out front like we were fixing to give out cash to all comers. Just stay away from him. Let the big guns talk from here on out. We can talk some more when you come in tomorrow."

"Okay, Boss."

"And Jamaica? Stay away from the pueblo."

As I hung up, Diane appeared in the doorway with a message slip in her hand. "They're not waiting on my narrative. My field supervisor is coming up from Albuquerque tomorrow," she said. "I better put on my asbestos underwear, 'cuz I know that guy. We've got some history. He's looking to burn my ass."

◄ 20 ►

The Invitation

That afternoon at the gym, after a hapkido sparring session with Diane that left me sore in the ribs, I came outside to find Mountain, once again tied to the hitch in back, fiercely defending the territory of my Jeep against a broad-backed pueblo man I saw only from behind. The fellow had both hands in the air and was backing away from Mountain, saying, "Okay. Okay. Okay." The wolf was at the end of his leash, the hair up on the ridge of his back just as it had been on the Gorge Rim trail the previous evening, when we'd seen the apparition.

"Excuse me," I called, making for my car as quickly as I could. "What are you doing there?"

Hunter Contreras turned to face me, his palms still up as if he were under arrest. He smiled apologetically. "Oh, hi, Jamaica. I saw your Jeep. It's pretty easy to tell yours now with that door off." He fished in his shirt pocket, brought out a scrap of paper. "I was going to leave you a note."

"Hold on," I said, putting my gym bag down and taking Mountain's fully extended leash in my hand, forcing him back toward the Jeep bumper in order to create a little slack. I knelt down and stroked his chest and whispered in his ear, "It's okay, buddy. It's all right. I know this guy."

Hunter waited, shifting his weight from one foot to the other. "That's a mean dog you got there. Lot of wolf in him, huh?"

I stood up again, but Mountain lunged once more.

Contreras danced backward, even though he was well out of the range of Mountain's leash limit.

"Yeah, he's a lot of wolf," I said, "and I don't know what's been spooking him lately. He's normally not aggressive at all. But he's been a little strange this week. What's the note about?"

"Oh!" Hunter recovered, still obviously wary of Mountain. "I was going to see if we could have a cup of coffee. Remember, we said we'd try to talk? My brother being the tribal governor, I was going to take your story to him, talk to him, see what we could do about . . . maybe getting you back on good terms with the tribe."

I picked up my gym bag and put it in the back of my Jeep. Mountain remained on heightened alert. "Thanks for the invitation, Hunter. I'm sorry to put you off again, but I have to go. I'm meeting someone. Besides, I've thought about it, and I don't know what else I would tell you. A little boy came to Momma Anna's when I was there on Saturday and said the buffalo had gotten out of the fence and were wandering up into the mountains. I went out there to take a look, and . . ." I started to say Jerome Santana's name, but stopped myself this time. "And someone was in the pen with the bulls. He wouldn't come out, even when I called to him. The gate was open when I got there, and the bulls started to run. They trampled him. That's the same thing I told Ruben Rael and Sonny

Warm Hands when they arrived a minute after the whole thing happened. It's the same thing I told Officer Lobato when she got there about two minutes later. It's the same thing I told Chief Moon Eagle when he showed up about ten minutes after that. And that's what I told the FBI and the BLM. No matter what kind of spin you want to put on it—and believe me, I really appreciate your offer to try—I just don't have anything else to say."

Hunter lowered his hands and put them in his pockets. "Well, let me think. You say a boy came to tell you about the buffalo? Do you know his name?"

I was about to answer him when a pickup careened across the gravel parking lot and Bone Man jumped out of the passenger side. He hollered a thank-you to the driver, slammed the creaky door, and came around the end of the truck just as the driver peeled away, no doubt grateful to be able to breathe clean air again.

"Hey, Hunter my man!" Bone Man called, a ludicrous grin on his face. "Jamaica, hey, *¿qué pasa*, eh?" Then he made an exaggerated lurch and raised his eyebrows. "Whoa! Jamaica! What happened to your face, dude?"

Neither Hunter nor I responded, so Bone Man went on without hesitating. "Remember I warned you about some big animal coming for you, right, Jamaica? The bones were right, man. The bones were right." He reached into his shirt, pulled out the bone necklace, and started strumming along it with his fingers. He closed his eyes and started bobbing and weaving back and forth.

Hunter spoke next. "I wasn't going to say anything, Jamaica, but that looks like it might be getting infected. You should maybe see someone about that, you know?"

I touched my fingers to the claw marks, which seemed to set the skin ablaze. It felt like small rivers of fire crossing my cheek.

Bone Man emerged from his trancelike state. He stuffed the necklace back into his shirt and made a peace sign at me with his fingers. Then he turned to Hunter: "Hey, if you see your buddy and mine, Ismael Wolf-skin, tell him I have some great stuff for him: another bear skull, some good teeth and claws, some pretty nice hides, too."

Hunter acknowledged him with a scant nod. Then, turning to me, he said, "Jamaica, tomorrow the journey is over for Anna's son. The family is gathering at Grandma Bird's on Thursday night for a feast. They want you to come. Because it's a ceremony for one who passed, we will be allowed to have a small bonfire, too, even though it's Quiet Time. Will you be there?"

"I don't know. I'm not exactly welcome at the pueblo these days. I don't even know how I'd get in, and if I did, someone would spy my Jeep and usher me off the reservation."

Bone Man had been listening as if he belonged in this discourse. "That's easy!" he said. "I always have my buddy meet me at the back gate on Rattlesnake Road. He picks me up in his car and drives me in. I go in and out all the time, even when it's Quiet Time."

"I could have Serena pick you up there at the gas station," Hunter said.

"I'm not so sure I'd be welcome," I said. "Even Momma Anna has been acting strange with me lately."

"Oh, come on." Hunter smiled. "You need to be patient with her. Our customs are different. When someone passes, it's a lot of work. Someone in the family has to stay with the body constantly until the spirit makes its journey. We have to go through a four-day cleansing pro-cess. Even the home has to be properly cleaned and prepared so the spirit will feel free to leave it. Anna's been through a lot, almost no sleep, very little to eat for days. But it's mostly over now. Just a few family things. I know everyone expects to see you. And maybe you and I can talk then."

Bone Man continued to grin at us, nodding his head as Hunter spoke.

Before I could answer Contreras, Diane came out of the gym and up to our gathering. Mountain wagged his tail affectionately, and she reached down to rub his neck. "What's going on?" she asked, scanning the two men.

"Let me introduce you to these gentlemen," I said. "Diane Langstrom, this is Hunter Contreras, the Tiwa language teacher at Tanoah Pueblo."

Diane extended her hand, shook Hunter's, and said, "Hello. Pleased to meet you."

"And this"—I held out my hand in a gesture of resignation—"is Bone Man."

Langstrom looked at the filthy hippie and tilted her head to one side. "I'm not shaking your hand," she said flatly. "You the guy who runs that roadside bone pile on the way to Santa Fe?"

"I do, yes," Bone Man said, nodding his head. "Me and some friends of mine."

Diane put her hands on her hips. "Do people actually buy that nasty old crap?"

Bone Man grinned, his teeth still rimmed with rotting vegetation. "They do," he said. "One man's crap is another man's treasure!"

"You got a license to sell merchandise there?" Diane pressed.

"A license? What are you, a cop?"

"Better still." She smiled. "FBI. And I'm keeping my eye on that sorry pile of refuse you call a business. I've heard you sell some illegal stuff there—eagle feathers, whole birds of prey. Is that true?"

"Not true," Bone Man said. "Not true, man. Now, if you'll excuse me, I'm going to take a shower." He turned and walked toward the gym door.

"Good damn thing, too," Diane called after him.

Hunter spoke up then. "Listen, Jamaica, I've got to run. Why don't you give me that boy's name and I'll see if I can find him, maybe talk to him?"

Diane bristled at this. She spoke in a warning tone. "We're taking care of that, thank you." I smiled at this proprietary defensiveness of Diane's, something we at the BLM found so typical of the FBI.

Contreras held up his hands in resignation. "Okay, just trying to help." He turned to leave, walked a few steps, then turned back. "Anyway, Jamaica, I'll have Serena meet you at the gas station Thursday night about seven thirty, okay? The family will want you there." He looked at Diane and made a little nod. "It was nice to meet you, miss." Without waiting for a reply, he spun and walked toward his truck, which was parked alongside the road about twenty yards away.

"That guy's a teacher?" Di said.

"Yeah, he keeps the Tiwa language going at the pueblo. A lot of parents don't teach their children their traditional tongue anymore. He got the program going through a piggyback grant onto Jerome Santana's computer lab for pueblo youths."

"So one of them was working to get the kids ready for the future, and the other was trying to keep them in touch with the past, huh?"

"Yeah, that's about how it was. You should see Hunter with kids. He's so good with the little ones."

"Why'd he want the Dreams Eagle kid's name?"

"He said he'd try to smooth things over with the tribe for me, take my story in again himself as one of them, a voice of reason against all this trumped-up crap about how I started the stampede. His brother's the tribal governor this year."

Diane didn't respond to this, but turned to fuss over the wolf. "You don't like the big Indian man?" she said, cooing to Mountain and rubbing his ruff.

"No, I don't think he does," I said. "And that's the second one this week."

◄ 21 ►

The Carving

When Mountain and I pulled up in front of my cabin, Kerry was already waiting outside, sitting on the porch, ruggedly good-looking in jeans and a denim shirt. He rose and smiled as we approached, but he winced when he saw my face, then kissed me delicately on the lips so as not to brush my wounds. "That's getting worse," he said.

I could smell his skin, warm from the sun, his hair. He reached one hand up and tenderly brushed my cheek with the backs of his fingers, his green-flecked eyes gazing into mine. "Did you see a doctor?"

"I will. I'll make an appointment."

"When?"

"Tomorrow."

"You promise?"

"I'll do something if it's not better tomorrow," I said, and slipped out of his embrace and into the cabin. I put my hat and my big elk hide bag on the table, picked up Mountain's water dish and filled it at the sink, then put it back on the floor.

Kerry moved to the table, pulled out a chair, and sat down. "You got out of that pretty neatly."

"I don't like to promise in case I can't follow through." I moved to the table, straddled his lap, and sat down, my face right in front of his.

He laughed, nuzzled my neck, nibbled at my ear. "I can't make you do anything you don't want to do. You're too damn stubborn."

"You love it." I ran one hand through the irresistible little cowlick at the hairline over his forehead.

"I do." He grinned. "I love it." He reached one arm around my back and slid the other hand along my thigh. We kissed. And kissed again.

The baking heat of the day was beginning to relent as cool, down-slope breezes fanned through the pines outside the cabin. Gentle gusts brought the sweet, woodsy fragrance of pine sap in through the windows. Clouds shadowed the sun, leaving the one large room in a delicate, soft gray light. A raven croaked in a branch somewhere outdoors, the porch roof creaked in a puff of wind. Mountain began to snore softly, lying on the cool floor.

Kerry stood upright, lifting me under my bottom so that we rose together. I wrapped my legs around his waist as he carried me to the log canopy bed, setting me down on the large, round aspen timber at the top of the footboard. I grabbed the corner pole with one hand to keep from falling backward. He never let his eyes leave mine as he unbuttoned my shirt, then pulled it off of me, carefully balancing me so that I wouldn't fall back. His eyes moved south to enjoy what he had revealed. His hands followed, one of them moving around to my back, where he expertly unhooked my bra with a gentle flick of his fingers.

He unzipped my jeans, then picked me up again, this time with one arm around my waist, as he used his free hand to tug the jeans down over

my hips, dragging my panties in tow. I liked this! I helped out by clutching my arms around his neck, wiggling so he could get my pants off.

Then the laughable part where we had to remove my boots so the
jeans could come all the way off, me clinging to the bedpost for balance
as Kerry gave up grace and began tugging at the heels of my boots and
the tight wads of denim around my ankles. "Damn it!" he said, grinning.

I fell back into the bed giggling, relishing the fun, eager to start the
passion in earnest.

But Kerry pulled up and looked at me. "Wait! Don't move!" He
bolted toward the door.

"What are you doing?" I said, raising up on one arm, feeling
abandoned.

"I want to take your picture, just like that, with the scar and everything. You look wild and beautiful," he said. "My camera's in the car,
just let me get it."

I shook my head with disbelief. I was primed for passion, and instead of consummating this, my lover had gone for his camera. An avid
photographer, Kerry's specialty was not portraits, but landscapes—the
beautiful places he patrolled as a forest ranger, rare and wonderful
glimpses of unspoiled natural beauty. He had sold some of these in gal-
leries, published a few in magazines. But he had also photographed me
many times over, especially with the wolf, just for his own pleasure.

Never before, though, in the nude.

I thought about this, decided it was kind of sexy that he wanted a
snapshot of me in the altogether, and was trying to think of the best
pose when Kerry came back through the door.

But he wasn't bearing a camera. In one arm, he clasped a large bundle of rags nearly two feet high; in the other hand, his rifle.

"Get dressed, babe," he said, his face suddenly sober. "This was on
the porch. A few feet from the door."

I got up, pulled the bedsheet around me, and went to the table where he'd set the bundle. Kerry went back through the door, Mountain trailing him.

I reached in my big bag and pulled out my handgun, then started for the pile of clothes on the floor at the end of the bed.

But Kerry was back instantly. He had his camera bag with him this time. He checked the safety on his rifle, then set it on the kitchen counter. Mountain wandered back inside and slumped down onto the floor. Kerry closed the door and locked it. Then he turned to me. "It's okay. Whoever left it is gone. There's no one in sight. Now, get back in the bed."

"But what's that?" I asked, pointing to the bundle. "I didn't hear anyone drive up. I didn't even hear footsteps on the porch. You'd think we would have heard something. Even if we didn't, Mountain should have. Do you think someone was watching us, through the window?"

"I don't know," he said. "I looked all the way around the cabin. I can see down the road. There's no one out there."

"I have to see what that is," I said, standing there draped in the sheet.

"It's some sort of statue or something," he said. "I could feel it through the cloth. It's not going to explode, it's not going to leak, and it's not going to go anywhere. So leave it for now and get back in the bed. Please?"

I thought a moment. "I can't. I have to see what it is."

He sighed. I started to unwrap the bundle. It was swathed in some kind of rough cotton cloth, like old feed bags. I unrolled several layers of this covering, revealing a crudely carved wooden santo, a statue of a saint like those sculpted by local villagers here in the northern mountains of New Mexico. The figure was that of a man in a long robe holding a heart-shaped totem to his chest with one hand, the other arm outstretched with the palm outward as if to push something away. His expression was stern and fearsome. Beneath his sandaled feet was a carpet of what looked like cactus thorns. The carver had inscribed the underside of the pedestal: *San Cirilio.*

As I held the carving up to look at it, a burst of light swept through the room. Kerry had snapped a photograph of me, the statue in my outstretched arm like Liberty's torch, the scars on my face toward the lens of the camera, the flash illuminating the whole scene.

◄ 22 ►

The Professor

Wiley Mason was an antique living treasure in New Mexico, especially in the Taos Valley. Still going strong at ninety years of age, he was known throughout the northern central mountains. People spoke with great reverence of this leathery, white-haired, wiry character whose body had shrunk from its former, formidable size until his head looked almost comically large, as if he were a cartoon of himself. Legend claimed that his eyesight was still sharp enough to spot arrowheads in the deep silt of desert arroyos, his bony legs still strong enough to carry him on arduous hikes, and his constitution still spry enough to sustain him through baking hot days on archaeological digs and bone-chilling nights on mountainsides, accompanying the local tribes on vision quests and ceremonial rituals.

His adobe home in a compound of buildings on forty acres in San Cristobal, north of Taos, was a mecca for seekers who came to learn of

Pueblo Indian mythology, native creation stories, and southwestern mysticism.

I had talked to his wife when I phoned to make the appointment, and she had assured me that Professor Mason would be most interested to see the santo that had appeared on my doorstep. She met me at the door and ushered me into the cool great room, shaded by a *portal* overlooking the San Cristobal Valley. While I waited for the professor, I perused the collections of artifacts, masks, books, and ritual objects displayed in glass cases around the inner walls of the large room.

"What have you brought me?" a sharp, trembling voice echoed against the walls. Wiley Mason made his way carefully down the two steps into the room, but then strode toward me with an oversized, outstretched palm.

I shifted my rag bundle to the crook of my left arm and extended my right to shake his hand. His grip was firm and strong. "It's a santo," I said. "It says 'San Cirilio' on the bottom."

"Aha!"

"You know about San Cirilio?"

"A little something. A little something. Put it over here." He gestured toward a table and moved some books aside to make room.

I set the bundle down and began to unwrap it.

Professor Mason pulled eagerly at the rags, as if he couldn't wait. When the carving was exposed, he reached into his shirt pocket and pulled out some spectacles and put them on. He picked up the santo and began to examine it from all angles.

"Uh-huh. Uh-huh. Oh, yes, yes. Yes."

I waited patiently, but he said nothing more.

Finally he set the carving down and looked at me. "Have you been in contact with a witch?"

I laughed, nervously. "A witch?"

He didn't seem amused. He tilted his head to one side and removed his glasses. "Has someone cast a spell on you?"

I started to laugh again at the absurdity of this, but the laughter died in my throat. It sounded instead as if I had burped. Finally I said, "Why are you asking me this?"

He pointed to my face. "How did you get that?"

I told him about Tecolote, and the vision I'd had at her house, but I was careful not to mention Esperanza by name.

"And this woman, you say she's a curandera?"

"Yes, that's what she told me. I don't think of her as a witch. I mean, I know she can do things, strange things. They also call her a bruja."

"Well, to some, witch and bruja are one and the same thing. Did she tell you she was a bruja?"

"Yes. And maybe I also heard it from someone else as well. But I know I heard it from her. And I know for certain that she told me she was a curandera. Why? Do you think she's the one who left this for me?"

"It's possible. If she's only a curandera, though, she cannot help us here."

"Help us? Help us with what?"

"If someone has put a spell on you, then she is probably just trying to protect you. She could have left San Cirilio for your protection."

"But why? I mean, what is this carving going to do?"

He took a deep breath as if to gather patience with my ignorance.

"Curanderas cannot afford to dabble in witchcraft, or their patrons will fear them and will not seek them out for *curas*. Instead, they can offer some protection, but you will have to seek out an *arbulario,* a true brujo or bruja, a witch who can undo the spell."

"What spell? You mean the scars?"

"Yes, the scars. And perhaps more than that. Have you been ill?"

"No."

"Has anything strange been happening?"

Now I laughed out loud. "Everything strange you could imagine. Strange things are the norm for me."

"Like what?"

I told him of the apparition I'd seen while running on the gorge rim, the pictograph that had vanished from the face of the rock. I told him about the prayer stick, the nachi.

"What do you know about this nachi?" Mason said.

"Nothing. I asked my medicine teacher about it, and she said to wait a few days and she would tell me what to do with it." I felt a pang of discomfort remembering Momma Anna's admonitions about the object. Then, reluctantly, I added, "She told me not to tell anyone about it."

The professor broke into a wide, toothy grin. "Well, you failed that assignment, didn't you?"

I shrugged.

"Tell me about the nachi."

I thought about showing it to him—it was outside in my Jeep. But I remembered Momma Anna's warning that it could hurt someone. I described it to him instead, and he scratched a few words on a little notepad from his shirt pocket. Then he made for one of the bookshelves against the wall. He pulled down a tome and wet his fingers on his tongue, then began riffling through the pages.

"Aha!" he said, bringing the book back to the table beside San Cirilio. "Did it look like this?" he asked, pointing a long, bony finger at an old, yellowed page with a fuzzy black-and-white photograph printed on it.

"The feathers were tied more in a crown around the top, not inserted into the sides of the stick like in this photo. And there were grooves and notches on the bottom of the stick as if some kind of writing were made on it."

Mason turned the page of the book to another photograph. "Notches like these?"

I bent over to look more closely at the blurred print. The professor handed me a magnifying glass. "Yes, with those same grooves."

"Did your medicine teacher tell you what this nachi was?"

"No."

"She didn't tell you anything?"

"Like I said, she just told me not to speak of it, that she would talk to me in a few days."

"Aha." He made another note on his pad. "And what color did you say the nachi was?"

"Blue on one side, yellow on the other."

"Blue? What kind of blue?"

"You know—what they call Virgin Mary blue around here. The same color as they paint their doorjambs."

"Oh dear."

"What?"

"Just a minute, just a minute." He thumbed through more pages of the large volume on the table. "And you said the man in your vision—the one you had at the curandera's house—you said he wore a whole bearskin, that his head was actually inside the mouth of the bear?"

I nodded my head.

"Not like this?" he asked, pointing at a reproduction of an old, faded black-and-white photo.

Just then the phone rang, and Wiley went to a nearby desk to answer it.

I studied the book. The picture showed a man with the top part of a bear's head for a headdress and his arm clad in the sheath of a cased bear's arm, the claws held upright for the photo, as if he were going to strike the photographer with them.

Mason spoke loudly into the phone, as if volume would solve the problem of geographical distance. "Yes?" He paused briefly to listen. "Well, does anyone there know where it is? He said he'd have it for me." Another pause. "No, no, he said he'd have it ready for me, so it must be there somewhere. You know what you're looking for, right? No, it's not a tape. It's a round silver disc. It looks just like the ones you play in that fancy car of yours, only there's probably no half-naked women on the label." He shook his head in consternation, then turned to look at me and rolled his eyes. "Okay, well, keep looking. It's there somewhere."

Mason hung up the phone and came barreling back to me. "Well, Ms. Wild, does that look like what you saw?"

"No," I said. "There were no parts and pieces. He had the whole bear on, and it was as if he lived inside it. I could hardly see him. His face was painted."

"Yes, tell me about that."

"It was black on one side and white on the other. And he had a strip of red cloth tied across his forehead. It showed like blood between the teeth of the bear. I thought what I saw *was* a bear until I looked more closely and saw the man's face in its mouth."

"And this pictograph you saw—the one that vanished. You say it was red, like the petroglyph that's stained over with red up in the ruins on Sacred Mountain?"

"Yes, red. A red bear. Part man, I think."

At this, Professor Mason snapped the book shut, causing the table to wobble a little. He started to walk for the steps into the room. "We're going to need tea," he said over his shoulder. Then he bellowed toward the entry hall, "Frida! Frida! Make some *poléo, por favor.*"

◄ 23 ►

No Good News

When Mountain and I arrived at the BLM, phone lines were ringing, Rosa, the receptionist, was talking into the receiver, and Roy was pacing anxiously in the lobby. When he saw me, he hurried over. "Give me the keys to your Jeep," he said, holding out his palm, a folded newspaper tucked under one arm. "We're going to have someone come out and take a look at it, see if it's worth fixing, or if we need to just pay to replace it."

I got out my key ring, started working the car key off. "I'll have to get my gear out of my Jeep." I was thinking of the nachi and the santo—both were in my car.

Roy petted Mountain impatiently. "You can get your things out of your rig when you're ready to leave; someone will have to give you a ride, you can take your stuff with you then."

The phones continued to ring. Rosa couldn't keep up. I tendered the key.

"Have you seen this week's edition of the Taos paper?" Roy asked. "It just came out today."

"No."

"They got a big spread on this mess, right on the front page. There's even a photo of you driving your Jeep with the door blown off. You look real mad in the picture. Looks like it was taken right out front."

"What?"

He opened the paper, pointed to the photo. "That reporter—Noah Sherman—he's the one who took it."

The headline read: TANOAH PUEBLO MAN KILLED BY RAGING BISON—CARELESS DRIVING MAY HAVE CAUSED STAMPEDE. Right beneath it, the shot of me—angry, speeding away from Noah Sherman in my banged-up Jeep with no driver's-side door.

The Boss folded the paper again and tucked it under his arm. "I hated to show you that, but I knew you were going to see it. I got a copy in my office. You can read the whole thing later." He gestured toward the reception area. "The phone's been ringing like that all day."

"Roy! Everyone in the Taos Valley will think I'm a murderer!"

He took my arm. "Listen, when you go in to that interview with that attorney, say as little as you can. Don't go elaborating about things. You stand by what you put in that report—you ain't got nothing more to add, you hear me?"

"Boss, what's going to happen to me? Whose side is this guy on?"

"That guy's not the only one you're dealing with. There's also an attorney from the Department of Justice involved now. So you just do like I said." He released my arm, patted my shoulder. "And let me keep Mountain in my office with me. We don't need to go calling attention to how unusual you are right now."

Wild Indigo

When I came into the conference room, the two attorneys, one from Interior and one from Justice, were waiting with a stack of manila folders on the table in front of them. For once, I took the Boss's advice to the letter.

◄ 24 ►

The Alliance

A gentle rain fell late that afternoon, cooling the air and creating towering double rainbows over Sacred Mountain. I left my Jeep at the BLM so the appraiser Roy had summoned could make a decision about what to do with it. Rosa, grateful to get away from the relentlessly ringing phones, gave me and Mountain a lift to the local dealership, where I picked up a loaner, a soft-top CJ. I transferred my gear—including San Cirilio and the nachi—from Rosa's car, and the wolf and I headed for home in our new ride.

Late summer tourists clogged the main drag in Taos looking for dining spots, and I found myself waiting at one of the few stoplights in town, right at the entrance to the plaza. A gazebo had been erected on the corner of the one downtown parking lot, the rim hung with chile *ristras* and painted gourds. Somewhere, chiles were roasting, and the pungent fragrance laced the air. The sound of a car stereo blasting a Stevie

Wild Indigo

Ray Vaughan tune emanated from beyond the square. A small herd of vacationers crossed at the light on foot, carting shopping bags and cameras, wearing hats that looked new and uncomfortable. Still more visitors looked at their watches as they waited in cars, unable to move at their accustomed pace through the narrow street that for centuries had been the *camino real* to the grand and beautiful Taos Pueblo, the highway to that best-known Tiwa village. As always, Taos resisted time and change—and for that very reason, it attracted these outsiders, who would then find themselves both charmed and a bit uncomfortable in the vortex between the past and present. The same wayfarer who felt the powerful draw of the ancient ritual dances at Taos Pueblo would pace impatiently on the primeval dust plaza there and complain that the travel brochure had promised the dances would begin at nine a.m., so where were they already, it was fifteen after?

In this smaller Jeep, Mountain sat in the passenger seat and stuck his nose out the window, taking in the sights, smells, and sounds. I smiled at him and reached to stroke his ruff. He began to wag his tail wildly and fixed on something across the street. He made a little yelp, and then jumped toward the window, which I'd raised to half-height in case he had an idea like this one. I grabbed his collar. "No, Mountain, no! Sit! Sit!"

The wolf continued his excited display. I followed the direction of his gaze and saw two old women sitting on one of the park benches on the corner of the plaza. These *mujeres* were talking earnestly and making animated gestures, their heads covered with blankets and turned toward each other so that I could not easily see their faces. But as I examined them further, I began to recognize first one, and then the other.

My hand shot to my mouth. I said aloud: "It's Tecolote! With Momma Anna!"

Mountain seized the moment and managed to instantly morph himself into a flattened shape and squeeze through the half-open window and out of the Jeep. At the same time, the light changed, and traffic charged forward in both directions. I slammed the CJ into park and jumped out the door, narrowly avoiding an oncoming pickup. Mountain lunged only a few inches ahead of the truck, and the driver jammed on his brakes, making a loud squeal. This same event was repeated in a dominolike sequence as motorists on both sides of the road hastened to undo their automatic reaction to a long-awaited green light. The wolf, frightened by all this noise and machinery, ran even faster toward the two women on the bench. I stood helplessly watching as drivers cursed and shook their fists. Across the narrow entrance to the plaza, I saw Tecolote raise one hand and reach with the other for Mountain as he approached. She seized his collar and then looked toward the cacophony of swearing and squealing brakes. She nodded at me, and I saw Mountain lie down trembling at her feet, his eyes wide with fright. I got back in the CJ and put it in gear, then signaled to turn in to the plaza—for which the driver behind me regaled me soundly with his horn. Just as the light turned red, I squeaked through the intersection and into the archaic village common, where I parked the Jeep in front of one of the adobe shops.

"He's a bad boy, I tell him," Tecolote said. "He says he is sorry, don't you, Montaña?" She stroked his back and neck.

Mountain still looked shaken by his near miss with the pickup. I went to him and he sat up and wagged his tail, his ears down with fear. My heart pounded in my chest, my mind having raced to the way my life would feel without this wonderful four-legged companion beside me. I bent down and put my arms around his neck and hugged him, stroking his long back. "Oh, buddy, you scared me there, you really did."

Mountain's tail continued to beat against the ground.

I stood up and looked at the two women.

Momma Anna patted the bench beside her and gave me a shy smile. "Sit down! Sit down!" she said, in the traditional welcoming tone.

I went through the necessary formality of taking each of their hands in greeting and bowing my head slightly to acknowledge their status as elders. Then, instead of taking the seat offered, I squatted on my heels next to Mountain and continued to pet him. "What are you two doing here?" I asked.

Tecolote said, "Do you think you could get us a tamale over there?" She gestured toward the sidewalk vendor across the lawn on the other side of the square. "Your teacher and I are starving here. We'll look after *el lobo* for you."

I stood up, resigned to my duty. "Red or green chili on top?"

"Christmas," they replied in unison.

When I returned from my foray to the tamale stand, Mountain had relaxed into a nap at Tecolote's feet, and Momma Anna was laughing about something, holding her hand in front of her face out of modesty. The women took the tamales with great glee and ate them from their paper cartons with plastic spoons. They both grunted approvingly and made comments about the good flavors. When they'd finished eating, Momma Anna gathered their utensils and cartons back into the bag and handed it to me. "Do you mind?" she asked, adjusting her blanket over her head and shoulders.

I took the trash and walked the few steps to the nearest receptacle. Then I returned to confront the two women as directly as I dared: "So, what are you two doing here together?"

Tecolote held up her palm as if to stop my questions. "Your teacher and I are consulting on a matter of great importance."

Momma Anna nodded her head with a shy smile. "It what I tell you."

"What you tell me?"

"You know—you must find out. I tell you find out."

I squatted down and looked directly into her face. "Momma Anna, when I was at your door yesterday with questions that might have helped me to find out, you wouldn't talk with me!"

"You bring that next other lady. I not know her."

"But she could help us, she wants to help."

"She not Indun. Not like us. Not like you either. You part Indun, part white girl, part wolf." The two elders looked at each other and laughed loudly at this.

I smiled, exasperated. "No, no, she's not Indian, but she's FBI, and she has a lot of resources at her disposal. And she wants to help."

"I cannot say things. People listen, there trouble. I must not talk, say name, that boy."

Tecolote interrupted. "Did you get a visitor?"

"A visitor?"

"*Sí,* a visitor."

"The santo? San Cirilio? Yes, I got him."

"Good. You keep him in the center of your casa, on your hearth. He protects from evil."

"Why didn't you at least knock on the door, say hello?"

Esperanza smiled at me. "I don't bring him to you, Mirasol. I *send* him to you."

"But who?—who delivered it?"

Tecolote smiled and patted Mountain, now resting with his head on her shoe. "San Cirilio is able to go where he will. Or sometimes San Cirilio is carried on the backs of *los lobos*. The old people over here say that he is a friend of the animals, and that he can talk to them. We used to have *lobos* here, but not too many no more. Maybe he finds some of those ones they bring here to live again in the mountains."

"But what do I do with him after I've put him in my house?"

Tecolote sighed. "You don't *do* with him, Mirasol. You let him *do* with you. He is the one who will *do*. To be in his presence is not to be taught, or made to do something. It is to be blessed with his beauty and his radiance. And his strength and protection. Let him do this for you."

Before I could respond, Momma Anna cut in, as if there had been no other matter under discussion. "You talk my brother Yellow Hawk. That the one teach young men, he teach my son."

I swung back to face her. "Teach him? Teach him what?"

"They have lot of training this time year. My brother—he peyote chief. He teach young men. He stay with them in kiva."

"So . . . your son, he was staying in the kiva? Training with Yellow Hawk?"

Momma Anna nodded. "They don't come up, only when moon is dark. We take them food, light fire in dark moon time. They lose weight down there, they need food. That Madonna, she not wait for him, make fire, take him food. She off doing what she please."

"Then . . . if the trainees are kept in the kiva except during the dark of the moon"—I tried to think of a way to put it delicately—"why was . . . your son in the buffalo pasture? In broad daylight?"

Momma Anna's eyes filled with tears. "I not know! You ask my brother. He maybe knows."

"But—I'm not even welcome out at the pueblo. Can't you ask him?"

"I try. He not come ceremony for my son—that when kiva doin's, and he not come. They done now, and still he not come comfort me. Now, no one knows, he's nowhere."

"Nowhere?"

"He not come home after kiva doin's. He maybe went Sacred Mountain, fast, pray. Many time elders do before journey, Indigo Falls. No one knows. He's nowhere." She paused a moment, then turned her head in contemplation. "Do you know man name Ron?"

"Ron?"

"I think white man, maybe poor, not clean."

"Who are you talking about, Momma Anna?"

"At my son house, I hear him talk phone. He walk away, I make busy like not listen. He talk quiet—say man name Ron. He say he go see Ron."

"Ron? Did you hear anything else?"

"I dunno."

"Why did you say you thought he was white? Poor? And . . . what did you say—dirty?"

"My son say that."

"Do you know anything else about this man Ron? When your son last saw him, where he met him?"

"I not know. You find out."

I stood up and shook my head in frustration. "I don't get it. You want me to find out about people I know nothing about, talk to people you yourself can't find. I'm supposed to find out stuff but I'm not welcome anywhere, nor will anyone talk to me. *You* won't even help me, and I'm in real trouble now—my job's on the line. Everyone's mysteriously dropping off packages, things I don't understand. I feel like I'm going in circles and I know less than anyone else!"

Tecolote took a harsh tone: "Stop complaining, Mirasol! At least these things that come to you are for your good. Many people are trying to help you. San Cirilio is trying to help you. You always go looking for wisdom, and then you complain about how much it costs."

Momma Anna broke in: "But what about the nachi? That maybe not good. Maybe someone send evil there. Old time, that for scalp ceremony, mean war. They have many old scalp in kiva, use that kind nachi for scalp ceremony. Nighthawk feather mean water. Somebody make war near water—maybe scalp you. Yellow, blue—mean meeting night-day, dusk. Or maybe summer-winter, meeting of two season. You got mark of bear, you under spell."

I threw up my arms. "Okay, stop it, stop it! I'm tired of all this spell stuff, and these cryptic messages and strange objects. Have you seen the Taos paper? Do you know what's really going on? They're practically calling me a murderer, and everyone in town is going to read that, if they haven't already."

Tecolote rose and took hold of my forearm, her gnarled fingernails digging deeply into my flesh. "Calm yourself, Mirasol. Do as your teacher says and sit here with us for a while. We have brought you some things to help." She pushed me back toward the park bench until I sat down.

At this, Momma Anna rose from her seat and reached beneath her shirt and drew out her *jish*. She untied the deerskin thong that held it closed and rummaged inside the bag for a chunk of brownish root, which she placed in my palm. She closed my fingers over it and said, "Burn half with red chile and salt. Carry other half next to heart." She thumped her chest and then held up her medicine pouch. "Like this. Then, after: take nachi that spring by you house, back where we find flower, wild spinach that next other time. Plant in wet mud, leave there. Make offering, corn-meal. Back away, don't turn back on it, keep face to nachi, okay? Do at noon, big light. No witch come out at noon. Tomorrow. Don't wait. Then, nighttime, you come pueblo for feast, bonfire. Serena pick you up, Hunter say you come."

Both women looked down at me. Tecolote spoke now: "Take these." She reached into the pocket of her dress and brought out a tied knot of brown cloth. "Together, it is a tea—put it all in the kettle, even the seeds. Boil it a little, then let it cool and drink. And you must close your curtains, Mirasol, lock your door. Sweep out any ashes from the fireplace. Put San Cirilio on the hearth, he protects you. I will ask an *arbulario* to lift the spell in a little time—perhaps three, four days, after all this is done."

Without another word, they turned from the park bench and walked across the street to a nearby alley. Momma Anna adjusted her blanket over her head, and the two women locked arms and disappeared down the narrow passage and into the haze of the ensuing twilight.

◂ 25 ▸

Yellow Hawk

The only time I had ever talked with Yellow Hawk was back at the beginning of the summer, on the evening of the big bake, the night before Momma Anna's grandson's wedding. A huge feast was held at Frank and Lupé's home, a ramshackle HUD house identical to the hundred or so around the outskirts of the old, walled village of the pueblo. The home, like most of the others, was built square in the middle of once-rich farm fields, now idle due to government subsidies that paid the Tanoah *not* to plant corn, after centuries of growing the sacred maize and centering their culture around its bounty.

As I drove up the long, deeply rutted dirt road through the field, I could see cars and pickups parked everywhere. Serena waved her hands wildly as she came down the lane toward me. "Wait! Wait! Park down at the end. Lupé will come get you when you can come up to the house."

I parked where she said and got out with a basket of gifts. Serena held her hands up and pushed away, gesturing for me to wait right by the car, so I did. She left me there and went back up toward the house.

It was nearly seven in the evening, and the blue sky was beginning to flatten in color. A faint pink glow began to hum on the horizon, telling of Father Sun's fatigue and willingness to perhaps surrender to the Moon another day of pueblo life. Horses flicked their tails in the nearby pasture, and dogs barked at the next house over, where elk antlers hung in clumps from the two posts marking the dirt drive. It was the time the Tanoah called Kapnákoyapana, Corn Tassel Coming Out Moon— roughly the same time we knew as the month of June. A magpie dropped to a nearby fence post and inspected me with suspicion. Momma Anna once told me the magpie was the consort of the Corn Girls, two sisters who—in a jealous struggle over his affections—ended up separating, and one went to the hole into the underworld that is at the mouth of the Indigo Falls. This beautiful planting/fertility myth told of Blue Corn Girl going after her sister Yellow Corn Girl, into the home of the ancestors, the House of the Dead. And then, just as Magpie came to find them, the two rose from beneath the waters again as yellow and blue corn ears, and spilled from the falls and down over the land to feed the People. It was symbolic of the journey the corn makes as it must offer its own life, in the form of its seed, to the underworld, thence to come up again to be in this life.

I set my basket on the roof of my Jeep and then leaned against it, drinking in the beauty of the evening. A half hour later, I had shifted positions enough times that my legs were tired of standing, so I opened the rear hatch and sat in the cargo area, which was coated with Mountain's hair, the windows smeared with his drool and painted with nose prints. He'd chewed away one of the net accessory holders meant for small items one might normally carry in the trunk. A host of bones, beef knuckles, and toys in various states of decomposition surrounded the big covered foam pad that was his car seat. Somehow I was comforted by all this, and I felt his presence in it. I missed my companion. I dangled my legs over the rear bumper and swung them back and forth like a child. It was cooling down, a beautiful evening.

After twenty more minutes, I wondered if I should just start the car and go home—no one could possibly miss me, as I had never truly arrived. And it was even feasible that Serena had failed to tell Lupé I was there. But it might be seen as an offense if I left; yet it was also unthinkable for me to approach the house when I'd been asked to wait. I finally decided to surrender to the fact that I'd be covered with wolf hair, and I pulled my legs up into the Jeep, turned to lean my back against the spare tire, and tried to get comfortable while I assessed the situation.

Lupé stuck her head under the back hatch and said, "Well, are you ready, White Girl?"

I straightened, started brushing fur off my dress, and stood up, banging my head into the raised hatch. I put a hand to my crown, winced, and stepped out of danger. "Ready?" I said.

"Yes. The elders got to talk with you, see if you can come to the feast."

I followed her up toward the porch on the front of the house, a narrow band of cement furnished with a long bench. Four old men sat smoking cigarettes, wrapped in their blankets. I recognized Momma Anna's brother Yellow Hawk as one of them. He held up a hand and waved for me to come closer. Lupé asked, "Do you have any tobacco?"

I stopped walking. "In the glove box of my Jeep, there's a medicine pouch. It has sage, cornmeal, and tobacco."

"Is it real tobacco, Indun tobacco?"

"Yes, that's the kind Momma Anna taught me to use."

"You go 'head," she said. "I'll get it and bring it to you."

I approached the elders with my basket. They all looked at me without speaking. I stood in front of them for what seemed an eternity, afraid to break the silence myself, in case it was some sort of tribal taboo for me to do so. Lupé reappeared and slid the bag of tobacco discreetly into my hand. She took the basket from me and went in the house, slamming the screen door behind her. I smelled coffee, chili, and stew, and maybe even barbecue coming from the kitchen door. I also smelled the sharp scent of burning cedar.

Yellow Hawk held up his hand. "How are you?"

"I'm good. Fine. I'm fine. And you?"

He nodded.

I offered the bag of tobacco. Lujan took it and held it up to examine it briefly. The others looked at it also, and two of them nodded. Yellow Hawk tucked the offering under his blanket. "Sit down, sit down," he said.

I looked around—then, for lack of a better option that I could see—sat down cross-legged in the dirt, carefully arranging my long dress modestly over my legs.

The elders nodded, clearly approving my choice of seating.

Yellow Hawk said, "Why you want be Indun?"

Stunned, I opened my mouth, but could not think of a thing to say. Finally, I recovered enough to mutter, "I don't want to be an Indian."

Grunts, nods, then silence from the old men.

A few minutes passed.

"We don't tell white people our ways. What we speak of, lose power. Our ways, our power. We don't talk about it."

It was my turn to nod my head.

A small, wiry man at the opposite end of the bench from Yellow Hawk spoke in Tiwa. They all grunted and nodded their heads in agreement.

Yellow Hawk smiled. "We speak Tiwa, this doin'."

I nodded again.

Yellow Hawk kept bobbing his head, his eyes fixed on me. Then he raised a hand and gestured to the others. In unison, they rose and went into the house. When the screen door closed, he said to me, "I am old. Anna old. We old now."

"No, you're not old." I smiled. "Grandma Bird and Grandpa Nazario are old. You are their son."

He was not impressed with my attempt to win him over with flattery. "They ancient," he said, and chuckled. "I am old."

I started to speak again, but he held up a hand to stop me.

"Every age has its people. And each time, there some thing the people must do, each age." He stopped to take out his tobacco pouch and roll a cigarette. The light was fading, and his dark skin under the shadow of the porch looked like worn leather.

Yellow Hawk lit his smoke and inhaled deeply, turning his head upward. He exhaled a long stream of sweet-smelling smoke. Then he looked down at me. "We not know, long time, what we need to do. I play as boy, do good thing I get smile, do bad thing I get whip. I learn do good thing that way." He smiled. "I ride horse, help my father plant, hunt, make drum, cut wood, dance, run race, run many mile every day. I learn as I do, while I grow."

From inside the house, quiet murmurs and whispers were accented only by the occasional ringing of a pot lid as a woman checked the consistency of the stew or gave the posole a stir. Gas lamps hissed, and the window and doorway began to glow golden against the twilight.

Yellow Hawk said, "One time, we not live outside wall. All the People live inside wall, in village—not like this house. We come out to field, here, like this, plant corn, every color corn. Blue corn for sky, white corn for cloud, yellow corn for sun, even red corn for earth. We not wear shoe with heel in village, only moccasin, show respect that way. Every baby wash first day in river, whole tribe come to welcome. Every death, whole tribe come to send spirit home. We speak only Tiwa, not white or Spanish. We live in house made of earth, our earth, Nah-meh-neh, our life, this Mother Earth. We bring wood from mountain, make viga, get water from river, mix straw with earth to make a home. We hunt, plant, go up mountain to many place, visit our ancestors, our gods, our shrines."

He waved his hand. "All that mountain up there our land, not just little bit like today. We have sacred place all over that mountain, gods, place make offering, do spirit work, place of old ones. Different place for different work, make different offering, ask different blessing, each one for different moon. Our way, our life—that our religion. We do all together, we share, we take care everyone. We don't have church, or wait for heaven, or even know sin. Our religion this earth, this village, the corn, our ways. Our language, Tiwa, that our religion, too. We keep our way sacred with our language."

Momma Anna stuck her head out the screen door, looked at me on the ground, and scowled. She spoke sharply to her brother in Tiwa, then closed the door.

"Our way always give, always share. Everything, share. When Spanish come, we say, 'Here, this land good, we share.' They take everything, make our people slaves, take our women and children, say we not speak Tiwa no more, have dance, ceremony. They take our ways. We hold on, keep dance in secret, hide our children. We tell them, 'Run! If enemy come, run to place where old ones live, hide and wait!' Those times, we speak Tiwa in quiet whisper, teach to children at night, in sleep.

"Now, today, when people come village, we still share, we say, 'Come, sit, eat.' Many time, they still try steal our ways, take picture of sacred dance, walk in house, no knock, ask question, very rude. Our way, no question. One thing now, we not share sacred tradition. No one tell these thing. Our doin's, we speak Tiwa. We speak these things outside, to others, they lose power, our ways die. Then we die. Already, our ways dying. No more living inside wall, in village. Everybody got car, job, drink water out a pipe, no planting corn, squash. No more go where old ones live, make offering, fast, pray. Not even our land up there, gov-'ment take away. I'm old. I still not know what our people must do, this age. Maybe we just die, some not know, some not care. I try keep our ways alive."

He pinched out his cigarette with two tobacco-stained fingers. He held up the remaining bit and began to chant softly under his breath in Tiwa. He stopped after a minute or two, then was quiet for a time. He got up from the bench.

I rose, too, brushing the dirt off the back of my dress.

"Our language last vein our life's blood, last thing keep us alive, last thing sacred not taken from us. You come inside. We speak Tiwa. I ask respect."

He opened the screen door and held it for me to go inside. "They say you live with a wolf."

"Yes, he's a real challenge. But I love him."

"Maybe you Indun, time before."

◄ **26** ►

Super Natural

On the way home from my encounter with the two *mujeres,* I had to stop for gas, since the dealership had left the CJ's tank empty and running on fumes. I started the pump and went around to the passenger side of the Jeep. Mountain stood in the seat and held his head out the window, sniffing the evening air. I pressed my face into the long ruff of his neck and nuzzled him. "No more jumping out of cars and running into traffic, okay, buddy?"

He wagged his tail at me and smiled. Then he pushed his neck against my face again, as if to reassure me. I reached a hand in through the window opening and began stroking his side and the ridge of his long back as far as I could reach. Mountain, even though still a cub, was a large bit of livestock. Pretty soon he would weigh more than I did, and he stood nearly three feet tall on all fours.

A brace of loud music and big-engine noise interrupted our snuggling.

I saw Gilbert Valdez's slick red Mustang pull up to the other side of the gas pump. The engine purred to a stop and the music died. Because I was on the far side of the car, Valdez couldn't see me. A woman got out of the Mustang's shotgun seat, and I saw that it was Madonna Santana. She reached into the back of the car and fetched out a shiny black leather coat and put it on. In defiance of tradition, and despite the fact that she was newly widowed, she wore makeup, her beautiful, long black hair was down and loose, and she was dressed in snug jeans and a cowboy shirt.

I came around the front of the CJ as Madonna was stamping her feet on the pavement, complaining that it was getting cold. Valdez was pumping gas into his ride. I nodded at the widow, and she looked surprised to see me. "Jamaica! Hi! How are you?" Right away, she noticed the claw marks. "What happened to your face?"

"Ah, it's nothing. I'm good, Madonna, I'm good. Listen, I'm sorry for your loss . . ."

She closed her mouth and lowered her head, as if ashamed to be caught out like this. "You probably heard that my husband and I weren't getting along."

"No, no, I guess I didn't know. I'm sorry to hear that. I—"

By this time Valdez came to join us. "Jamaica! Did you get a new car?"

"For right now, yes."

"Yeah, probably going to need one after what I saw," he said. "Oooh! Ouch! What did you do to that good-lookin' face of yours?"

I gave an exasperated sigh. "It's nothing, I just got scratched."

The three of us stood there in awkward silence.

"Well," I said, "I have to be going." I headed to the pump to take out the nozzle and close up the cap on the tank.

Valdez went inside the station, but Madonna came up to me and put her arm on my shoulder. "Jamaica, this is not what it looks like," she said. "We work together at the casino."

"Yeah, I know."

"He's just giving me a ride home after work."

"Okay." I put my hands in the back pockets of my jeans.

"There was trouble in my marriage. A lot of people were talking about me and Gilbert. But it's not like that. He's just giving me a ride home."

"I thought you were supposed to refrain from driving inside the pueblo during Quiet Time if you possibly could."

"We are. But some of us—like Gilbert—get special permission because of what they do. I can't drive there now because I'm no big shot. But Gilbert runs the casino, so he can drive, as long as he stays out of the old part of the village. He's giving me a ride home so I don't have to walk. It's three miles to my house! It would be dark by the time I got home to Angel."

"How's Angel doing?"

She frowned. "He's not so good. He wants to be alone all the time. He won't even go stay with his grandma Anna when I'm at work. I don't know what to do."

"When I was by the other day, he kept telling me he was a good boy. But he seemed pretty upset."

Tears glistened in Madonna's eyes. "I know."

Valdez reemerged from the station with a bottled soft drink. "Well, am I a lucky son of a gun or what? Two of the most beautiful women in New Mexico, right here waiting on me!"

"Listen, I better go," I said, and I moved to open my car door.

But Madonna reached out and put her arms around me. "Just don't think bad things about me, okay, Jamaica? It's not like everybody's saying."

I hugged her back, genuinely, and said, "You do the same for me, okay? Don't believe what they're saying about me. I hope you'll give yourself a little time to heal, to grieve. Be good to yourself."

"You, too," she said, and moved away.

"Hey, did your dog do that?" Gilbert asked, gesturing at his own face in reference to the marks on mine.

I got in the driver's seat. I smiled at Mountain, and he smiled back. "He's not a dog. He's a wolf."

I drove away.

By the time Mountain and I got home, the sun had almost set, and the shadow of the tall mountains to the west of the property left my cabin in dark shade. I took the wolf for a brief romp through the sage and scrub piñon so he could do his business, then we headed inside. I filled his water and food dishes and put them down for him on the floor, and he began to crunch away at his meat-laced kibble. I hurried to turn on lights in the one big main room, which comprised my living quarters, and even in the pass-through closet and the small bathroom that had been added, shed-style, on the back of the house by the owner some years ago to make it viable as a rental property. I did as Tecolote had told me and covered the windows—which required me to tack up sheets and towels, because I had no curtains. I'd never wanted to hinder my beautiful views, nor had I been concerned about privacy, since I lived in such a remote place, on such a large parcel of land.

After this chore, I swept the ashes out of the woodstove. I covered the metal ash bucket and set it out on a flat stone about ten yards away from the house so any live embers could safely cool before I emptied them on the land. The evening was chilly, so I laid a new fire and lit it. Then I brought San Cirilio into the house, unwrapped his rag coverings, and placed him on the slate tiles near the woodstove, which was as close to a hearth as I had. I realized I didn't know what to do with the nachi until tomorrow, so I left it in the car. After Momma Anna's description of its purpose, I decided it wouldn't help matters to bring it into the house.

As I busied myself with these activities, my mind fretted over my brief encounter with the widow Santana and Gilbert Valdez. Madonna's worry over what I might be thinking of her, the shame and embarrassment she displayed, even her attractive but plainly modern, white woman way of dressing—all of these evoked strong sentiment in me. In eschewing tribal customs and defying societal expectations, she seemed as determined to escape her own life—who she was—as Jerome Santana had been four days ago in the buffalo field. In breaking the strong fence of custom and tradition that may have enclosed and—at times—stifled her, she also destroyed the very thing that protected her. Now she seemed to me like a misguided lamb among the wolves, and Gilbert Valdez was definitely a predator.

For my own part, I longed for something Madonna Santana was eagerly discarding. I could not imagine that anything would be worth more than belonging to an extended family, a tribe.

After I'd prepared the house, I remembered Tecolote's admonition to lock the door. But as it was Kerry's custom to come by for frequent, unannounced visits after his long shifts at the Ranger District in Tres Piedras, I wanted to wait until I was ready for sleep to take this precaution. I turned next to the items the two *mujeres* had given me. I filled a cast-iron kettle with water from the tap and set it atop the woodstove to make the tea using the things Tecolote gave me. While I waited for the water to heat, I turned to Momma Anna's little chunk of root and remembered her voice: *Burn half with red chile and salt. Carry other half next to heart.* I examined the small bit of woody, brown tuber she'd given me. Then I got out my book on native herbs and plants and looked for its likeness among the photos and descriptions. I wasn't sure, but it seemed most like the root described as *cachana,* or "witch root," which botanists had not identified, and whose source was a carefully guarded secret among Native American shamans, even such that its distribution among native peoples was harshly regulated by them. The author of the book speculated that the rhizome might grow in the Jemez Mountains, a range south and west of my cabin. A caveat in the root's description said the herb should be administered with utmost care because it was extremely dangerous if misused. I gathered the items I would need: a knife and a small cutting board, a large abalone shell I used for burning sage and cedar for smudge, wooden kitchen matches, some red chile seeds, and salt. Momma Anna had given no recipe of proportions, so I decided I would try to use equal amounts of each ingredient. I wiped my abalone shell out and placed a good pinch of the chile seeds and the salt in the center. Then I took my knife and began shaving away at one end of the root, creating short strands of dry, woody fiber. I put these atop the other items in the shell, and then measured out another pinch of seeds and salt, and shaved more of the cachana. Momma Anna had advised me to use half of the root, so I continued in this way until I felt that I had done so. A small heap of debris rose from the shell, like the makings of a tiny ceremonial bonfire.

Before I could strike a match to this concoction, my kettle began surging steam. I opened Tecolote's small cloth bundle and saw sunflower seeds in a nest of dried herbs, and green and brown and yellow strands of what might have been flower petals, stamen, and pistils. The seeds made me think of the old bruja's nickname for me: Mirasol, which means Sunflower. When she first called me by this moniker, she said it was for the flower that "grows where you grew, tall—like you—with yellow crown." I lifted the lid on the kettle and threw the contents of the bundle inside. I watched the seeds float and spin in the bubbling water, the herbs take on the liquid and drop to the bottom, and the strands I thought were flower parts disintegrate. The liquid boiled for a minute or two, and then I poured some off into a big coffee mug. The smell of the broth was tantalizing: sharp like citrus, with a woody, mushroomlike undertone. I brought the mug to the table to let it cool, as the curandera had instructed. Then I turned again to my smudge mixture. Holding the abalone conch in one hand, I struck a match with the other and held it to the base of the material piled in the shell. The root took the flame instantly and began to hiss and shrivel, giving off an astonishing amount of smaze for such a little heap of fuel. The chile seeds popped and withered and turned black, and the blend of ingredients danced with green-tinged flame. The smoke was acrid and my eyes began to water and sting. My nose recoiled and I thought I might sneeze. Suddenly, I couldn't breathe.

I wanted to set the conch down; it was burning my hands. Foul vapors obscured my view of everything. I couldn't see the table: I reached out to place the shell on its top but I felt empty space. The heat from the smudge seared my palms. I swung to one side and tried again to find the tabletop, and I released the scorching bowl to spare my hand any further damage. I heard a crash as the abalone shattered against the floor.

Still unable to breathe, and coughing now, I made for the door, or where I thought it should be. Just as I was about to reach for the knob, I felt a blast of both noise and air, and I heard the door slam back hard against the wall, as if something—or someone—had fairly exploded into the room.

Mountain and I were running, only not on the gorge rim as we so often did. This time, we were on the slopes of a sharply escalating ascent. There was a feeling of urgency—we had to get somewhere in a hurry, or get away from something. We were not running for joy and pleasure but perhaps for our lives—or someone else's. Mountain was out in front of me, but he stopped frequently and turned to encourage me on. His tongue hung several inches out of his mouth from exertion, in spite of the intense cold, and he looked at me with anxious eyes. He turned onto a trail that led farther up the alp. "No, no," I told him, "not that way. We want to go down. We want to go down the mountain, we want to go home." The wolf looked torn between his instincts and mine. He reluctantly turned back and took the lower trail, but he didn't run ahead as before, staying just behind me instead.

A cold mix of rain and sleet began to pelt us, and I could hardly see the trail. The ground was wet and slippery, and several times my shoes slid and made my stride erratic. I had to get down the mountain, I had to get both of us down the slope as fast as I could or something unimaginably horrible would happen. I tried to run faster but my legs were cold and unresponsive. My foot lodged on a root and I tripped and fell face-first, downhill into mud and musty detritus, which smelled sharply of orange and also earthy, like mushrooms. I tried to pick myself up but my arms wouldn't move—I couldn't raise them from the ground. I cried out in pain. Mountain lay down beside me and nuzzled my neck, his breath heavy and moist. He beckoned me to climb on his back, to take hold of the long ruff of mane at his neck and ride on him. I managed to grasp a fistful of fur. Instantly, I felt him lifting me as he rose, and I was somehow small enough to ride him, to ride on his strong back, his thick coat surrounding me and keeping me warm, my only connection that one handful of hair that bound me to the back of him as he loped effortlessly away from danger, away from the cold, away down the mountain to safety and home.

Kerry's hand on my face felt warm. I looked at him and smiled. "Oh, you're here. I must have had a bad dream."

He wrinkled his brow. "You all right?"

"I'm okay," I said, stretching, checking every part to see if it worked. I sat up, looked around. I was on the floor near the woodstove. The house was cold, the door standing open.

"Can you move? Can you get up?"

I rubbed my eyes, then took a deep breath. "Yeah, I'm okay." I pushed myself to my hands and knees, then rose to my feet.

"Good," Kerry said. "C'mon then. We have to get Mountain to town now. He's barely breathing."

◄ 27 ►

Cry, Wolf

One vet in Taos contracted with the Division of Wildlife to see animals brought in with injuries or illnesses. Kerry got the man out of bed and down to his clinic to tend to Mountain. "Has he been poisoned?" the doctor asked.

"No. I don't know. I—"

Kerry interrupted. "We don't know what happened; we just found him this way, lying on the porch in front of the door."

"How long's he been like this?"

I shook my head. "I don't know."

The vet gripped Mountain's large chest with his hand. "His heart's barely beating. You stay here with him a few minutes. Let me make a call and get someone down here to help me."

I pushed my head into Mountain's neck, willed him to breathe, his heart to beat. I smelled his wild scent. "C'mon, buddy, you can make it," I sobbed. "You can't leave me here. I need you."

Kerry rubbed my back as I continued to bury my face in the wolf's fur. "You saved me," I whispered. "You got me down the mountain. Now, get on *my* back and ride. I'll carry you, I'll get you back to safety. Come on, just let me bring you home again."

A sour cup of coffee and two bottles of water later, the vet sent me and Kerry home. "He's ingested something, would be my guess, something that's either drugged or poisoned him. We don't have much in the way of fancy diagnostics here like they have in Albuquerque. I'll do some blood work, run a few tests. Until we know more, we can only watch him, keep him hydrated. It's touch and go. Nothing you can do here, might as well get some sleep. I'll call you if anything develops."

"But I don't have a phone!" I said.

"Not even a cell phone?"

"No, they don't work out where I live. I'm almost off the grid."

"Well then, you call me. I'll be up with him through the night. You go to the nearest phone in a couple hours and we'll touch bases like that until we see a change. How's that?"

Back in my cabin, I found the cracked conch shell on the floor in front of San Cirilio, its contents dissipated from the flames. On the table sat Tecolote's infusion in the big mug, cold now. I sniffed at it. It still smelled good, even enticing. I was thirsty. Kerry coaxed a fire in the woodstove while I deliberated whether to drink the tea: *Is that why things went wrong, because I didn't drink it after burning the root?*

Then I remembered the root! The other half was missing, not on the table, nowhere to be found. I was supposed to put the other half next to my heart, but perhaps Mountain had gotten hold of it and eaten it. "Take me to the café on the highway," I told Kerry. "I have to use the phone right away."

In the middle of the night, I rose from the bed, carefully taking Kerry's arm from around me and placing it on the pillow. He muttered something and dropped back into deep sleep. I pulled my Pendleton blanket from the chair and cloaked myself with it, went to the table in the dark and felt around until I found the mug of Tecolote's tea, picked it up, and took it with me. I went outside, to the place where Mountain and I so often sat at night, looking up at the stars. I lowered myself carefully to the ground, so as not to spill the contents of the mug. It was very cold out, and I gathered the blanket tightly about me. I felt the emptiness of Mountain's absence, remembering all the times he'd stayed beside me, watched for coyotes or mountain lions, or run in place and whimpered in his dreams while I tried to work out the meaning of my day's events, or some other pressing matter. I sniffed at the tea again and the smell was still inviting, so I took one small sip and waited.

Nothing.

I took another sip. The drink was delicious and felt soothing to my throat, which was sore and raw from the smoke of the witch root.

I waited.

Still no effect, other than that the tea seemed to be quenching my thirst, when all the water I'd consumed earlier in the evening had had little effect.

I continued to sip the liquid as I watched the stars and huddled under my blanket. I felt a small warming in my chest as I finished my cup, but no other noticeable side effects. I did, however, feel great sadness and fear about Mountain, and I began to cry. "Great Spirit, Mother Earth, and Father Sky," I prayed, "please don't take my great heaven beast, my soul mate, my wolf companion from me. He's all the family I have, and I love him beyond measure. Please help him to heal and recover. I love him. I need him. Aho."

◄ 28 ►

Wicked Things

I dreamed again of Mountain and woke before dawn, sobbing into the bedcovers. Kerry stirred and rolled over, and I got up to write down the contents of the dream:

> At first, Mountain came to lie down beside me as I was doing something; he just wanted to be near me. I noticed him and felt good that he had come to be with me, and I paid attention to his beauty and felt comforted by his presence.
>
> Then we were running together on the side of a steep slope. A bad storm was coming. I was trying to find our way home, and I wanted to take the lower of two paths, but Mountain struck out on an ascending one. I called him back, but he looked at me and waited, wagging his tail, as if to say, "Come on! This way!" I had to coax him several times before he would

come join me on the downward path. "This is the way home," I kept telling him, but he lingered and stalled and didn't want to run with me on the trail I had chosen.

I started some coffee brewing, and Kerry got out of bed and came up behind me. He put his arms around my waist and nuzzled his face in my neck. "You need to shave," I said. "You're rough as sandpaper."

He rubbed the side of his jaw with one hand. "Sorry."

I turned to face him. "You slept last night. You actually slept."

He grinned. "I know. Hey, babe!" His tone was strange.

"What?"

"Have you looked in the mirror?"

I brushed my uncombed hair with my hand. "No, why?"

"Take a look," he said.

I made for the bathroom, and he followed. Standing at the sink, I examined my reflection. The marks on my cheek had faded overnight, only faintly pink now instead of the virulent red they'd been for days.

"What happened?" he asked.

I touched my cheek—no burning. "I don't know. Maybe Tecolote's tea."

"You drank that? You're braver than I am. After what happened, I wouldn't have touched that concoction."

I continued to scrutinize myself in the mirror.

Kerry watched for a few moments, then said, "Babe, I know you love that wolf better than anything or anyone in this world."

My eyes grew moist.

"You've got to be hurting bad. Why don't you talk to me?"

"I dreamed about him." I clutched at my chest, grabbed a handful of my T-shirt and twisted it into my palm. "It was like something I saw when I was . . . when I passed out after burning the smudge."

"What was it? What did you see?"

"We were climbing a mountain and he wanted to take a trail leading farther up but I knew we had to go down. There was something urgent about it; I knew we had to get down the mountain but that wolf wouldn't come with me."

Kerry turned me around and looked at me, his hair still disheveled from sleep, a line on his face where the pillow had wrinkled into his cheek. He gathered me into his warm chest. "Boy, when it rains it pours, huh? So many tragedies in just one week."

"I don't even have my job to do so I can occupy myself," I said. "I feel like I've wandered into a nightmare, all this strange stuff that's been happening to me. I don't feel grounded, I can't . . . I want Mountain!" I broke into a sob.

Kerry squeezed me tighter. "Listen, I'm going to drive down to the café and use the phone. I'll take off work today and stay with you."

"No, no, don't do that," I said, pulling away from him. I looked into his green eyes. "I may need you more if—if . . . Mountain . . ."

"I'll be here if that happens."

"Go. I'll be all right."

He hesitated. Then he gave a little snort. "You're so stubborn."

Alone in the cabin, I felt Mountain's absence so painfully that I wanted to do anything to distract myself. I drove up the highway to the café to call the vet. "His heart's just barely beating," he said. "He's not conscious, but he's hanging on. We'll just have to see what the day brings."

"Isn't there anything you can do? Pump his stomach? Anything?"

"It's not that root thing you thought it was. We drew some blood. He's been given atropine, a near-deadly dose. The only thing we can do is wait."

"Atropine? What's atropine?"

"It's a highly poisonous crystalline alkaloid—comes from the belladonna plant, and some other plants. It prevents the response of various body structures to certain types of nerve stimulation. It can be used in very small amounts to relieve spasms, or to lessen secretions, even to dilate the eye. But your wolf here has received a big dose of it, and it's keeping his heart from performing like it should. Stuff's concentrated in his bloodstream, no use pumping the stomach. I don't think he ingested it by mouth. Like I said, all we can do is wait. But I think it's only fair to tell you, it doesn't look good. He might pull through, but there's a good chance that even if he does, his heart—or even his brain—has been damaged. He may not even regain consciousness. Best thing is that he made it through the night, he's still fighting. Like I said, all we can do is wait and see."

I got in the car and drove on down the highway. Inside my chest, I felt like a powerful fist was grabbing my own heart and squeezing out all the life. A fearsome, dark loneliness—like a patient and familiar enemy—edged in around the corners of my life, ready to strike again now that my four-legged sentry was not there to defend me, to love me, to stand beside me.

I drove through the canyon of the Rio Grande, along the river. As I traveled, memories of Mountain rose to greet me. I passed a place where we had crossed to the other side last May. We'd had an unusually dry winter, which meant almost no snowpack melt that spring. The mammoth stones in the riverbed rose above the water and we could step from one to another. Right in the center of that wet highway, like a clown, Mountain stopped and perched all four of his massive paws on one rock no larger than a basketball. His big body couldn't balance on so small a center, and finally he teetered and fell into the water. I laughed at him, and he rose out of the river and began galloping around the reeds and shallows, splashing great waves of water on me and everything around him. He grew so excited with the shock of the cold water that he sped up and began circling in and out of the trout pools along one bank until he finally fell into enough depth and current that he was forced to swim. I laughed and laughed at him, and he made sure to repay me as soon as he got out by forcefully shaking every ounce of liquid out of his coat and onto my dry clothes, rubbing against my legs, and wagging his wet tail into my body.

As the canyon narrowed, I saw a tiny trail we had taken once on a hike. I was searching for petroglyphs that day, and we found many of them for me to photograph. But near the summit of that climb, we were rewarded with a much greater prize: the nest of a pair of golden eagles spread across a flat of rock near our route to the top. We stayed a distance, but as I was climbing through a crevice of two large stones nearby, I found a perfect tail feather—a good omen indeed. It was unlawful to take it, so I made a small cairn of stones and planted the plume in the center—a shrine to the beauty of the place. Mountain and I lingered on a high ledge watching for the eagles. They came, after fishing in the river, with trout dripping from their beaks. On the stone floor near their nest, they ripped the fish apart and then took turns feeding a pair of fledgling young. Using a zoom lens, I photographed them. But the best treasure I gained that day was a beautiful black-and-white photograph of the wolf that I took from the top of the canyon, his mane rippling in the wind, a big smile on his face, the Rio Grande winding for miles like a silver ribbon below him. I called the picture *Mountain on the Mountain*.

Suddenly, I felt a wave of guilt that I hadn't been able to protect him and care for him as I'd pledged to do. I'd failed him—such a beautiful, magnificent, innocent animal.

I reached the tiny village of Agua Azuela, parked the CJ, hiked behind the ancient adobe church, and started up a winding goat path on the south-facing slope. I sought the only healer who perhaps could help in this instance.

Tecolote was waiting on the *portal* as I came around a bend in the trail. She waved at me. "Come! Come, Mirasol! I made you tea!"

At her crude plank table, I sipped the warm liquid without concern about whether or not I would experience any strange visions or out-of-body episodes. It wasn't courage, but rather surrender to a sense of overwhelming fatigue and sadness.

For once, Tecolote was quiet, not chattering at me like a bat. She was intently focused on her task at hand—rolling some herbs up in tiny pieces of fabric, then tying them with bits of thread. She had at least a hundred finished ones in a pile in the center of the table, all made of solid-colored fabric, some red, some turquoise, and some white.

The tea was soothing. I felt my body relaxing.

Some time passed with neither of us speaking. The kettle on Esperanza's hearth hissed steam. I could hear birds singing outside in the chamisa bushes. It seemed so peaceful here, the sun coming in the open doorway and warming my left side.

Finally, I let out a heavy sigh.

"Don't worry, Mirasol. I am sending you something for Montaña. We will do all that we can, you and me."

I sighed again. I tried hard not to cry. "I . . ."

"Shhhhh. There is no need to talk about it. He is almost too beautiful to speak of anyway. We will do all that we can."

"He . . . someone poisoned him."

Tecolote stopped working and looked at me, tipping her head to one side. "Do you know what I am making here?" She opened her wrinkled palms to encompass the pile of cloth bundles.

"Prayer ties?" I asked.

"*Sí! Bueno, bueno!* You got it right."

"For Mountain?"

"And for you, and that boy, and maybe for the others."

"What boy? Kerry? What others?"

"Shhhhh. Drink your tea, Mirasol."

"But why are *you* making prayer ties? Isn't that a Plains Indian practice?"

"Many wise teachers came through here over the years. Do you know the village of Las Trampas?" She pointed a bony finger out the door and toward the east.

"On the High Road? Near Truchas?"

"*Sí, sí,* that one. It is named for some long-haired white men who set traps, caught animals, and sold their hides many years ago."

"Fur trappers?"

"*Sí,* trappers."

"Go on."

"Go on? You are giving me orders now?"

"No, I'm sorry. I mean, please tell me more."

"*Las trampas,* they knew a little bit about healing—not like a curandera, mind you, but they knew a few small things. They had medicines we didn't have over here, salves and things. They knew how to pull out a bullet and pack the hole it made in the body with herbs that killed the poison. They knew a lot about sewing up wounds—they used horsehair instead of sinew, and this made only tiny holes, which healed nicely and didn't attract poison and decay. And they knew a few other little things."

"But how do you know about all this? That must have been well over a hundred years ago!"

Esperanza smacked the table hard with her hand. "Have you no manners, Mirasol? You interrupt me when I am telling you a story for your own good!" Her eyes were as wide as an owl's.

"I'm sorry."

"Drink your tea!"

"I've finished it."

Tecolote hissed like a snake. She reached over the mound of prayer ties and snatched up my cup. "You are always wagging your tongue, asking foolish questions." She went to the hearth and spooned some herbs into the mug and added some of the boiling water, then hobbled back to the table. She slammed the cup down in front of me, sloshing a little of the liquid out onto the wood surface. She pointed at the cup. "Now. Your *taza* sits waiting for you to empty it again. Do not interfere any more until that is no longer the case." She looked around a little, then snatched up a piece of turquoise fabric. "Now, where was I?"

"*Las trampas,*" I prompted.

"Ah, *sí.* They knew a little something about *mal ojo y mal puesto.*"

"Evil eye? And . . ."

"*Sí,* the evil eye of witches, and the illnesses they can cause from outside a person. *Las trampas* had a *libro negro,* a black book of many spells and *remedios.* They wrote down the *curas* in there for many things, especially Indian things. They put in there the teachings from many places where they traveled, things they gathered over many years. They also lived with an old *pujacante,* a Comanche witch. The people over here let *las trampas* take beaver and elk and bear and many lions, even *los lobos* like your beautiful Montaña, for their hides. In return, we asked them questions and learned their secrets. But, you know, *más sabe el diablo por viejo que por diablo.*"

"What does that mean?"

"The devil knows more because he is old than because he is the devil."

"I don't get it."

She sighed. "How do you say it? Experience is the best teacher?"

"Oh."

"*Las trampas* had experience of Indian witches."

Tecolote went to a nail on the wall beside the door and selected several long filaments of braided sinew. "Tie these on this," she said, and showed me how to twist one of the strands of sinew around the neck of one of the prayer bundles. She looped another fabric pouch onto the same cord. And another.

We worked in silence, making long strings, each with a dozen prayer ties. When all the bundles were attached, we had ten ropes. Esperanza wrapped them in a coil like a lariat and handed them to me. "You are going to need something more," she said, and she went out the door and across the *portal* to the side of the house. I stepped outside to see where she went, but she was nowhere in sight. A minute later, she reappeared holding up a speckled egg between her thumb and forefinger. She trundled inside, set the egg down carefully on the table, and picked up some of the red cloth and tore off a large piece. She wrapped the egg several times over in the cloth, then went to the hearth and took a metal cup off a hook where it hung by its handle. She pushed the egg inside, then went back to the table, tore off another piece of red cloth, placed it over the top of the mug, and tied it tightly around the rim with a piece of sinew. "This you must not break!" she said, her voice shrill. "Take it." She held out the cup.

I spread my fingers and grasped it across the rim. Just as I thought she'd released it, she grabbed the handle and shook the cup up and down, almost causing me to lose my grip on it. I gasped.

"Good!" she said. "It won't shake around and break in there."

I breathed out hard, my nerves rattled. "What am I supposed to do with these things?"

Tecolote strode right to me, almost touching my chest. She looked up into my face. I could smell the scent of earth and clean sweat on warm skin, the tea on her breath. Her head was twisted to one side, with the ear nearly parallel to the ground. She stood less than shoulder height to me, and yet I feared having her at such close range. She reached out and plucked the ropes of prayer ties out of my hand. "*Abaje la güeja.* Bend down!" she barked.

I lowered my head, and she hung the ties around my neck. "Spend these like gold, Mirasol. You will know when you need to use one." She grabbed the wrist of my outstretched hand, the one that gripped the egg in the cup. "This *huevo fresco* is for that lovely *lobo*, Montaña. Tonight, you will break it into the cup beside where he rests. Leave it overnight, and in the morning, if we are very lucky, there will be an *ojo* in the cup, too. Then he will be healed."

I stood for a moment, then made to leave.

"Wait!" Esperanza cried. "There is one more thing." She went to the *nicho* in the wall, where dozens of candle flames danced before santos and *bultos*. She removed a sunflower from a pile of offerings. What looked like a piece of bacon encased the base of the long stem on the bloom. Tecolote tapped the wrapper. "This keeps the blossom from drying out." She handed it to me. "When you get ready to make your journey, take this off and let the flower dry as it will. You keep it with you—this is good medicine for you."

"My journey?"

"*Nunca hay caballo ensillado que a alguno no se la ofrece viaje.*"

"What does that mean?"

"It's an old vaquero saying. There is never a saddled horse that does not offer a journey to someone."

I shook my head, perplexed.

"Never mind, Mirasol. Just be careful. You will need to be very careful."

I went back to my cabin and tried to busy myself with chores. It was unseasonably warm, and a wind blew out of the southwest. I checked the level of water in the cistern to see if more needed to be hauled for my household needs. It had been a dry monsoon season, so I wasn't even catching any water off the roof to supplement what I was using. I made the bed and washed up the coffeepot and cups. I took a small hand ax and attacked a few splits of wood to make some kindling for starting fires in the woodstove. I straightened up the ends of the wood-pile and sharpened the ax. Around the perimeter of the front half of my cabin lay a perfect, half-circle, connect-the-dots arrangement of huge bones—an elk tibia, the femur of a calf, knuckles of cow and antelope—Mountain's gallery of prized possessions, all arranged at the outside circumference of the circle he could reach while hooked to the porch post, via a large stainless steel eye bolt, by the lead of stout airplane wire and carabiners. I gathered the bones up, one by one, so the coyotes and mountain lions wouldn't steal them, and I piled them on the porch beside the door.

Finally, at about a quarter to noon, I decided to follow the procedure Momma Anna had prescribed for dealing with the nachi.

I got the package and my medicine pouch out of the car and hiked up the slope behind my house and back down into the draw to La Petaca. The heat of the day coaxed a sweat from my pores, and my skin glistened by the time I got to my destination. Shaded by old, twisted junipers and piñons, all was cool and quiet near the stream except for the singing of water as it traveled over the stones. I found a soft, silty place along the bank, unwrapped the paper from around the prayer stick, and stuck it into the mud. I had to apply force to get it to stay; it wanted to lift up and travel with the current. I pushed until nearly half the shaft was under the ground. Then I opened my medicine pouch and took out some cornmeal. I offered it to the earth and sky, then sprinkled it over the nachi. Then, as Momma Anna had instructed, I kept facing it and backed away, carefully feeling behind me so I wouldn't run into a low-hanging tree branch. I threaded my way through the trees until I could no longer see the nachi, then turned and jogged up the slope and back down to my cabin.

◄ **29** ►

High Tech

I decided to enlist a new ally to gain access to the pueblo that afternoon, so I went to the BLM to use the phone. Then I headed for the Tanoah Falls Casino, just on the outskirts of the rez. When I walked in, the jingle and clang of slot machines set up a din that made my head spin. Bright lights flashed through the dimly lit space, and a wide aisle led toward the back of the building. A few customers, mostly native, sat reverent before their chosen electronic deity, cups of quarters in their hands like offerings. In the rear, a red neon sign in the shape of a buffalo skull hung on the wall. Beneath it, fry bread and Indian tacos were served at a diner-style counter. I spotted my confederate as she handed a check to a man wearing a shirt that read SOUTHWESTERN DAIRY.

Madonna gave me a subtle wave, then climbed stairs to an office above and behind the café area. She returned with a leather jacket over her arm. "You won't need that," I said. "It's turning into a scorcher."

"Really?"

"Yeah, and there's a hot wind along with it. Nothing like it's been the past few weeks."

When we got outside, Madonna waved me around to the back of the building. "I could get in a lot of trouble for this," she said, aiming the remote at Gilbert Valdez's car and disarming its alarm system.

"You're already in hot water," I said. "You don't seem to mind it."

By this time we were sitting in plush leather seats. Madonna turned the key and the motor roared to life. She turned and looked at me, close quarters. "You should talk," she said. "You're always in some kind of predicament or another. I saw you on the front page."

"Yeah, I guess everybody's seen it by now."

"Not here at the pueblo," she said.

"Why not?"

"They mentioned my husband by name. Saying the name of one who recently passed calls to their spirit, keeps them here. So they won't allow the paper out here until after he's made his journey."

As we drove the back way into the pueblo, I grilled the widow with a host of questions that had been running through my head.

"What was your husband doing in the days before his death?"

"He was doing religious training in the kiva."

"He was there night and day?"

"Yes, constantly."

"Huh. I thought Jer . . . I mean, your husband—I don't know, somehow I thought of him as more of a modern guy—a force for change in the tribe to be more viable in today's world. It surprises me that he would embrace this kind of training."

Madonna suddenly reached over and pushed my head toward my lap. "Get down! There's George Dancing Elk! If he sees you, we'll both be in trouble."

I sucked in my breath and tried to flatten my upper half over my thighs. Out of the corner of my eye, I could see Madonna wave and give a halfhearted smile. "These windows are so dark, I don't think he even saw that it was me, let alone you."

"Can I get up now?"

"Yes. Go ahead."

"Okay, let's talk about your husband's friends, associates, anyone he spent time with."

"Well, he was training with his uncle, Yellow Hawk Lujan."

"I know. Apparently no one knows where he is right now."

"I heard he'd gone fasting on the mountain. I guess some of the old ones do that before the journey; I don't know. I've never been to the Indigo Falls."

"What?! You've never made the trip up the mountain with the tribe?"

"No. This isn't my tribe, Jamaica. I don't even speak the native language here. I'm from Cochiti Pueblo down south. I have never been invited to ride up the mountain to the Indigo Falls."

"Oh, I didn't know."

"This is a small pueblo. There are only so many families. Some of the young men and women have to marry outside the tribe to avoid inbreeding. It is common that a member of the pueblo will marry someone from outside."

"But then, you aren't included in the ceremonies?"

"Some of them. And sometimes after a long time in a marriage, a few chosen ones will be included in nearly all of them, the ones who learn the language. But I have never been invited. And I don't speak Tiwa. My son will take my place, and my husband's place, in all tribal activities now. These are Angel's people, and this is his home. The house we live in is his house. I am here only to care for him."

After this, a pregnant silence. I almost dared not speak again. But I had to ask a few more questions. "So, before all this kiva training—what can you tell me about your husband's life, his routines, the people he hung out with?"

She sighed. "I might not be the best person to ask. We fought a lot. He would go away angry. He drank, sometimes a lot. I stayed away sometimes, too, when I knew he'd be home with Angel. But mostly he was at the computer lab. He practically lived there."

"Was he working with the kids all that time?"

"I don't know. I just know that I could almost always find him there if I wanted to."

I thought about that for a moment. "Do you know anything about a man named Ron who might have known your husband?"

"Yeah, Ron . . . what was that he called him? Dirty Ron? Crazy Ron? I can't remember, he had some nickname for him."

"So who is this guy?"

"I don't know, but I think he had something to do with the computers my husband bought for the lab."

"And you don't remember the nickname?"

"Ah, shoot! I know it—I just can't recall it right now. It was just some little name my husband called him. He would get ready to go out in the evening and say, 'Well, I have to go meet Shabby Ron,' or whatever it was. And off he'd go to the lab. I never met the man."

"If you remember the name, will you jot it down and tell me? Maybe

I can contact this guy and find out anything he might know. This Ron—whoever he is, it doesn't sound like someone from the pueblo."

She laughed. "No. My husband did not have too many friends here. When his family was on the war council a few years ago, he made many proposals to the tribe. He and his brother, Frank, tried to institute some changes that made them very unpopular with a lot of the elders. Yellow Hawk tried to mediate, but there was a big power struggle. They ended up having a lot of bad feelings all around. That was the year the casino got built. Even though my husband wanted a lot of modern changes—English literacy programs for the elderly, medical training for those who take care of the old and the sick, business training and assistance for entrepreneurs in the tribe, and computer training for the young people—he was *against* the casino. All his family was. They felt it was an unhealthy move for the tribe, all for the sake of greed. In the year they served on the war council, everything they tried to do was voted down. There are still hard feelings."

"Do you mind if I ask what the trouble was between you and your husband, Madonna?"

She bit her bottom lip, her eyes glistened. "I don't know exactly where to start. This was not his first marriage. He has sons almost as old as me. They're always in trouble, and they always need money. My husband couldn't say no to them."

I nodded my head.

"I am not a saint either, Jamaica. I suppose you already know that. I had a daughter before we were married, by another man. I was not married then, I was only a child myself. My daughter lives with my mother at Cochiti. She will be fourteen next month—she'll be the same age as I was when I had her. She already had her Becomes Woman ceremony and everything, where she had to grind corn for four days and everyone went from house to house singing her name. I went there for the ceremony, and I felt ashamed that there was no father there to sing for her. I missed my people then, and I felt like I lived in three worlds—my home at Cochiti, my life here, and the modern world we have to live in now in order to survive. It's not easy when you have all that to deal with.

"But . . . I guess I don't understand some things about the way people live here. My husband seemed like a pretty forward-thinking guy. We both agreed that we live in modern times and can't go back to the past, so we're not going to live as if we're trying to ignore progress. But he started building that house five years ago, and nothing is finished in it. I wanted nice things, and he told me I was being greedy. I was lonely at home with Angel all day, so I went out and got a job. My husband never forgave me for that. But my job made it possible for us to have a new car, some nice furniture, good clothes. I want Angel to have nice things, too."

"And you fought about that? About money? And things?"

"Yes. And about what a woman is supposed to do in this world."

"So . . . your spouse wanted you to assume a more traditional role as a wife?"

She snickered. "That's putting it mildly."

"Even though he wanted so much education and economic viability for the young people of the tribe?"

"It doesn't make sense, does it? Well, the lab is just right over there."

Ahead of us was the Indian Center, a beautiful new building where important community events transpired: lessons in basket weaving and micaceous clay pottery making, lectures on care for diabetes and high blood pressure, and food stamp and surplus product distribution. Here, federal employees worked to serve the tribe in a variety of programs. Because the pueblo was closed, the Indian Center was vacant, or at least its parking lot was empty. Madonna pulled around into a dirt lot behind the big building. The computer lab was a portable metal classroom set on dirt among the sagebrush, made level by concrete blocks and some railroad ties. A family of tumbleweeds had lodged beneath the wooden steps up to the door of the lab. The wind buffeted and caused the steps to creak. It was hot, and the blowing dust felt like it was sandblasting my skin as I got out of the car.

"Looks like there's no one here. You're lucky this is Quiet Time, and computers and things like that are forbidden right now. Normally, this place is full of kids, no matter what time of day. Only time my husband could find any peace to work here was at night, so that's when he came to write programs, grants, lessons for the young people, things like that. He said it was the only time he could hear himself think. I brought some keys from the house—we'll just have to see if one of them works."

Inside, the space was divided into two sections. In one half of the room, a few rugs were spread on the floor and a half circle was made of large woven pillows adorned with images of turtles, bison, horses, and wolves. A painted gourd rattle, with a hawk talon for a handle, and a blackened micaceous pottery smudge bowl sat in the center of a rug. On the other side, a row of computers squatted like one-eyed gargoyles on desks made from doors and sawhorses. Above these, on the wall, spread a display of students' computer artwork. Vivid, primary colors illuminated the name *Aerosmith* across one large sheet of paper, done in a futuristic font with a host of graphic arrows going outward from the band's name in all directions. A cubist face of a brave in red and green war paint stared out from another piece of paper. Another entry in this exhibit was a long, winding red-dirt road with a platoon of red chess pawns placed along its length. A giant white hand reached down to reposition one of the pawns. At the bottom, the title of the piece was *The Red Road*.

I turned to Madonna, who was shuffling through some papers on a desk. "Is this what your mate was teaching? Computer graphics?"

She looked up at me. "Actually, I think that was just the students playing around with some of the programs. I think he was teaching them basic computer applications—you know, word processing, spreadsheets, presentations."

"But there's a lot of artwork here."

"I know. A bunch of the kids liked to hang out here and do that stuff. It was kind of like a club. They came every day after school. My husband said it kept them out of trouble. He encouraged anything that made them computer literate."

I walked to the desk where she was riffling through papers. "Is this where he worked?"

"Yes. He did his grant writing here, and he designed programs and developed learning exercises for the kids to do."

I pressed the power key. "Mind if we look at his hard drive and see what's on there?"

"No, I was just looking through these papers . . . sometimes he would write letters to Angel in Tiwa, on the computer. He wanted his son to know his native tongue as well as how to operate a computer. He would write short notes to him in the tribal language. Sometimes he'd print them out with a little picture, but sometimes he'd tell Angel to check in his file on the computer, that there would be something in there for him. Angel comes here with his Head Start group in the mornings."

"Angel comes here to study Tiwa with Hunter Contreras?"

"Yes."

"Do you know a kid named Sam Dreams Eagle?"

"Know him? He's Angel's best friend. Even though Sam's a couple years older than him, they play together all the time."

"Does Sam come here for Head Start, too?"

"Well, he used to. Now he's in elementary school. But I heard his old granny sent him and his brother to the Indian School in Santa Fe this week. Probably got too much for her to deal with—she's hard of hearing, you know, and I think she's losing her sight, too. Angel keeps saying that Sam ran away. He doesn't understand why his friend had to leave."

By this time the display was up and the cursor prompted for a user password.

"I know this." Madonna smiled. She typed quickly. "Angel told me one night when I was putting him to bed and we'd talked about secrets. I shared one with him, and he shared this one with me."

Once I had access to the computer's desktop, I pulled out a chair and sat down.

"That's funny," Madonna said. "Usually there's a picture of an angel right there on the desktop, right in that corner. That's an icon for his file. It's not there now. In fact, there used to be a lot of stuff on the screen when you first booted up, shortcuts to files with pictures and documents in them. It looked like a comic book. Now it's all blank!"

I scanned the contents of the hard drive. "Everything's been deleted. Nothing but native applications, no document files, no picture files, nothing. It looks like there's nothing on this computer that wasn't there when it came out of the box."

Madonna drew up. Her face looked stern. "What happened to my husband's letters to Angel?"

"I don't know." I looked around. "Could they have switched the computers around? Could another one of these be the one?"

"No," Madonna said. "See that microphone resting on the top of the monitor? He used that to record little messages for Angel. He had voice-recognition software—none of the other computers had it. He worked with that software for a long time on the computer at home to get it to work with his native tongue."

I checked the list of recent applications on the hard drive and saw SpeakAloud. I tried to find the application but had no success. "Maybe he has another code or a password on this."

"If he does, I don't know it."

"Does anybody else use his computer here? Any of the kids? That Ron guy?"

"I don't know. I don't think so. You saw that I had to use a password to log on. Unless somebody knew it, I don't think they could even get to the desktop."

"How about Contreras? Does he use computers when he teaches the kids the language?"

Madonna laughed. "Are you kidding? It's a miracle that guy will even allow Indians to drive cars around here. He doesn't want much to do with anything that's going to change the way the pueblo has been for the past few centuries. If he could, he'd turn back the clock and I'd be chewing a buffalo hide to soften it tonight—after I served dinner and washed everyone's feet."

I looked through the items atop Santana's desk: a pile of papers including a PC supply house catalog, files of grant paperwork for the computer literacy program, letters to the high school requesting that students be given opportunities to use computer equipment; a stack of blank data CDs; a ream of printer paper; and some sticky notes. Above the monitor, tacked to the wall, were a list of the students' names and phone numbers, a photo of Madonna with Angel as a baby, another photo of Angel on the lap of a department store Santa Claus, and a group shot of the Head Start kids sitting in their semicircle on their pillows, with Contreras at the hub, his back to the camera. I turned and looked toward the area where the small children studied their native language. It was as if the photo were taken right from in front of Santana's desk—everything lined up perfectly in the picture just as I saw it from where I stood.

"Did your partner and Contreras get along?"

"Oh, I think they had their differences, but they worked them out. I know when Hunter was looking for space for his language program, my husband really wanted them here. They could have used the Indian Center—which has much nicer rooms—because that program is federally funded. They wouldn't have had to share a room like this. But Hunter didn't want any of the white people who worked there to overhear the language and maybe learn some of it." She chuckled at this. "My husband made the high school kids come one day and move all the computers over against one wall to make space for them. And he wanted Angel in the program, too."

"Can I see your computer at home?"

"Oh, we don't have it anymore. I sold it."

"You sold it?"

"Yes. After a point, my husband was always working here, never at home. He didn't use it anymore. I figured we could use the money."

◀ 30 ▶

Looking for Clues

When I returned to town, I stopped at the vet clinic to see my beloved Mountain. "My name's Steve," the tech told me, offering his hand. "I'm the one taking care of your wolf today. He's still not conscious, but his pulse rate has stabilized and we're not as worried about respiratory failure—at least for right now. We're just hoping he'll come out of this coma. We've moved him to one of our large cells with its own run. We put him right on the floor, and even for a while packed him with some ice. It's so hot today, and it's cool on that concrete slab. Atropine affects the body's ability to regulate temperature, so we have done everything we can to keep him cool. He's just resting, and we're checking on him every half hour or so. We have him on some IV fluids to keep him from getting dehydrated. There's nothing else we can do."

"Can I see him?"

"Sure, c'mon back."

Wild Indigo

In gray light a beautiful carpet of blond and black fur lay completely inanimate against cold cement. The tech opened the cell gate and I went in. I touched Mountain's face. I could hear small breaths. I put my hand to his chest. A weak heartbeat. I sat on the floor and looked at him, touching his feet, his legs, his face, his ears. I raised one of his lifeless paws and pressed it over my face. I always loved the way his pads smelled, wild and warm and wolflike. A place on his foreleg had been shaved, and a bandage secured an intravenous valve connected to a long plastic tube leading to a bag of clear liquid that hung from the wire cage wall. I maneuvered myself behind him and lay down, pressing my body into his back. I could feel the weak whisper of life within him, fighting for a foothold. Tears poured from my eyes and I felt like my chest would split open. I pushed myself closer and ran my fingers through the long, beautiful ruff at his neck. I stroked his side and buried my face in the back of his head. I willed my heart to open and beat for both of us, my lungs to breathe enough air to feed his body, too, my spirit to dive into the uncertain abyss between life and death and find Mountain, lift him up, and bring him home again. I thought for a brief moment that if he died, I wanted to die, too, to go with him and never be apart from him again. And I cried aloud, such a wail that Steve opened the door and looked in on me—then said nothing and closed the door again.

A voice woke me. "Ms. Wild? We're about to close for the evening. I thought I'd let you know. You're welcome to stay—I'm going to sleep on a cot here in the surgery room and keep an eye on Mountain. In fact, we're about to hook up another IV to give your wolf some liquid nourishment. But I thought you might like to know we're closing up the clinic and everyone else is leaving."

I lifted my arm from around Mountain's neck. I felt his nose, and it was dry, but there was a little breath coming out. "What time is it?"

"It's seven. The doctor has already left for the day."

"I have to go somewhere. But I'm coming back when I'm finished."

"Well, okay, I guess that would be all right. Just knock at the back door, around behind the building."

I knelt on the concrete floor and lowered my face into the crook of Mountain's neck. "I'll be back, buddy, as quick as I can. Wait for me, okay?"

I stopped by the market just as Jesse was locking the door. "*Buenas tardes*, Jamaica!" he said. "Hey, got a new car?"

"I'm sorry to ask this, Jesse, but could I come in and just pick up a few things, really quick?"

"I guess so. Hey, where's Mountain? Isn't he with you?"

"He . . . I . . ." I closed my eyes and tried to compose myself.

Jesse opened the door and stood aside for me to enter. As I walked through, he patted me on the back. "There, there, now. Tell me where El Lobo is. I want to know."

"He's at the vet. I think someone poisoned him." In spite of myself, I started to cry. "I don't know if he's going to make it."

"Damn! Who does a thing like this? I hear about it every other day here in Taos—somebody's always either shooting a dog or putting some antifreeze down to poison it. How did it happen? Did someone come all the way out to your place out there, or what?"

"I don't know. I don't know. Just . . . will you ask your wife to pray for him?"

"You damn betcha! I'll have her go down to the *sanctuario* this evening and light a candle. Maybe I'll even go with her. You go ahead and get what you need—I have to get something out of the back."

I wandered around trying to find some things to take to the family feast at the pueblo. I finally settled on a bagged salad mix, some cherry tomatoes and cucumbers, a can of black olives, a bottle of lemon vinaigrette, and some cold, peeled, precooked shrimp from Jesse's meat cooler. As hot as the day still was, I thought a cold shrimp salad would be a good dish to bring. When I got up to the register with my basket of items, Jesse stood over a huge parcel on the counter wrapped in butcher paper. "No charge tonight," he said. "I already counted up the register. I don't want my accountant to get confused." He began stuffing my items in a paper sack.

"No, I . . . Just let me write you a check and you can put it in tomorrow's earnings."

"No, I ain't gonna take your check. You got enough going on, just get on out of here."

"Jesse, you don't have to do this. I want to pay you for these things."

"Go on, now," he said, shoving the sack in my arms, "or you gonna make me mad. You don't want to see me mad, I'm telling you."

I sniffed back more tears. "Thanks, Jesse. You're a dear." I put an arm around the man and gave him a hug.

He was clearly surprised, and a little embarrassed. "Go on now," he said. He followed me out of the store with his large parcel, barely able to hold it up with one arm while he locked the door. I was loading my groceries into the back of the CJ when Jesse came up and tossed the big paper-wrapped bundle onto the rear deck. "That's for Mountain," he said. "It's part of a side of elk. He's going to need his strength when he recovers. Red meat is good for that. Don't worry, it's frozen. I predict by the time that thaws out, you'll have El Lobo back home and he'll be as good as new."

My mouth opened but I couldn't speak.

"Don't say nothing to my wife about that," Jesse said as he walked toward his pickup. "She don't need to know that I got a crush on some wolf. It would make her jealous, and I wouldn't be able to live with her like that."

At the gas station in Cascada Azul, I went to use the pay phone and called the ranger station in Tres Piedras. My voice came out in a whisper. "He's still alive."

"Where are you?" Kerry asked.

"I have to go to the family feast at the pueblo. Then I'm going back to the vet clinic. There's a guy there named Steve—he's going to spend the night and watch Mountain, keep him hydrated. I'm going to spend the night there, too, after the feast. I brought some things."

"I'll come when I get off work. Do you need anything, babe?"

I gulped. "I need Mountain." My voice was a soft cry.

"I know, I know. I'll be there as soon as I can, okay?"

Waiting for Serena, I remembered the maxim about being on "Indian time." When Momma Anna invited me to come to her house, or anyplace else for that matter, even when I arrived on or before the specified time, she would always say, "You're so la-ate!" in her singsong Tiwa greeting. But if she were to meet me anywhere outside of the reservation, I might wait as much as an hour and a half, and when she arrived, she might not say anything—or she might tell me the story of what she encountered along the way, as if this were explanation for why I was made to linger alone for so long.

I sat in the CJ in a corner of the lot, the windows down due to the heat. A car pulled up and unloaded a passenger. I saw Bone Man emerge, then open the back door—and out tumbled Bob Marley, his golden retriever. Bone Man reached into the backseat and pulled out a large duffel bag. The car pulled away.

Aw, jeez. Of all the times to have to deal with Bone Man.

It didn't take long for the hippie to spot me, and I saw recognition in his face soon thereafter. He made a beeline for me. "Wow, dude! You got another car! Hey, your face looks all better, too!"

Sensing that I might be trapped if Bone Man came up to the driver's-side door, I got out of the Jeep and came a few steps toward him. Bob Marley ran to me and deposited a huge loogy of slobber on the thigh of my jeans. "So, what you got there, Bone Man? You moving or something?"

He looked behind him, his face confused. Then the lights came on. "Oh, you mean the duffel? Dude, this is some great stuff. Wanna see?"

Before I could think of an excuse not to, Bone Man had pulled a rolled-up army blanket out of the bag. He proceeded to unfurl it, then to lay out some items in a rough display. He had an assortment of crudely taxidermied parts and pieces, mostly bear—faces, paws with claws, a cased arm of a bear like the one I'd seen in Professor Mason's book, and a variety of animal tails and paws, from coyote to badger.

"What are you doing with all this stuff?" I asked.

"Indigo Falls time, man. I do a lot of trading at the pueblo this time of year so they can get their medicine right for the journey."

"Yeah? What do you trade for?"

"Cash. A few other things."

"Like what?"

"You won't bust me if I tell you?"

"I'm not the DEA, Bone Man. I'm a resource protection agent. Unless you're trading in endangered species or doing harm to the land, you're out of my ballpark."

"Dude, I'm always careful about that shit. I don't want to bring bad juju to myself." He snatched a lynx paw out of Bob Marley's jaws. "Stop that! You know you can't eat this stuff!" He started to roll up his wares in the blanket again. "Okay, I think it's probably safe to tell you—but just in case, I want you to know that I'm a member of the American Indian Church so you can't bust me for this."

"For what?"

"I get peyote and sometimes some jimsonweed, too. I use it for ceremonial purposes only."

"Yeah, I bet."

He stood up, stuffed the roll back into the duffel. "No, it's true. I'm a seeker. I'm always looking for visions. That stuff helps me get my *sight.*"

"Okay, whatever, Bone Man."

He pulled the drawstring on the duffel bag and tied it. "I probably won't get any jimsonweed this year, though. That stuff has to be doled out by a shaman, someone who really knows what he's doing, or it can poison you. The medicine man who administers it is gone."

"Gone?"

"Yeah, they say he left his horse standing out in the yard and just walked off without him. I guess the horse nearly died—it didn't have food or water and was tied to some tree for a couple days."

My heart beat so hard I could hear my pulse in my temples. "What's the name of this shaman?"

"Yellow Hawk. He's the peyote chief. He's the head of the church right now, too. He's the only one who can administer the sacrament—at least right now—well, there was this one dude before him, he's my buddy Ismael. But I guess he got deposed or something like that, and he's not supposed to do it anymore. So now Yellow Hawk's the only one."

I forced myself to breathe. "Do you know where he's gone to?"

"Dude, nobody does. Nobody's getting the sacrament for their vision quest. It's got the whole tribe worked up."

"Excuse me," I said, fishing in my pocket for change. "I have to make a phone call."

Diane answered her cell phone. "Langstrom."

"Hey, have you heard anything about a missing person out at the pueblo?"

"Not that kid again, right?"

"No, I'm talking one of the tribal elders. His name's Yellow Hawk Lujan."

"We usually get our Missing and Endangered reports from the sheriff's office. Have you talked to them?"

"No, and I'm at a pay phone, but I know a guy who would know what's up at the S.O. Do you know Jerry Padilla?"

"Horny guy, always slobbering over your tits?"

"Yeah, that's him."

"I could call and see what he knows. Why?"

"I think there's some foul play here. Yellow Hawk was giving Santana religious training in the kiva before he died. He's also the peyote chief and the leader of the American Indian Church. You remember that hippie guy I introduced you to, Bone Man?"

"Gawd. That guy stunk, how could I forget him?"

"Well, he says that Yellow Hawk administered the peyote and the jimsonweed at the pueblo, and now he's gone. My medicine teacher, Momma Anna, is his sister, and she also said that Yellow Hawk had disappeared."

"Well, I guess I can check and see if there's an MEP report on him. I'll call Padilla."

"And, Diane?"

"Yeah?"

"Somebody poisoned Mountain."

"Son of a bitch! Is he . . . ?"

"He's at the animal clinic in Taos. He's barely hanging on."

"What happened?"

"I don't know exactly. It's—I'll have to tell you about it another time. I'm waiting to get a ride into the pueblo right now."

"Oh, no. Not again."

"It's okay, I've actually been invited to the family feast. They're having someone pick me up at the gas station—you know the one in Cascada Azul where you and I talked the other night?"

"Yeah. Just the same, be careful. Where can I reach you if I get any information on this Yellow Hawk guy?"

"I'm going back to the vet clinic after the feast. I'll be there with Mountain."

"Okay, well, I'll get back to you then."

"Wait. Diane?"

"Yeah?"

"One more thing. Is there any way you can check and see if Sam Dreams Eagle is really at the Indian School in Santa Fe?"

"Why? You think he's rolled up in this?"

"I'm sure of it."

"How do you know?"

"I just have a big damn buzz."

◄ 31 ►

Family Feast

In the small kitchen of Grandma Bird and Grandpa Nazario's adobe home, the stove exuded a tremendous heat. Stoked with wood, there was a pot on every burner, and the oven was full of feast dishes. I found a large plastic bowl on the shelf and started assembling my shrimp salad.

Momma Anna appeared over my shoulder. "Why you bring that?" she grunted.

I turned and gave her the formal greeting of respect. Then I answered, "It's a shrimp salad. I thought something cool would be good— it's been so hot today, and that warm wind . . ."

She looked at the bowl as if green slime were swimming in it. "Why you bring that? You know what we eat! We eat meat. We eat chili, posole, stew. Not shrimp salad! Indun not eat shrimp salad."

All the women in the kitchen stopped to observe this discourse. They stared at me.

I hung my head, trying to appear ashamed, but in truth I was angry. I swallowed, then said, "I'm sorry. I'll take it back with me; we don't have to put it on the feast table."

Momma Anna gave another grunt and moved through the crowd of cooks to the stove, where she tasted her red chili with elk meat. "Indun eat meat," she said again, not looking at me. Then she turned to a forty-gallon drum that was lined with a black plastic bag. She reached into the sack and pulled out round loaves of Pueblo bread that had no doubt been baked by the women long before dawn this morning. When she had placed about a dozen of them on the table, she and Yohe began slicing the bread.

After what seemed like an interminable silence, the other women resumed their cooking and preparations for the feast.

I stepped out the back door of the kitchen to catch my breath, wishing I had my car so I could leave. *I wish I hadn't had to ride here with Serena. Now I'll have to wait until she's ready to take me back.*

The men were stacking wood in a square tower on the hard dirt for a small bonfire. They talked softly among themselves and laughed. Anna's son Frank looked across the yard at me and gave me the slightest nod. His uncles Eddie and Pete were splitting wood. Both much younger than their sister Anna, they were quite near to Frank's age. Several teenaged boys stood under the brush arbor and laughed and pawed at one another. They looked at me and scanned my figure. This was no place for a woman. I went back inside.

By now, the ladies were ready to serve. The same table, constructed of plywood and sawhorses, held steaming dishes of food, baskets of prune pies and cookies, and plastic pitchers of Kool-Aid. These filled the center with barely enough room for the foam plates that rimmed the outer edges of the table. Heaping platters of roasted pork, stewed beef and vegetables, and sliced elk meat exuded an earthy scent. Big casseroles of sweet potatoes, *supa,* posole, and red chili added color and spice. A towering tray of sopapillas and the sliced loaves of the horno-baked bread spread so wide that three women had to work to rearrange the dishes already on the table to make a place for it. Momma Anna took my hand and pulled me toward the kiva fireplace in the corner of the main room. "Your face all better. You do what I tell you?" She clutched her *jish* through her shirt, referring to the root she had given me.

"I did, Momma Anna, but something went wrong."

"What went wrong?"

"I don't know. I ended up on the floor, passed out, and Mountain . . ." I had to stop and swallow hard to keep the emotion down. "He ended up poisoned somehow. He almost died, he may still—"

"What poison? Who?"

"I don't know, I was burning the—the root you gave me, and it all happened then."

"Where the wolf now?"

"He's at the vet clinic. He's so weak, Momma Anna." I could feel tears welling.

"What happen?"

"I don't know. He's in a coma."

"Coma? What that?"

"He's not awake, he doesn't respond. He's just barely alive, not aware. The vet said someone gave him atropine."

"What that?"

"I don't know—a drug of some kind. I thought maybe he got the other half of that root you gave me. I can't find it."

Momma Anna opened her mouth in shock. "You lost your cachana? How you do that?"

"I was burning some with the red chile seeds and the salt, and then I passed out on the floor. When I woke up, Mountain had been poisoned. I thought maybe he had eaten the root."

"No, no, that not what cachana do—maybe you breathe too much, but it not poison. Sound like someone give that wolf *ololiuhqui*."

"What's that?"

"Only medicine man can give. Very deadly if not done right. My brother Yellow Hawk only one right now can do it."

Just then, Grandpa Nazario rose and held his palm up in the air, signaling the beginning of a prayer. Yohe hurried outside to gather up the men. They filed in quietly, removing their hats, squeezing against one another and the walls of the room.

Momma Anna let go of my arm and worked her way through the crowd to her father. She whispered in Nazario's ear. He nodded. Then Anna took one of the gas lamps down from its nail hanger on a viga that spanned the roof. She lit the lamp and held it up as Grandpa prayed.

I had been to many feasts, and as Grandpa Nazario prayed in Tiwa, I knew he was calling the ancestors. He was naming them all, inviting them to feast with them, and asking for their blessing on the gathering. We stood, hand in hand, for what seemed like a half hour while this incantation went forth. Then someone passed me a large glass of water. I took my sip and passed it on, as I had been taught to do. We all drank from the same cup. When we were finished, Auntie took a plate and put a tiny bit of each food from the table onto it, making an offering to these ancestors that were just summoned. She started to take the dish toward the kitchen, and I knew that she would then take it outside—to the sunset—where she would leave it for the spirits to feast upon. But before she could work her way through the gathered crowd, Momma Anna handed the lamp to someone and said loudly, "Wait. Look what my daughter bring." She pressed her way into the kitchen and emerged with my shrimp salad held above her head. She set it proudly down on the table, pushing aside one of the Styrofoam plates to make room for it. "I not eat anything but this. My daughter make this shrimp salad for feast."

A pinch of lettuce was added to the spirit plate, everyone grunted in agreement that it looked good, and the feast began, with the elders and little children eating first while the others waited on them.

When most of the family had eaten, Serena, Yohe, and I sat down to have some food. The table was still full of young folks, and Hunter sat at the far end from us, teasing the teenaged boys and making them laugh. Serena said, "You know my dad prayed for your wolf tonight."

I turned to face her. "He did?"

"Yes. Anna told him, right before the prayer, that your wolf is sick or dying or something."

I lowered my head and pushed a forkful of posole around the plate. "Yes, he's in a bad way. But I'm grateful for the prayers."

"We will all be praying for him. And for you. You didn't eat hardly anything. Lucky the old ones already ate and didn't see you. Otherwise, they'd make you eat. You just been playing with that little bit of food on your plate."

The front door opened, and tribal police chief Epifanio Moon Eagle and another man I didn't recognize stepped into the room. Moon Eagle was nodding his head, bowing and smiling, greeting all the family, when his eyes lit on me. His face grew stern and he said something to one of the women in Tiwa. A small crowd gathered around him, and there was much chatter. Momma Anna was wringing her hands and pushing her lips out in a scowl as she argued with the policeman.

I stood up, wondering what would happen to me.

But Hunter got up from the end of the table, made his way through the welcoming committee of women, and spoke to Moon Eagle. I saw him gesture with a wide sweep of his hand, as if to take in the scope of the whole family. Then Contreras made another gesture toward Grandma Bird and Grandpa Nazario, who were sitting on the edge of the bed alongside the woodstove. Moon Eagle finally nodded his head, relenting. The women busied themselves with rewelcoming him— Serena got him a plate, Yohe took his hat, and Auntie ushered him to one of the benches at the plywood table.

I sat back down, not certain what to do.

Moon Eagle dipped a sopapilla in some red chili and looked across the table at me. "You got a reprieve tonight. I guess the old ones all want you at their feast, so I'm gonna turn my head, pretend like I didn't see you. I hope you didn't drive here and somebody spots that broken-up Jeep somewhere and reports it."

"I didn't drive," I said. Then I picked up my plate and cup and started for the kitchen. But I stopped alongside Moon Eagle and bent down to speak quietly to him. "Do you know anything about what's happened to Anna's brother Yellow Hawk?"

Moon Eagle swung his big frame and looked directly at me. "They say he left his horse standing out in the yard, tied to a tree, and went off to fast and pray."

"Don't you think that's odd—that he would abandon his horse like that?"

The chief blotted the chili from his lips. He ran his tongue over his teeth. "Do you know Yellow Hawk?"

"A little. I met him once at a family wedding, and I see him some-times on feast days. We've only spoken once."

"But you know he's the peyote chief, right?"

"Yes, someone told me that."

"Well, they don't get to be peyote chief by walking the straight and narrow, if you know what I mean."

"I guess I don't follow you."

"I mean, Yellow Hawk is an old man. He gets a little absentminded. He's done a lot of ceremony in the past few weeks, done a lot of sweats, taken some herbs."

I thought for a moment. "I think people are worried about him."

Moon Eagle turned back to his plate. "Well, if they are, they should talk to me about it. Now I'm gonna have a little more of this red chili, if you don't mind." He turned back to his plate.

Most of the women were working in the kitchen, so I went to join them. Momma Anna handed me a bucket and told me to go for more water. I headed out the door and walked along the adobe wall to avoid the men at the bonfire out in the yard. The night was black beyond the gas lamps in the house and the sparks of the little fire. I felt around and finally found the rail for the steps over the wall and took them carefully down to the dirt alley below. I crossed to the corral and then searched in the dark for the pump. It took me a while to find my bearings. I pushed the lever up and down to prime the pump until the water began to flow. As I was filling the bucket, I noticed a light from the top of the wall. Serena called to me in a forced whisper, "Jamaica! Come quick!"

I fastened the handle down on the pump shaft and hoisted the heavy bucket. I trudged across the alley, trying not to slosh too much of the liquid out, and then I muscled my way up the stairs with the heavy load. "What?" I asked.

Serena lowered her small flashlight. "The governor is here. Eliseo Contreras. Anna told me to keep you out of sight so he won't see you. He's come to pay respects to my family. He's Hunter's brother, you know. Hunter likes you so much, he won't mention that you are here. But we have to stay away for a little while."

Serena took the bucket of water to the kitchen and then we went back over the wall to the corral with a basket of food. We got in Serena's truck and she drove to the home of Jerome and Madonna Santana. "I know my sister is angry with her—that's why Madonna didn't come tonight. But she is still my niece," Serena explained. "And little Angel is my godson as well as my great-nephew. I want him to share in the feast for his father's homecoming."

We took the basket to the door. Serena opened it without knocking and called out, "Angel! Madonna! It's your auntie Serena."

Angel came bounding down the stairs, wearing his earphones and carrying his portable CD player. He paused on the bottom step, pressed a button on the device, pulled the earphones out, and gave his great-aunt a hug. "Mommy just called," he said, clearly excited. "She's done working, and she'll be home in a few minutes!"

Serena made her way to the kitchen, where she took the plastic bowls and bags out of the basket and began warming food. "You set the table," she told me.

A glossy wood table dominated the small, unfinished dining room. Pink insulation and bare studs lined one wall. The other walls had been drywalled, but not mudded and taped. Angel pulled some place mats out of a drawer and helped me find paper napkins and flatware.

By the time Madonna walked in the door, we had a banquet set for the twosome. Angel knelt in one of the upholstered captain's chairs and played with a spoon. Madonna's eyes glistened as she took in the spread of feast dishes.

"My nephew has made his journey," Serena said. She took a small dish and prepared another spirit plate, just as Auntie had done at Grandpa and Grandma's. As she took it outside, Madonna went to her son and they embraced.

"Let's all say a prayer," Serena said when she returned. We joined hands at one end of the table and Serena started the Lord's Prayer in English. Madonna and I joined in, but little Angel wiggled and squirmed as he stood in the chair.

"You should join us," Madonna said, inviting Serena and me to sit down.

"No, we can't stay," her aunt answered. "There are lots of dishes to be done at Mom's house. We better get back. I just didn't want you and Angel to miss the final feast." She went to the kitchen to get her basket.

"Oh, Jamaica," Madonna said. "I remembered what my husband used to call that guy: *Seedy.*"

"Seedy?"

"Yeah, that's it."

"Why? Was he down on his luck or something?"

"I don't know. But he always smiled when he said it, like it was a joke."

"Huh." I moved toward the door.

Angel got down from the chair and took my hand. "You 'member, you told me to keep looking for my friend?"

I squatted down to his level. "Yeah. Did you find him?"

"Uh-huh."

"See? I told you that would work."

"But now he's gone again."

"Well, maybe you'll find him again."

"No, he runned away."

"He ran away from you?"

"No, he runned away from *everyone*. He runned up the mountain to hide."

Madonna interrupted: "I told you, Angel, Sam's old granny sent him and his brother to school in Santa Fe."

"Nuh-uh!"

I took Angel's hand. "Well, let's hope so. You go over and ask his grandmother in the morning, okay?"

Serena came to the door with her basket. She hugged Madonna and little Angel, and then I did the same.

"Thanks again," Madonna said before closing the door.

Later, after all the tribal guests had left Grandpa and Grandma's house and the dishes were washed and put away, I went out the kitchen door to spread the dish towels and rags over the adobe hornos to dry. The sky was sprinkled with stars, the moon not up yet, and the last few embers of the bonfire crackled in the dirt across the yard. It was only a little cooler outside than in the house. I stood and felt the breeze. Frank Santana came over to me. It was the first time I'd gotten to speak to him since his brother's death.

"I'm so sorry for your loss," I said.

"Thank you. My brother is home now, he's made the journey. I wanted to thank you for the basket you brought by the house."

"Oh, it was nothing."

"The wind has changed direction," he said. "It's coming out of the east now. My mom says that's a sign something bad is going to happen."

I blew out a breath. "I don't think I could take anything else bad happening."

Frank looked at me. "I heard Grandpa pray for your wolf. Someone said he is dying."

I shuddered. "God, I hope he doesn't die. I don't know what I will do if he dies."

He reached out a hand and put it on my arm. "Sometimes Creator wants one of our family to come home. That's what happened with my brother."

I shook my head. "Do you really believe that, Frank?"

He looked away. "I don't know. That's what they teach us. It sounds good, anyway."

I took a risk: "What if I told you I thought something was strange about your brother's death? That it didn't feel right to me?"

Frank was quiet.

"I'm sorry," I said. "I didn't mean—"

"No," he interrupted. "Let's walk over here a little ways." He pointed toward the brush arbor, now empty. We strolled to the structure and sat down in two of the lawn chairs underneath the thatch of cedar branches across the top. Frank pointed to the eastern sky. "My uncle said that group of stars over there is our ancestors, looking down at us."

"Which uncle?"

Frank leaned in close to me and almost whispered, "The one who is missing. Yellow Hawk. George Dancing Elk found his horse next to his house, nearly dead. He had saddled it and made ready for the journey, but he never rode out. People say he walked up the mountain, but I think something is wrong there, too."

"Where do you think he is?"

"I think he must be on the mountain; he's not here. But I don't think he went on his own. He wouldn't have left his horse like that. That's not like him."

"What do you think happened?"

A large plume of sparks and small embers erupted from the bonfire, and the men gathered around it cheered. In the spark-light, I saw a few of them holding beer bottles, hiding them against their chests in the crook of their arms. Alcohol was forbidden on the reservation, and was even more taboo during Quiet Time.

"I think," Frank whispered, "my uncle knows something. When you find my uncle, he can tell us the answers."

"When *I* find him? Why me?"

"You can go up the mountain, right? Beyond the reservation, it's federal land, isn't it?"

Here, a legal battle had been broiling away for decades. The U.S. government had claimed the land comprising Sacred Mountain in the early fifties, only to have the court overturn it a decade later, thanks to the Native American Defense Initiative, which fought legal battles on the part of the continent's original peoples. Appeals and counterappeals had held the matter in limbo ever since, but a portion of land—including the area surrounding the mouth of Indigo Falls—had been wrested back from the feds and granted to the pueblo in perpetuity. Members of Tanoah Pueblo still made the journey to the Indigo Falls every autumn, following the same route their ancestors had for centuries. But, according to the current legal status, the BLM and U.S. Forest Service oversaw a large parcel of the wilderness area that included the course the ancient trail took between the reservation and the falls. Lines drawn on maps did not dissuade these people from making their annual pilgrimage. Nor was I prevented from following the path, since it was federal land, at least up a part of the trail. The glitch, however, was that no white man was allowed on the sacred ground at the mouth of the falls. And the Indians fiercely protected that sanctuary.

"Why don't *you* go up the mountain and find him?" I asked.

"We don't make the journey until Saturday. We have preparations until then. By that time, it may be too late. My uncle could starve to death or die of thirst. The wind is changing, so the weather will change, too. He may die of exposure. We cannot leave until after the second sunrise from now. You could go tomorrow."

"But he surely knows how to survive up there! He's made this journey before, hasn't he? Doesn't he go up there to fast and pray?"

"He didn't take his things. They were still with his horse. He left his blanket, his jerky, his water, his totems. He can't survive without them; he's old."

"But we don't even know if he's up there."

A large shadow blocked the light of the dwindling bonfire. Hunter Contreras spoke from the shadows: "What are you two doing out here?"

Frank stood up. "Talking about how the wind has changed."

I rose, too.

Hunter said, "Yeah. Maybe it will cool off again. This heat today was bad." He waved a big hand at me. "C'mon, Jamaica. Serena says she has to get the kids to bed, so she wants to take you back."

◄ 32 ►

Animal Wisdom

In the cold gray cell in the back of the animal clinic, I laced the end of one of the ropes of prayer ties through the gate and stretched it to another segment on the side wall, fastening it there like a garland. I carefully untied the red cloth from the top of the cup, unwrapped the egg, and broke it into the mug. I set it in the corner. Then I knelt on the floor. I unwrapped a bundle of offerings and laid them out before Mountain. His favorite squeaky toy: a bright-colored rubber porcupine almost the size of a football. A huge bone. A bandanna that Momma Anna had given him for Christmas. A stuffed toy pheasant with a torn beak and a coat matted with dried drool. A black rubber Kong toy. A little plush hedgehog that made a grunting noise when squeezed. A T-shirt that I'd worn several times without washing, which would comfort him because it was permeated with my scent. And the last pair of my panties that he'd shredded—I'd searched through a bag of household trash to retrieve them.

Wild Indigo

On the floor before me, Mountain was stretched on his side. He was so beautiful, even in a coma. I spoke softly, caressing his shoulder. "A lot of people are praying for you, baby wolf. A whole roomful of people prayed for you tonight, and they will keep on praying for you." I thought of Grandpa's fervent prayer in Tiwa, and of how Hunter had told me that the language brought the People in and out of existence from nothingness—just by the vibration of the spoken words. I hoped that those prayers in Tiwa were creating enough vibration to keep Mountain here. I lowered my head and kissed his face, feeling his warmth, smelling his wild aroma. I let my tears fall into his mane. I raised back up to my knees and began stroking him from one end to the other, including his long, beautiful, bushy tail.

I closed my eyes, one hand on his chest, and I prayed—turning my face to the sky as I had seen the aunties and grandmas do at the bake, when they blessed the bread. I said no words, thought no thoughts, but prayed with all my heart. Then I moved behind Mountain and again lay on my side, pressing my body into his back, one arm around him and the other cradling my head. And I lay there in the dark and cried. Perhaps what hurt the most was the dark feeling growing inside of me along with my fear and grief: that if my beloved wolf chose to take the path up the mountain and beyond the ridge, that I might want to go with him rather than stay in this life.

I sang through my tears:

> *Stars shine on us,*
> *Wind sings to us,*
> *Moon smiles on us,*
> *You and me.*
> *No more lonely,*
> *We are family.*

I opened my heart
And in you came
You gave me wild,
I gave you tame.
No more lonely,
You and me.
No more lonely,
We are family.

I woke when I heard Kerry come in. I sat up.

"How is he?"

I petted Mountain's side. "No change."

Kerry squatted down and touched the back of his hand to the wolf's cheek. "Hi, big guy," he said. He fondled one tufted ear.

I let out a sigh. "I guess I must have dozed off. What time is it?"

"After midnight." He checked his watch. "Almost one. Sorry I'm so late. Some jerk tourists decided to have a campfire in this weather—high winds and warm temperatures. I had to go up there and put it out and cite the campers."

"It's okay. I needed the rest. I haven't been getting much sleep."

Kerry reached up and took my chin in his hand. "And how are you, babe?"

I tried to smile but my face wouldn't respond. I sniffled. "My heart is breaking. I'm afraid."

He rocked onto his knees and leaned over the wolf to embrace me. "I know."

Steve opened the door from the lab in the back and stuck his head into the hall between the cells. "Jamaica, phone."

Diane didn't waste any time. "The Dreams Eagle kid is missing."

"What?"

"After I talked to you, I called your pal at the S.O.—Padilla. Boy, what a piece of work that guy is. Anyway, he called out to the pueblo and I guess it took him a while because of some feasts and religious rites or something, but he finally tracked down the tribal police chief. Moon Eagle went to that house that you and I were at the other day and pressed the old woman we met to talk—you know the one who couldn't speak much English and acted like she couldn't hear? Evidently, she fessed up that she's been worried about the boy's safety, so she started telling everyone he was in Santa Fe at that Indian School there. She was trying to get him and his brother placed with a sister in Oklahoma, and until she could get it worked out, she was keeping the kids locked in the house. But little Sam got out and ran off. She hasn't seen him since yesterday."

"Oh, God. Now what?"

"Well, Moon Eagle had to file an Amber Alert because it's a child. And an MEP form with the S.O. Amber Alerts come to the FBI, so I was sitting here waiting when it came across the wire."

"Well, what's going to happen now?"

"Nothing much until morning. We got the alert out to the media, but who's watching television or listening to the radio at one o'clock on a Friday morning? If they had any sidewalks in the State of New Mexico, they would have rolled them up at twilight. We have a child endangerment specialist coming up from Albuquerque. The tribe is doing a search on their reservation, but last report I got, the grandma doesn't have any idea where the kid would have gone."

"I do."

"I beg your pardon?"

"I think I know where he went."

"Well, tell me then. Let's find him."

"We're going to have to go get him. I'll tell you all about it in a second, but let me ask you a couple things first. Did you find anything out about Yellow Hawk Lujan?"

"No MEP has been filed with the sheriff's office. Padilla asked Moon Eagle about it, but nobody seems that concerned about the old guy. I guess he's prone to taking off without notice. That's all I got on him. And anyway, a missing child takes priority."

"Okay. Did the grandmother say why she was worried about the boy? Why she was hiding him and telling everyone he was away at school in Santa Fe?"

I could hear Diane rustling papers. "Let me see what the report we got says . . . I guess she got a visit from some guy she didn't trust, somebody name of Wolfskin, he was asking about the boy."

"Ismael Wolfskin?"

"Yeah, you know him?"

"No, but I know someone who does."

"Who's that?"

"Bone Man."

"Aw, Gawd. Not him. You're gonna make me go pick him up? He's gonna get shit and animal innards all over my car!"

"Go get him, Diane. I got a lot of stuff to do to get ready."

"Get ready for what?"

"I'm going up Sacred Mountain to the falls."

"You think the kid's up there?"

"I'd bet money on it."

"Well, if we're going to have a search and rescue, that's the state police's deal—we'll have to get them on board."

"If we try to get them involved, we're going to get bogged down in red tape and two different nation's governments—Tanoah Pueblo's and the USA's. We'll stand around arguing while the kid gets eaten by a mountain lion or dies of starvation. You can tip them and let them get started with the debate, but I'm going up the mountain at first light."

"I'm going with you. Let me go get Stinkbone. And I'll throw some things in my car and get ready. Whatever we know, whatever we find out from questioning that bone guy, I'll brief the special agent who's coming and the state police, but you're not going up that mountain by yourself."

Kerry had been listening. Without a word, he headed out the door into the alley to his truck.

"I won't be going alone," I said. "I'll meet you at the gate to the buffalo confine at four a.m." I hung up the phone.

◀ 33 ▶

Saddling Up

The BLM kept horses and trailers at a small stable in the canyon to the northeast of town. When I worked as a Range Rider, before being assigned as liaison to the pueblo, this livery was my garage. Since they hadn't changed the combinations on the locks, it was easy to get horses for me, Kerry, and Diane.

As we loaded the trailer with tack and the horses, Kerry asked, "Don't you need to call Roy?"

"I'm gonna call him," I said.

"Yeah, but when?"

"As soon as we're loaded."

"You're taking what?" Roy barked into the phone.

"I've got three horses, a trailer, and the tack we need."

"Jamaica, I suspended you! You can't take the BLM's horses anywhere."

"I'm going up Sacred Mountain. You're going to get a call in about a half hour anyhow, from the state police. There'll be a search and rescue. I'm just getting a head start while the bureaucrats try to get mobilized and argue about jurisdictional authority."

"What search and rescue? Who's up there?"

"It's the kid—Sam Dreams Eagle—the one who told me about the buffalo being out of the fence on Saturday."

"Holy Christ! Let me get my britches on. Where you starting from?"

"I told Diane Langstrom I'd meet her at the buffalo pen. Kerry's with me, too. The trail to the falls goes right up from there."

"Let me slug down a cup of joe and I'll be right there. We'll talk about it."

"I can't wait, Boss."

"I ought to fire you for this, you know."

"I know."

"They got most of the mountain closed down for two weeks now because of the Indigo Falls ceremony. Trails will be blocked up above, and probably they'll have 'em guarded."

"I know. After the news breaks, will you let any Forest Service or BLM folks up there know?"

"I can try, but you know how it is up in high country—cell phones and regular radios won't work. Anyway, I doubt anyone's up there right now because of the closure."

"Okay. We'll just have to take our chances."

"Well, git on up there and find that kid. I'll see what kind of a story I can make up in case anyone finds out I let you have the horses."

"Thanks, Boss."
"You be careful."

When Kerry and I pulled up on the BLM side of the buffalo pasture, we saw flashlights moving like fireflies in the field between the pueblo homes and the bison area. Before we could coax the horses out of the trailer, a cluster of figures came toward us, their lights making small, moving pools on the ground. Hunter, Serena, and two of the teenaged boys I'd seen at the feast came up to investigate us. "Oh, it's you, Jamaica. What are you doing here?" Serena asked.

I hesitated a moment.

Before I could think of a good answer, she explained, "We're out here looking for one of our children from the pueblo. He's a little boy who plays all the time with Angel, named Sam. Everybody's out looking everywhere for him." She waved at the two youths, and they took off back across the field to resume their search.

"We're here to help," I said. "We'll go up the trail a bit, look on this side of the reservation—on the *federal* land," I emphasized.

"You can't go up to the falls," Hunter warned.

"Yeah, I know. We're just going up a little ways—I mean, he's a seven-year-old kid, how far can he have gone?"

"You think he went up toward the falls?" Hunter asked.

Serena seemed incredulous. "We're not supposed to leave for two sunrises!"

"Oh, I don't know," I said, giving Kerry a look. "I have no idea, really. We're just going to check in the foothills here bordering the reservation. I figure this is something we can do to help. By the way, this is Kerry Reed, with the Forest Service. Kerry, this is Momma Anna's sister, Serena, and her boyfriend, Hunter."

The men shook hands, and Serena smiled, nodding as she said hello.

Kerry said, "Yeah, we thought we'd just ride around a little, see what we could see. If there's anything else we can do to help . . ."

"No," Hunter said. "I better let my brother know you're here."

"Okay, if you think you need to," I said cheerily, starting to unload the tack. "Tell him we're staying on the BLM and Forest Service land. I don't think he'll be able to say much about that."

Contreras didn't respond. I got my pack out of Kerry's truck. My CamelBak was less than half full. Mountain and I had drunk most of the water when we'd had our last run on the canyon rim. I shook my head. "Damn."

Contreras noticed my concern. "Is something wrong?"

"Oh, I forgot to fill my water bladder last time I used it."

"I'll get you some water," he offered. "There's a pump over there across the field." He held out his hand to take my pack.

I hesitated. "You're not going to run tell the tribal council that I'm here? Take my pack so I'll have to wait, then get me all balled up in a bunch of red tape?"

"I will need to tell my brother at some point, but as you say, there is nothing he can do so long as you stay on federal land. I just know he would want to be informed that you're here. But I can tell him after daybreak."

"Right. Well, when you do, be sure to mention that we're staying on federal land."

He gave a feeble smile. "I didn't mean I was going to try to make trouble for you, Jamaica. At least let me get you some water. You might need it. No one should be out without water in this country."

I looked at Contreras. He had always been kind to me, kinder than most of the pueblo residents, many of whom treated me as if I were about to steal their children. "Okay," I said, handing him the pack. "I appreciate it. Kerry, do you have enough water?"

Kerry held up his pack. "I could use topping off," he said, patting the bladder in the back.

Hunter took the packs and jogged away to fill them.

"You got some jerky or bread or something?" Serena asked. "Something for food? I could get you some jerky."

"I have some energy bars, maybe some nuts and trail mix in my pack. I'll stick them in my saddlebags," I said.

"Yeah, me, too," Kerry said. "And I always have jerky." He went to the door of his truck and pulled out a plastic bag of dried meat. "Thanks for reminding me."

"I'm going to get back to the search," Serena said. "You let us know if you see anything, okay, Jamaica?"

"Hey, Serena," I said, "before you go, can I ask you something?"

"Sure."

"Do you know Ismael Wolfskin?"

"That old man? He's real old. I don't think he can see too well anymore. He lives with his daughter on the other side of the pueblo, but he still walks down and bathes in the river every day, on the other side. He's Winter."

"Winter?"

"Yeah, we're Summer, our family, south side. But like Hunter—he's Winter, north side. Why?"

"Oh, I just heard someone mention him at the feast, I think. I wondered who he was."

"Yeah, they say he was once a very powerful medicine man. I heard talk that when he was a young man, he used to be one of the Blue-Legged People, the clown society—but we haven't had them for a long,

long time, not since I've been alive—most of them have passed beyond the ridge, even those who can still remember them. They were a Winter kiva; they don't use that one anymore, it's a shrine. He doesn't take part in the dances these days, or drum or anything, but he still leads the Scalp ceremony. That is an honor until one dies. And he used to be one of the peyote chiefs. Grandpa Wolfskin is one of those elders, like my dad, who speaks a language even older than Tiwa—they would speak it in the kiva to one another when they were planning what they would do to the younger men, so none of the young guys could understand them." She laughed a little at this. "I think that old man had to stop doing ceremony—they made him quit because he gave somebody too much . . . too many herbs one time, or something like that. They say he's gotten mean, and his mind isn't right. I don't know exactly how old he is, you know they didn't used to bother with birth certificates for Indians. But he's older than my dad, and Grandpa's about ninety-six. Well, I better get back now. Let us know if you find Sam, okay?"

While we had a moment alone, Kerry and I checked our arms and ammo. Each of us had a rifle and a pistol. I'd always carried both when I rode the open country in my former job. I remembered how in those days I used to bury extra ammo, water, gas, blankets, even canned food rations and double-bagged horse feed out in the remote places, and then mark them on a map in case I ever needed extra supplies. Those items had saved my butt a few times. In fact, I was pretty sure there was a cache of mine on the other side of the falls, on the northeast aspect of this same mountain—a place I'd ridden range about five years ago. I grabbed my BLM uniform belt with my knife, my pistol in its holster, and the extra ammunition clips. I thought I probably didn't need the collapsible nightstick and cuffs, but they were attached, so I left them there. I put the belt on, then pulled on my hooded sweatshirt to cover this, and because it was a little cool in the predawn—though still much warmer than usual for this time of day, and year. I put my headlamp on my ranger hat.

As we were bringing the horses out of the trailer, Diane pulled up. "You tell your boss what you're doing?" she asked.

"I did." I worked a bit into the piebald mare's mouth. "You tell yours?"

"Yeah. What did Roy say?"

"He said he ought to fire me. Yours?"

" 'Bout the same. Been awhile since I rode a horse. Hope I remember how." She checked the clip in her own gun and holstered it on her belt.

"We'll be trail riding," I said, checking the girth strap on the roan gelding. "Horses know what to do when there's a trail, you don't even have to drive 'em. We won't be doing any fast or fancy stuff."

"Good deal."

Kerry came up and hoisted a saddle on the other mare, a bay filly named Ruby, about three years old. "Hi," he said.

"Kerry, this is Diane Langstrom. Diane, Kerry Reed. Diane, you ride this gelding—according to the sign that was on his stall, his name's Sonny. He'll be the easiest to ride, I bet. All mares are bitches, so they take some handling, and besides, you're definitely not ready for this filly—she'll give you a hard time."

Hunter came loping across the field with a pack over each shoulder, his flashlight in his hand, bobbing light ahead of him. In spite of his size, he moved with amazing quickness and grace. It reminded me of the footraces they held every summer at the pueblo, an event where everyone—youths and elders—could run with others their age. The young and able showed impressive speed and stamina, and even the aged were surprisingly strong and spry. They ran the racetrack in the pueblo for ceremony twice a year, but they ran for miles and miles in preparation for the event. It was said that the men in the village used to run a hundred miles in those races in the old days.

As he drew close, the horses volted and jibbed. The gelding snorted, the mares whinnied. Kerry and I moved to quiet them. Hunter pulled up short and took note of Diane's presence. "You going, too?" he asked.

Behind the horse where Contreras couldn't see, I waved a hand to get Di's attention and widened my eyes, giving her a note of caution.

She played it cool. "Might as well," she said. "I don't know what I'm doing, and I can barely ride a horse, but I guess I'll string along with these two."

"You need any water?" Hunter asked. "I just filled their packs. I could get you some, too."

"No, thanks," she said. "I brought some bottled water. I'll toss a few of 'em in a backpack. All right, Jamaica, tell me what to do."

I got the ropes of prayer ties out of the truck and tied them onto the strap on one side of my saddle. Then I took the sunflower Tecolote had given me and unwrapped the gooey stuff at the base of the stem. I tucked the bloom into my pack, just behind the water bladder. I put the pack on, fastened the waist and sternum straps, and clipped the bite valve onto the chest belt so that I could simply lower my head, grab the valve with my teeth, and take a drink of water without having to use my hands. I watched Kerry do the same. We mounted up. I noticed Contreras was still there watching us. "Serena went back to the search," I said.

He stood at the exact place where I had called to Santana just days before, hoping to save his life. He held one hand high, palm up, feeling the air. "Wind's died down," he said. "Sky's sinking, heavy. Could be rain. Or even snow."

"Snow!" Diane said. "It's been so hot the past day and a half. I'd welcome snow."

"Let's go," Kerry said, turning his horse.

"Thanks for the help, Hunter," I said.

I switched on my little LED headlamp and took the lead on the trail, Diane falling in behind me and Kerry bringing up the rear.

◀ 34 ▶

The Lay of the Land

Tanoah Pueblo lies at the mouth of a wide, flat valley at the foot of Sacred Mountain and the southward joint of the Rockies. Where the People live, and have lived for at least a thousand years, the land is kissed by the sun and riddled with springs and brooks fed by mountain snowmelt. In these watercourses, old cottonwoods stand with gnarled authority, their trunks wide and weathered. For much of the year, their leaves shimmer in the sunlight, and then turn pumpkin-colored in late autumn before they fall to the ground. Chokecherries and wild plums rise in hedges along the banks of streams. Only a few fields of hay and alfalfa are still farmed by the tribe, and these solitary gems stretch bold and green under a beautiful blue sky. Gardens of squash, chiles, and corn grow from water diverted through *acequias*, and sheep and horses graze in rich fields of ricegrass, wild spinach, and green shoots of native asparagus, watercress, and the indigenous mint called *poléo* used to make cures and teas. Even in winter, the sun shines on the pueblo, and the days are generally pleasant because of this. The tribe lives in a beautiful oasis of light and water, shielded by the mountain and nourished by the springs. In contrast, just a few miles to the west, an enormous high desert covered with sage and chamisa, broken only by scrub piñon and juniper in coarse outcroppings or deep arroyos, stretches for miles without interruption.

Just as stark a contrast from the soft and gentle valley was the trail up the mountain toward the Indigo Falls. In the foothills, a spare forest of juniper and piñon marked the interface, but as the way ascended, the flora changed to ponderosa and lodgepole pine, spruce and cedars, and even higher, aspen. In the dusky dawn light, the long views from the valley across Grand Mesa diminished to the section of path before and behind us, with occasional glimpses through the trees at a sea of pinetops below. The trail wound along a singing creek, and as the forest deepened, the light lessened.

As Hunter had said, the sky was sinking. A close, silvery mist hung about us, and the air grew cooler as we advanced upward. The canopy of pine boughs made the pathway dark. Along the edges of the stream and around the bases of tree trunks, huge, colorful mushrooms grew—some the size of dinner plates, and in a variety of shapes and hues. I saw great red domes spotted with bright white polka dots; twisted, bonsai-like wood mushrooms; blue, alienlike tall stems with little Chinese hats; and enormous pale yellow saucers—all fungi reveling in the dark, moist riparian oasis of this mountain brook.

We passed a branch off the main trail, a narrow footpath that led into thick forest. We'd agreed to get out of sight of the pueblo before we attracted any more unwanted attention, and then find a place to stop and regroup. I could hear the loud chattering of a raven up ahead of us.

"At least it's not hot like it was yesterday," Diane said from behind me. "I'm actually a little cold."

"Think it's safe to stop now?" Kerry called from the rear.

I found a wide place under a dense canopy of trees and hawed the filly to the side. Kerry and Diane pulled in beside me.

"What's our plan here?" Kerry asked, unfolding a Forest Service map as he chewed on a stick of jerky. "I noticed we passed a little path that cut off to the east back there. Should we split up, or do you think this kid has gone up higher than this?"

I took a drink of water from my bite valve. It tasted stale. "I don't know. He's old enough to have gone on several of the pilgrimages by now, so he probably knows the way." I leaned over to look at the map. "There are quite a few places, up above, where the trail divides—I know because I've worked the other side of this mountain." I pointed to a faint dotted line on the map. "If he's following this track, he could end up anywhere after it forks up ahead if he stops or gets lost. But if he sticks to the path to the falls, he's going to have to go clear up to the top—here"—I pointed again—"and follow that ridge to the rim of this box canyon back in here to the falls. I'm guessing the Indians come up *here*, then dip down into their land *there*, at this place near the source. There will probably be some kind of gate or marker where Indian land begins, and the trail will be closed there."

Kerry studied the map. "There's no way a seven-year-old can do that. Especially not on foot. I don't even know if we can get back in that canyon on our horses. They must leave them here"—he pointed to a stretch of flat mesa on one side of the summit—"and then walk in the rest of the way to the falls. I can't see how a little kid could even make it up to where the trail forks. It's just too far."

Diane used the opportunity to remove her pack and dig out a wad of denim. She unfurled a jean jacket, pulled it on, then wrestled her way back into the pack. "How do you know the kid's up here, anyway?"

"A child told me," I said. "Sam's best friend, Angel."

"Angel Santana?" Diane said. "Son of the recently deceased?"

"That's right. He told me last night that his friend had run up the mountain to hide. I'd talked to you before that, had you checking at the school in Santa Fe. So later, when you told me that Ismael Wolfskin had been looking for the Dreams Eagle boy, and that the grandma said he'd run away, I figured Angel's story was right. And now I'm not so sure that Sam's alone up here."

Kerry snorted. "Wolfskin? That old guy Serena was talking about? Doesn't sound like he's any likelier to make it up this trail than a little kid."

"No, think about it, guys," I said. "Wolfskin's not alone in this. Santana gets drugged by somebody—let's say it's Wolfskin—and he gets put out in the buffalo confine where he gets trampled to death. First of all, it sounds like the old guy couldn't have gotten Santana out there on his own. And the only witness may be this little kid, Sam. But why would Wolfskin, a guy who's no longer practicing peyote chief, give drugs to Santana in the first place? Somebody else maybe used the old shaman to do it. Serena said she thought she'd heard his mind wasn't right. Maybe someone manipulated him."

"What's the motive?" Diane asked.

"I don't know."

She threw her head back in exasperation. "Great."

"I think it has something to do with Santana's computer lab."

"Why?"

"Well, for one thing, his computer there has been wiped clean."

Diane drew up. "How do you know that?"

"I got in there yesterday; his wife helped me. We booted his hard drive. All the files have been erased. And both the widow and Momma Anna talked to me about some guy named Ron . . . 'Seedy Ron,' I think he's called."

"Seedy Ron?" Kerry said. "What kind of a name is that?"

"Maybe someone associated with that filthy hippie you had me looking for," Diane said. "I went out to his rotted-out Winnebago on the side of his bone pile. No one was there."

"So you didn't get any information on Wolfskin?"

"*Nada*. We ran the name, no record. And it's not like the bone peddler has a job or a phone where I could track him down and question him. You think he's in on this some way?"

"I don't know. I just thought he might be able to tell us more about the old shaman."

"What about that Yellow Hawk guy? Think he's involved?"

"I do, but I'm not sure how. He disappeared the day after Santana died. I think there might have been foul play—I went by his house on Sunday to leave a small gift of condolence and found his horse all packed and saddled, ready to go. Later, I learned that Yellow Hawk had gone missing and the horse was left there until it almost starved. Doesn't sound like he made a quick getaway, but more like someone interrupted him when he was trying to leave."

"I got nowhere on that one, too," Langstrom said. "Moon Eagle said nobody had filed a complaint, and that the old guy was prone to wandering off for days, so no one was all that worried. He got right on the missing kid, though."

"Momma Anna asked me to find out about her brother Yellow Hawk. And her son Frank asked me again at the feast tonight—or was that last night? Is it officially morning yet?" Suddenly I felt the fatigue of two nights with almost no sleep.

"I think so," Kerry said. "Doesn't look much like it, though. It's been getting darker since the sun supposedly came up. The sky looks saturated, and the trees block most of the light."

"So, what's our plan here?" Diane said.

Kerry put a finger on the map. "The trail divides right up ahead. I don't think a seven-year-old kid could make it much beyond that on his own. If that far. We could go up to that fork, try to split up and come back down in a spread pattern, but we'd have to come through some thick woods."

"I don't know what you were thinking. If he ran up here to hide," Langstrom added, "it would be almost impossible for us to find him anyway. It's dark, the visibility is getting less and less by the minute with this sinking fog. If he doesn't want us to find him, I don't know how we could. I thought you had some kind of insider information or something, Jamaica. We're not ready for a search like this. We need dogs, a search and rescue team."

"I think I know where we'll find him," I said.

My two companions looked at me in silence.

"I think he's gone around the other side, to the top."

"Another way into the falls?" Diane asked.

"An old way."

"Well, if we keep heading upward, we're going to get up to the road in to the falls, and the trail will be blocked. You think we should keep riding up that direction?" Kerry said.

"I do." I pointed to the map. "The trail winds around the mountain to the northwest at first, but after it splits off and goes up to the falls, there's this other track that leads around farther and back toward the east, all the way to the top."

"And you think a kid could make it up there on his own? That's got to be almost ten miles! We're talking about a seven-year-old boy."

I remembered Hunter Contreras running at lightning speed across the field to bring us our packs filled with water. "Pueblo boys train from as soon as they can walk to run in their footraces. I've heard they used to be able to run for a hundred miles at maturity. I'm not sure how far Sam

Dreams Eagle can run, but I know he was training for the footraces. He told me so."

"Well, I doubt the little guy got that far, but we won't find him sitting here. Let's go." He folded up the map and stuck it in his jacket pocket, dug his heels into his horse, and the mare started up the trail.

Diane followed after. "I meant to ask," she called back over her shoulder from ahead of me. "How's Mountain?"

◄ 35 ►

The Fog

The mist began to settle on us as we moved upward, into darker and deeper woods. My sweatshirt felt damp and heavy, like a cold, reptilian skin clinging to my own. With my throat still sore and raw from the smoke of the cachana root, I felt insatiable thirst, and my infrequent sips from my water bladder seemed only to increase the sensation. I tried to measure my drinking so my supply would last, but I felt like I could easily down it all at once and still want more. My lips were dry, and the skin of my throat felt like rough paper. My tongue ached for water.

Ahead on the trail, visibility decreased to a matter of feet, with low-hanging branches looming up and surprising me, forcing me to duck at the last moment or crash into them, stinging my face. Kerry warned of these a few times, but soon the mist covered even the sound of his voice, and there was nothing but my own senses to alert me.

At the same time, the sound of horse hooves on the trail seemed amplified, their shoes striking an occasional stone like a ringing gong, and the pounding of the dirt and pine needles like the beating of giant drums. The spotted brown rump of Diane's horse ahead of me churned in a rhythm of muscular locomotion. Our saddles creaked in a call and response, like a leather chain gang at work. Ruby, the excitable filly I rode, flared her nostrils and held her head back, easily alarmed by any unusual sound or sight. Her breath came and went like a pulsing steam engine, her neck and withers quivered. We dropped into a little gully, and going up the opposite bank, she made to break full out into a gallop, then fought the bit, gnashing her teeth as I tried to rein her in.

A soft rain began to fall. The tiny drops made little splatting sounds as they hit my sweatshirt and jeans. I pushed my hat back off my head and let it hang down my back from the thin leather thong used as a chin cord. I sought the raindrops to moisten my face, which felt hot and inflamed. I was so thirsty! I wondered if I was running a fever.

I heard Kerry call "Hoah," and I saw his black-and-white jib a little as Diane pulled in beside him. I came alongside the others.

"The trail forks here," Kerry said. "Shall we all go left, or do you think there's any value in splitting up, checking out the other way, just in case?"

"I'm going left," I said, "toward the falls. And I don't think Diane rides well enough to go on her own. If you want to check out the trail to the east, you can, but she needs to stay with one of us."

"I'm okay either way," Diane said.

"Why don't you two ladies head up toward Indigo Falls? I'll take the right fork and follow it for a little bit to see if there's any sign of the boy. I won't go far—in this fog, it's too hard to see much anyway, and I don't think we should get strung out too far apart. But I think we ought to at least scout the trail for tracks or any other sign. I'll take no more than an hour, then I'm coming up this way, right behind you." He pulled the map out of his pocket and unfolded it again. He checked his course, traced a line on it with a gloved index finger. "Here, you take the map," he said. "I can find you, if you take the trail straight up. It's all lefts, just remember that. You guys got ponchos in your packs? It's starting to rain some now."

"I don't want mine," I said. "I like the rain. The moisture feels good."

"I don't have one," Diane said. "I'll use yours if you don't want to. I'm getting soaked."

I reached down and unloosed the strap holding the prayer ties. I removed one rope of them and handed it to Kerry. "Here. Take this," I said.

"What's this?" he asked, taking the strand with a gloved hand.

"A rope of prayer ties. Tecolote made it."

"What do I do with it?"

"Spend it like gold," I said. I reached with my fingertips to touch him, and he reached back. Our eyes met.

"Be safe, babe," he said. "I'll be right behind you."

"You ride ahead of me," I told Diane. "That way you can set the pace, and I'll keep an eye on you in case you have any trouble."

"Sounds good to me. It's all lefts, right? That's what Kerry said, wasn't it?"

"You got it."

We plodded ahead up the narrow trail, dodging low-hanging limbs. The rain continued to fall in a fine mist, and the tree branches shimmered with moisture. Diane stopped; her horse stamped.

"What is it?"

"Come see," she said.

I slid out of the saddle—my butt felt as if it had been flattened in a tortilla press. As I dismounted, I felt a swirl of vertigo, the tree branches spinning above me, the ground coming up to meet my boots too soon. I clung to the saddle horn and recovered my balance. I walked up to take a look.

Diane had dismounted, too. Ahead, in the middle of the path, a pile of stones made a tall pyramid, and the trail widened into a circle around it. From every crack and crevice in the structure prayer sticks, tiny versions of my own nachi, protruded. I saw feathers of every kind and color, in a variety of ties, splints, and mounts—some dangling from strips of sinew or leather thong, others cut into chevrons and wedged into splits in the sticks like an arrow, still more in crowns or tied to their masts. I spotted feathers of loon, blue macaw, duck, eagle, lark, oriole, bluebird, the green feathers of parrots, vivid pimiento-colored plumes from some other tropical bird. The ends of turkey and raven quills emerged from under stones placed on the ground around the shrine.

I went to my saddle bag and got out my medicine pouch. I offered cornmeal to the five directions, then—as Momma Anna had taught me—circled my head with the pinch of meal and let the dust fly from my fingers. I heard tiny crystals shatter and the sound of glass cutting air. I looked at Diane. "Did you hear that?"

"Hear what?"

"You didn't hear that?"

She twisted her lips to one side. "I don't hear anything. Are you okay? You looked like you had a hard time when you got off your horse."

I listened, hoping to hear it again, to prove it wasn't just my imagination. "Yeah, I kind of lost my balance there for a minute. I think it's because I haven't been getting much sleep. I'm so worried about Mountain"—I drew in a breath—"and I haven't had anything to eat today."

"I'm with you there. You suppose there's a little café up ahead that serves lattes? Maybe some breakfast burritos?"

I smiled at this. "I have some energy bars, a little trail mix."

"Thanks, I'll wait. You know, that wolf of yours is probably awake now, wondering what the hell you're doing halfway up a mountain in the cold rain instead of there with him."

I felt a wave of guilt. *Why did I leave him? What am I doing here?*

Diane read my expression. "Hey, hey. I didn't mean it that way. He's going to be all right, that's all I meant. I just have a feeling he's going to be all right. We're here to find a little kid, right? Hey, Jamaica, are you okay?"

"I'm all right," I said. But I was thinking, *What's going on with me?* I felt drugged. Was that possible? I put my foot in the stirrup and climbed back into the saddle. "Let's get going."

After the shrine, we began seeing turkey and raven feathers hanging from tree branches, one so covered with these that it reminded me of a Christmas tree bedecked with ornaments. Little cairns of stones appeared like sentries alongside the path. The rain picked up. Diane pulled the poncho hood over her head. I drew up my hat by the leather cord and put it on. Little rivulets of water began to run alongside the trail.

It was getting colder. Ruby tucked her head and plodded up the track. Her breath was steaming in thick clouds from her nostrils, then dissipating into thin purple wisps that hung like ghosts around her face until they were shredded by long needles of steel gray rain. Time seemed to be slowing down, stretching. I could follow the progress of a thin stream of drizzle from the brim of my hat as it elongated, hoping to stay united, unable to elasticize enough to traverse the distance to my thigh unbroken, and then finally bursting in the middle, separating into hundreds of tiny, isolated droplets. I thought of Mountain and me—separated—and felt unbearable sadness. *Peyote, I'll bet. It's really kicking in now.*

Sonny halted ahead of us. Diane raised her voice against the rain. "Hey, I'm going to put a coat on. Jamaica? Don't you think you ought to put your parka on? You're getting soaked!"

I glanced around me. Threads of moisture hissed toward the ground in slow motion. I heard the rain drumming on the tree branches. I dropped my head and looked at my sweatshirt. The gray jersey was dark and saturated in places.

"Isn't that your parka rolled up under your pack?" Di asked, already off her horse and changing. "C'mon, put it on, woman! It's getting cold out here."

We huddled under some pine boughs and I peeled off the drenched hoodie. Underneath, my damp T-shirt clung to my breasts. I shivered. I shoved one arm into my parka, then Diane helped me find the other sleeve and pull it on. I zipped up, put my hat on, and pulled the hood up over that, smashing the brim slightly.

"Do you think we should look for some cover?" Diane asked. "Maybe wait this out a little?"

"No." I headed for Ruby, put my foot in the stirrup. "We need to go on."

As we rode ahead, the rain began to pound louder against the tree limbs, onto the trail. Ruby slowed, her footing slipping now and then on rocks and slick mud. I couldn't see but a few feet ahead of me. I passed under a low-hanging branch. The distinctive, blush-tipped tail feather of a red-tailed hawk dangled in front of my face. I pushed it aside with my hand and rode on.

Suddenly there was an eerie stillness. I could see silver wires of rain driving around me, the vapor of Ruby's breath in the cold air, but all was silent. Small stands of aspen among the pines alongside the trail seemed so full of presence that they shape-shifted into groups of people, holding stock-still to avoid attracting my attention, keeping some ominous secret among their silent hearts. I could almost hear them breathing, whispering among themselves as we approached. I sensed that these threadlike fingers of rain were reaching from the clouds to probe our shapes so that they might discern the identity of these intruders into their domain. I felt the hairs rise on my arms, my skin tingle. We were encroaching on sacred ground.

My sense of sound had been briefly suspended, but suddenly I heard again the thunder of the downpour as it battered the mountainside. I saw Diane atop Sonny, stopped before another pyramid of stones. Strips of colored cloth were tied in the trees above it—red, turquoise, and white, the colors of the prayer ties Tecolote had made.

My stomach began to heave. I didn't have time to dismount. I leaned over Ruby's side and vomited. Water and thick mucus and a little posole.

"You're sick, aren't you?" Diane said. "I could tell. You've been acting funny."

I wiped drool from my mouth onto the sleeve of my coat. "I feel better now." I leaned over the side and puked again: dry heaves, a little water and stomach bile. I drank from my water tube to rinse my mouth. I could tell from how hard I had to work to get the liquid up to the valve that my pack bladder was near empty.

"Maybe we should go back."

"No," I said. "He's here. I know he's up here."

Diane eased Sonny around the shrine. "I hope they don't have any snipers watching down the trail."

"Wait!" I said. I carefully guided Ruby under one of the low-hanging branches. I reached down to the strap where I'd secured the prayer ties to the side of the saddle. As I moved my arm, I saw wisps of red energy follow it like vapor trails. I procured one of the ropes of ties and unloosed it. Reaching as high as I could to the limb above, I tied the end of the string of sinew into the tree.

"Is that for protection?" Langstrom asked.

"I hope so."

◀ 36 ▶

The Fork in the Trail

The rain began to let up a little and turned to a blanketing mist. The horses strained against the sharp ascent of the trail. I pulled the hood off of my hat so I could regain my peripheral vision. Diane stopped again. An iron pole gate stretched across the track. A sign suspended from the center read FOREST ACCESS CLOSED UNTIL SEPTEMBER 6 FOR TANOAH PUEBLO INDIGO FALLS CEREMONIES. TRESPASSERS WILL BE PROSECUTED.

"What shall we do?" Diane asked.

I felt light-headed. "We'll have to get off the horses and walk them through the trees and around that gate."

"I got a bad feeling about this," she said, swinging her leg over the saddle and down.

We led the horses around the gate, over slick, wet ground and slippery pine needles, through dense stands of conifers, and up a steep slope to the path on the other side.

"I'll take some nourishment now," Diane said, breathing heavily from the sharp ascent we'd just climbed.

We tied the horses and took off our packs. My behind was glad to get out of the saddle. I opened my pack and removed a zippered plastic bag of energy bars and small pouches of trail mix and dried fruit. I tossed it at Langstrom.

"Well, Jamaica," she said as she retrieved a nut bar from the sack, "you sure know how to show a girl a good time."

"Yeah, I excel at outdoor entertainment," I said.

Diane took a few other items and returned the bag to me. I stared at the contents. The energy bar wrappers glowed like neon lights.

"Aren't you going to eat anything?" she asked.

"Not right now," I said, wincing. "My stomach is still kind of upset."

"You sure you're all right to go on?"

"Gotta do it," I said, and returned the food pouch to my pack, strapped it on, and climbed back on Ruby.

A few hundred yards up the course I felt a shift in the atmosphere. The drizzle continued, but the air felt light, like clouds surrounding my body. I felt as if I were floating.

Ruby smelled like a wet goat. The saddle seemed to be cawing like a crow with every shift of her hips. When I stared in one direction, I could make out the individual drops of mist as they fell from the sky, follow their journey as they traveled slowly to the ground. I heard the trees murmuring.

Again, Sonny's rump appeared stock-still in front of me. I came alongside and saw two massive trees across the trail, not blowdowns or slash, but deliberately cut to block access. A large sign read KEEP OUT. TANOAH PUEBLO RESERVATION LANDS. NO ONE ADMITTED. TRES-PASSERS WILL BE PUNISHED BY DEATH, ACCORDING TO THE LAWS OF THE SOVEREIGN NATION OF TANOAH PUEBLO.

"Something's wrong," I said.

"Damn straight. I'm not going in there without a search warrant and a lot of other white people with guns and ammo."

"No," I said. "This was too easy. We should have had a problem getting up here without being turned back."

"Hmmm. I guess it does seem odd. I've always heard the trails were heavily guarded this time of year."

"Yes, and remember when Contreras told us he was going to tell his brother, the governor, that we were out here on the mountain? That would normally spark a militia into action. The minute they knew I was on the reservation during Quiet Time last Saturday, they sent out folks to keep me from getting to Santana's body and put me off the rez. I was surrounded almost the moment he died." I swallowed, coughed, almost choked. I felt as though I had a small bird fluttering its wings in my throat.

"You all right?"

I nodded my head, coughed some more. "Could I have some of your water? Mine tastes sour."

She got a bottle out of her pack and handed it to me. "Well, what do you think happened? Why didn't they come up after us, and why isn't there anyone here at the fork in the trail to protect their shrines?"

"I don't know," I said, "but we're riding on." I unstrapped the prayer ties and took out another strand. Again, I felt the beating of tiny wings against the walls of my throat. I coughed and coughed.

"Listen, I'm getting concerned about you," Diane said. "What's going on?"

I opened my mouth as wide as I could. A Rocky Mountain bluebird flew out, winged its way into the clouds of moisture above us, and vanished into the air. I turned to look at Langstrom. Her face was full of concern. "I don't suppose you saw that?" I asked.

"Saw you coughing? That's what I'm talking about. You're coughing, you're throwing up, you don't seem well. I think we should head back down and get you to a doctor."

I cleared my throat. My tongue felt like a slick stone pressed into the bottom of my palate. I couldn't lift it to speak. I slid off my horse and took the string of prayer ties to the sign and tied it to one of the large lodgepole legs. I got back in the saddle.

Diane shook her head and blew air out of her nose. "Okay," she said, and turned away from the sign to where the trail forked to the left. "I don't know where I'm going, or if you'll even be alive when we get there, but I guess we'll ride on."

The track we followed showed little use. Stones and limbs littered the path, and branches grew close overhead so that we frequently had to dismount and walk. The way narrowed to little more than a game trail as it wound around the mountain to the north and then to the east. We climbed sharply. Then the trace played out. Diane stopped, looked at me for direction.

"Look for a place to leave the horses," I said. "We'll go the rest of the way on foot."

As I tethered Ruby to a pine, I felt her nervousness and fear. A surge of guilt swept through me, as if I were abandoning her.

As I had Mountain.

Suddenly I felt a hot poker in my chest and a searing pain emanating from it in wide circles. My torso and legs grew hot, my arms were burning, my hands and fingers, even my toes, were on fire. A thought ran through my mind ahead of the blazing heat: *This must be what it feels like to be electrocuted.* I drew in what I thought would be my last breath, opened my eyes, and the heat was gone.

I saw Diane looking at me. "Where were you just then?"

"You mean . . . ?"

"Yeah. You took a little trip somewhere and left your body here. I've been talking to you for five minutes. Did you hear anything I said?"

I shook my head. "I'm sorry. No."

"It's something in your water, right? That Contreras guy put some kind of hallucinogen in your water."

I swallowed. "Yeah. I don't feel it all the time; it flashes in and out—I'm thinking I had some built-in immunity to it or it could have been worse."

"Why didn't you say something?"

"Because I didn't think you would stick with me. I thought you'd insist that we go back."

"Damn straight I would have."

"Well, we can't go back. And it's no use going back now anyway—as far as we've come, it would be no easier than going on."

"Fine. Great. Just great. I've got a ticket on the Magical Mystery Tour. Well, while you were out there in the ethers that last time, I was saying how we should have brought flares, a GPS, things like that. Other than your forest ranger, nobody knows where the hell we are. Including us."

"No, I know. I know where we are."

"You do? Well, good. Maybe you'll take the lead now, Miss Acid Head."

"Yeah, I will. Miss Acid Head?" I grinned.

She glared. "You could have told me, you know. Before we got this far."

"I'm all right."

"Yeah, that's what you said before."

"No, I am. It's wearing off. I'm all right."

"If you say so."

"I do. Now, bring your pack, all the water you have left, anything you have. We have to be getting close to timberline. The air is getting rare, and I feel that cloud deck bearing down on us."

"I'm right behind you. Where we going?"

"To the place where the old ones used to live."

◄ 37 ►

Unkind Ground

We came into the elbow of the box canyon from above, hiking over wet red clay and slick slabs of stone that looked like elephants' backs. As we approached the rim campsite, I heard the wash running. Large pools of liquid collected in rock depressions. Above us, the sky looked like an oyster—heavy, wet, glistening silver gray. We moved through clouds of mist looking for a good place to ford the wash, which gushed along at an amazing speed toward the edge of the gorge.

"Take your boots and socks off," I told Diane. "Roll your jeans up if you can, tie your bootlaces together and sling them around your neck, and we'll hold on to each other to keep from getting caught in the current." We tucked our pistols into our backpacks, and Diane helped me to wedge the rifle between my pack and my back, its stock and barrel resting on the straps.

We stepped together into the flow, our feet sinking into cold, slippery mud, our arms locked together for support. The bottom of the wash felt like an undulating snake, shifting and squirming beneath us. A constant roar told of the crashing and tearing of water forcing its way against rock, tree, and earth. Thick, reddish-brown water pummeled our ankles, next our shins, our calves, and then our knees. The flood was deeper than I'd thought. A sudden crack, like a rifle shot, and a long juniper limb came surging toward us, its green foliage bright against the muddied deluge. The thick end of it smacked hard into the side of Diane's knee. She went down, and nearly pulled me over with her. I reached with my free arm to grab her biceps and I braced my feet in the mud. My left arch found a stretch of flat stone embedded in the wash bottom, and I pushed against it for leverage. Diane sped away with the current as far as her arm could stretch, turning to one side, scrambling. Her head and one shoulder disappeared beneath the flood for an instant as she flailed with her arms and legs to find a hold. Her backpack twisted and bobbed atop the surface. I saw her boots race away on the angry torrent.

"My boots! My boots!" She thrashed with her free hand, trying in vain to reach them as they sailed off.

"Stand up!" I screamed, pulling hard on her arm. "We've got to get out of this current!"

"But my boots!"

"Come on!" I nearly dragged her the rest of the way across the wash.

We stood on the bank, assessing the situation. It was cold, and Diane's clothes were soaked. Her boots had flown downstream so rapidly that they were no doubt at the bottom of the canyon by now. Her pistol had been in her pack and—even though she'd gone under briefly—had been spared from getting waterlogged because the pack had floated.

I rummaged in my own ruck and found a pair of running tights, an extra pair of socks, and a hooded T-shirt. Diane stripped down under a tree and then struggled to pull on the clothes over wet derma. I saw her skin—which was blue with cold—grow scales, her back sprout a dorsal fin. Her short, slicked-back hair made a cap on her head, and her eyes seemed to bulge out beneath a sloping forehead. Gills formed on the sides of her face and fanned open and closed. She looked like a dolphin. I strained to call my mind to clarity while I retrieved my handgun from the pack. I holstered it again on my belt. "Maybe we can each wear one of my boots."

"You kidding? Your feet look like they were bound when you were young, they're so small. I couldn't even get my toes into one of your boots."

"We could cut the toe out so you could use the sole and the uppers."

"I don't see how tearing down the only good pair of boots we have between us is going to help."

I thought about it. Diane was probably right. With clothes on, she looked human again, but her voice sounded high and squeaky, like the dolphin's.

I peeled off my parka. "You take this," I told her.

She didn't hesitate to grab it and put it on. She shook out the rain poncho she'd borrowed earlier, spraying water everywhere, then folded it up and tendered it to me. "This will keep you a little drier, anyway."

"You can't go barefoot," I said. "The rocks will tear your feet to ribbons, the cacti, pinecones, all of it—you'll have bloody soles inside of a few minutes." I looked at what we had between us, inventoried my pack in my mind: my medicine pouch was soft deer hide, which would wear through in only a little more time than a sock. Besides, there wasn't much leather there anyway. My backpack was made of some sort of waterproof nylon, and Diane's looked to be of a similar material. Perhaps we could cut one of our packs apart and wrap her feet in the fabric. Too thin.

"Damn it! I don't see how you can go on without something on your feet."

"I'll try it barefoot. How much farther?"

"No, it's no use. We have to climb down into that gorge. There's no way you can do it without something to protect your feet." Then I had an idea: my water bladder! It was made of thick, pliable vinyl. It wouldn't be punctureproof, but it would shield her feet some. I'd drunk it dry anyway. I opened my pack and pulled out the plastic vessel.

"What are you doing?" Diane asked.

"Making you some moccasins," I said. "Only, since we don't have any buffalo leather, we're doing it the modern way. These will give you a little protection, though I doubt you can climb in them." I used my knife to cut the bladder down the side seams, creating two rounded rectangles of vinyl. "Put your foot here," I said, laying one of the plastic pieces on the ground.

She put one foot in place. "How are you going to fasten these onto my feet?"

I stopped to think. My head was swimming. The episode in the wash, the roaring of the water, the constant drizzling mist, and the eerie gray light—I felt nauseous again, and I thought I could hear voices, drumming and chanting. I took a deep breath and waited, listening. Suddenly I knew what to do next. I took my knife to the corners of my poncho and cut two large squares. I folded the material into thirds to make insoles. I took two of my ropes of prayer ties from around my neck. I heard Tecolote's voice: *Spend these like gold, Mirasol.* I cut away the prayer bundles and placed a long rope of braided sinew under each "shoe." Pointing to one, I told Diane, "Step on this." When she did, I pressed the vinyl around her foot, and she bent down and helped me hold it in place. I wove the sinew around her toes, then over and under her foot again and again, then behind the heel, securing the wrapping with a tie around the ankle. "Try that," I said.

Diane strode a few paces, circled around a bit, and came back. "It might work," she said, "if I'm careful." We outfitted her other foot. She stamped around a little, trying to see if the foot-wraps would work themselves loose. "Pretty clever," she said.

"Those won't do for climbing. And the sinew will wear through sooner or later. But they might last for a little while," I said as I pulled the altered rain garment over my clothes, then strapped my pack on over it.

We loaded up and started off along the rim. Diane soon moved with speed and confidence. "I'm glad I have these. They're actually staying on just fine. I'm amazed."

I held up a hand. "Stop! Do you hear voices?" I half-feared I was having another hallucination.

She raised her head and held perfectly still. "Yeah, I thought I heard something. From down below, right?"

I listened, too, sniffed the air as Mountain would when something strange alerted him. The voices had ceased.

We walked on a little, then I heard someone cry out, far in the distance. "There it is again!"

Diane stopped abruptly. "I heard it, too. That sounded like a man—maybe calling for someone else—but I couldn't make out what he was saying. Maybe it's someone looking for your little guy."

"We'd better hurry, then."

We skirted along the rim until I found the way down into the canyon. "This is some dangerous climbing," I said. "It's nothing but slick rock all the way. There's no way you can do it in those makeshift moccasins."

She looked down. "Jesus! It's got to be a six- or seven-hundred-foot drop to the bottom! How far down do you plan to go?"

"There's a ruin. Well, there are lots of them in this canyon. But where I think the kid might have gone—it's a couple hundred feet down, then over, then back up again to that wide ledge there, then down again, and over. It's a long, arduous climb."

We stood at the edge in silence. I shivered. "You take my rifle, and cover me from up here."

"Cover you? I'd be happy to, but it's going to be hard to see around all those ledges and overhangs, even if it weren't for all this mist. There are times when I can hardly see twenty feet in front of me as it is. I'm not letting you go down there by yourself, it's too dangerous."

"Just do it, Diane. Take the rifle and try to keep sight of me. And one more thing." I felt around in my shirt and found the map, pulled it out and spread it open against a nearby stone. "See this place here?" I pointed to a site on the northern aspect, on the way to the four-wheel trail coming up the mountain from the other side. "There's a twisted old juniper about forty feet west of the trail here—it looks like a big old bonsai, really picturesque. It stands there all by itself, no other trees around for about a dozen yards. Step out twenty paces due west of it, and there's a cache buried there under the silt. There's water, some food, blankets, ropes, some horse feed, and maybe even some ammo—I don't remember. But if you need it, it's there." I watched a small bonsai sprout from the place on the map, then quickly folded it to make the apparition go away.

"Thanks for the info, but I won't be going anywhere until you come back up."

"I'm just saying it's there. Remember it."

Diane tucked the map into the pocket of the parka. "Okay. Forty feet west, then twenty paces west of the tree."

"You got it." I started to lower myself into the gorge.

"I don't see what good this will do. You're going to need help. You're not right . . . you're having hallucinations. I don't want you to go down there alone. Wait until your forest ranger comes, and let him go down with you."

"Just watch my back."

On the climb down, it started to rain gently. The rocks and ledges were slick and cold. The temperature dropped. In spite of the hard work of climbing, I was chilly. I worked my way past the numbered digs, the dwellings with the corn silos, on toward the ceremonial ruin. A cold mist hung like clouds lodged in the gorge, obscuring my view of all else but the next rock in front of me. Once, I thought I heard an animal panting. The thick vapor that surrounded me muffled even the sound of the waterfall created by the flooded wash. I moved down-canyon, climbing over slide areas, across the ragged ledges, and through narrow passages where twisted junipers clung to the walls of the ravine, permitting me to step through their branches when there was no other solid footing. A few times, I stopped to look up toward the rim, hoping to see Diane, but the fog was so thick that I could only see a few yards above me.

I felt an outrageous thirst, and my stomach threatened to send up any juices that might remain. I stopped on a flat rock, clutched my middle, and bent over, hoping to get it over with. I heard feet scrambling behind me, small rocks stirring and then plummeting down the side of the cliff. I straightened and turned to heighten my radar. More scuffling, another rock clipping each stone face in sequence as it fell, *click, click, click*. And heavy breathing. Close.

I started around the giant boulder that would lead me to the ledge to the ceremonial ruin. My feet wouldn't cling to the wet basalt, and I began to slip. I clutched with my hands for a purchase, and met with sandpaper grit as the rough surface abraded the skin of my palms. As I slid, I twisted to try to get my backside against the rock face, and my left knee hit a hard out-jut of stone. Pain shot up my leg, through my bones. I saw the leg of my jeans turn red, felt the warmth and wet of blood soaking into the denim against my skin. In the distance, I heard men's voices calling, something in Tiwa. They sounded far away, up-canyon, perhaps near the high lagoon under the cliff overhang.

I turned again and tried to pull myself back up. My bloody knee rang with pain when I put weight on the leg. Again I heard panting from behind me, and small rocks bouncing as they dislodged and toppled to places below. I forced myself to ignore my injury, pulled my body up on a sheet of rough granite, and scrambled up to the high shelf that led to the ceremonial ruin. I stopped to catch my breath and saw a trail of blood drops on the stone below me, thinning with the mist and rain.

Now the hard lift lay before me. I hoisted myself by my arms, and as I jumped, a sharp pain tore through muscle and bone and caused me to cry out in agony. The toe of my right boot swung high and clung to the shelf. I heard footsteps somewhere near, the wheezing breath of exertion. I hung in terror for an instant, and then I strained and struggled and wrestled my body onto the ledge.

Before I could raise myself from my prone position, I felt hands grab at my waist. I turned to see Hunter Contreras below me, grasping at my pack. "What are you doing?" I wrestled to free myself of his grip, and to rise to my knees, but he held a firm grip on the belt of my pack.

"Is the boy up there? You can't go up there!"

"Let go of me!" I pushed at his hand, and he tugged hard, almost pulling me off the narrow ridge. I strained back toward the cliff face.

"I'm not letting you go up there. If the boy's up there, I'll go. Leave him alone."

I pushed myself upward, almost to my knees, but Contreras jerked again on the belt of my pack and pulled me down onto my chest, nearly sweeping me from the ledge. My fingers clutched at the stone. My left knee throbbed. I pressed the length of my right side into the cliff and reached for my knife. I couldn't get it out of its sheath. I worked my hand under my abdomen and unfastened the pack belt.

"Come down here!" Contreras tugged at my pack.

I slid my hand farther up my torso beneath me and fingered the sternum strap. "How did you get here?" I asked.

He stopped pulling for a moment and smiled. "We have a few secrets, even from your government, who supposedly owns this land. You know nothing about this ground. This is our sacred place. We teach our children about it. Our ancestors walked these ledges long before you whites set foot in this country. We know every rock and pebble, every root of the Standing People, every way the water flows."

I flicked the clasp on the sternum strap.

Contreras yanked again on the pack, and it gave little resistance. He teetered backward, and caught himself. "Come down here now!"

I rolled slightly away from the cliff face, raising my shoulder and sliding my right arm out of the strap.

Hunter could see now what I was trying to do, and he groped for my arm. But I scooted into the cliff wall, and the big man lurched and grasped, ultimately latching on to the only thing he could reach—the pack. I extended my left arm and the ruck slid off my back, over my shoulder, and away from my body as Contreras, pulling hard, fell backward from the force of his own motion. His massive shoulders led as he toppled in reverse, like a giant tree. I heard a hard thud as flesh struck stone, but the Indian made no noise, no cry of complaint or fear. I heard nothing more, no scrambling, no movement. I placed my palms under my shoulders and raised up to look over my slender perch, but I could see nothing below me but thick vapor. I listened. No sound.

"Hunter?" I heard my voice echo in the gorge.

"Contreras? Are you down there?"

There was no answer. I gasped. "Oh, God."

I raised to my knees, then turned myself carefully against the cliff face and worked my way across the shelf to the ruin. My leg was swelling in my jeans and the denim felt like a tourniquet, squeezing off the blood supply. My thigh throbbed.

Again, I heard panting behind me. Had Contreras gotten back up from his fall? Or was it an animal? I started to pull myself up to the floor of the ceremonial site when something struck my shoulder hard, a stone, which then fell on my hand and smashed my fingers. "Oh! Damn! Ouch!"

A voice came through the haze. "Wolf girl?"

"Yellow Hawk?" I hauled myself into the ruin. The peyote chief crouched in the corner, his arms outstretched, shielding something behind him. He wore only a threadbare T-shirt and jeans, and his skin was scratched and scraped everywhere, his face and arms were bruised. He looked thin and gaunt. I held my hands up to pacify him. "Don't throw any more rocks, okay?"

He nodded, and I took a moment to check my shoulder, which had taken a good blow. I massaged the injury as I moved carefully toward Yellow Hawk.

He shifted to the side, and I saw a small mound beneath a plaid flannel shirt and a jean jacket. "This boy need help," he said. He pulled back the shirt slightly to reveal Sam Dreams Eagle's head. "He is cold and hungry."

The boy barely stirred, making a small whimper. I dropped to my knees beside him and placed the backs of my fingers against his cheek, which was cool to the touch. The child shook with cold, his teeth chattered. I felt his carotid artery for a pulse—it was weak. "He has hypothermia. We have to get him out of here. Now." I shrugged out of my poncho and draped it over him.

Yellow Hawk looked at me, his face worn and worried. "I cannot." He looked down at his bare feet. They were bruised and bloody, the toes blackened. One foot was swollen to almost twice the size of the other. He pulled up the leg of his jeans to reveal a shard of bone protruding from the skin at the ankle.

"Oh, God," I said. "How long ago did that happen?" I put a hand to his ankle, looking for a pulse.

"They take me to mountain, take away moccasin so I cannot leave."

I touched the black toes. Gangrene.

"Who brought you here?" I said, feeling for a pulse higher in the leg. His legs were blue, the veins swollen, inflamed.

"My people take me, Indigo Falls. I am ashamed."

"To Indigo Falls? And you got away and came here? With the boy?"

"No, I swim. Boy run, this place, where old ones live. I tell him, 'If they come for you, run! Run to where old ones live!' He is good boy. I swim here."

"You swam here?"

"Time before time, river flow here, old ones live here. River change, go back through mountain, flow down, into valley. People move, build home out of earth, our home now. Our story tell all this. But some story older than our language, in time-before tongue. Only few old ones speak now. Story tell of way of changing river, hole through mountain, through House of Dead, through Eye of Great Spirit. No one know—if we go through, will we live? I swim."

"You went through the mouth of the falls, you swam through the mountain? Where? To that lagoon over there?"

He nodded. "Long time, no air. No light. I am ready die anyway, I am ashamed."

"Why are you ashamed, Yellow Hawk? You came through the mountain to protect little Sam. There's nothing to be ashamed of."

"I am ready die, not this boy. Not you. I know now what I must do, my time, my life. I save our language, save the People from their self. But you must save this child. And you. I am already dead."

"No, you're not. I'm going to try to figure out how to get some help for all of us here, just let me think. In my pack, I had a space blanket, one of those folded foil sheets. If I could get down there and find it, it might help Sam until . . ."

Yellow Hawk pointed a finger behind me, his eyes two black saucers.

I turned just as Hunter gained the shelf. A grit-packed, bloody bruise etched one side of his face. "You got away, old man," he said. "If you'd just stayed put, you'd have been safe, we would have brought you back home, and all this would have been done. Same with the boy."

I shifted my right side away from Contreras and felt along my belt for my holster. The sky rumbled, and a heavy rain began to pour.

Yellow Hawk used his hands against the wall to raise himself up on one foot. He spoke in Tiwa, shouting above the din of the pelting rain. Then he reached into his shirt and pulled at a piece of leather thong. He drew up the lacing; a shiny CD was strung from it. The old chief spoke in English now. "I tell my nephew, be willing die for what he did. I give him medicine, take him Bison People for judgment. I am ashamed, my nephew. Now I am ready die, too. All for this." He brandished the CD in front of him as he spoke, then released it and hopped alongside the wall, using his hands against the rock to bring him closer to Contreras. "But this boy, this wolf girl. They—"

"Wait!" Hunter lunged at the old man, grasping for the CD, and the two began to struggle. "Give me that, old man," he grunted. "That has to go to the Scalp House for ceremony. Nobody else has to die, just give me that."

I quickly released the snap on my holster and pulled out my gun. Yellow Hawk's body wavered between me and Contreras as the men grappled for the shiny prize, the old chief surprisingly resilient against Hunter's youth and size. They rocked against the stacked rock half-wall, the top stones jarring loose and toppling down into free fall. Contreras slammed Yellow Hawk back against the cliff face, and I saw the old man's head snap on his neck, but he pushed back, launching his long, wiry body into Hunter's chest like a projectile. "This will not go to Scalp House, be a war prize," he said, grasping at his chest and holding up the shiny disc. "This thing bring the People sickness. First, my nephew. Now you and others drawing power from this. You make old witchcraft, kind the People put away long time ago because it evil." He pointed to the red-stained petroglyph of the man/bear figure looming behind him. "You use evil, try harm this wolf girl. You bring wrath of Red Bear—mark her face, try take her spirit time and again, but this wolf girl strong—I see all this in vision. I will take this with me," Yellow Hawk said, blood trickling from the corner of his mouth. "This the thing I must do!"

"You're not taking it anywhere," Contreras said. "Give it to me." They smashed into the wall again, and the rocks gave way, collapsing. The wrestling twosome hung half over the ledge, their heads and shoulders suspended over nothing more than fog and space as the rain pounded on them. Yellow Hawk, on top, managed to draw back onto one knee.

I focused my pistol on Hunter's chest. "All right!" I yelled. "Stop it, both of you. Contreras, get up."

The two men turned to look at me in surprise, their faces streaming with moisture, their long hair slicked to their heads and dripping. Yellow Hawk put one hand on a patch of standing rock wall and pulled himself upright. Contreras slid on his back until he was on firm ground, then rolled to his side and came up. As he rose, he lunged at Yellow Hawk and grabbed for the CD, still tied around the chief's neck.

The old man started, clutched at the leather thong, then turned his head to look at me. As soon as his eyes met mine, I knew his mind. I charged forward, but too late. Yellow Hawk dove to the side, over the cliff, as Hunter lurched—too late to stop him—and the old man flew downward, like a hawk swooping out of the sky toward its prey, disappearing into the mist.

Contreras fell to his knees, almost drawn into the fall with the chief. "Aaaaaaagh! Look what you've done!" he screamed. He grabbed one of the stones from the rubble of the wall and hurled it at me, knocking the pistol out of my hand and into the corner firepit. I scrambled after the gun, but Hunter grabbed my feet and dragged me toward him. Marbles of ice began pummeling us, stinging my hands and arms. "We need that for ceremony!" he yelled. "Nobody else had to die, if you just would have stayed out of it! We were handling it ourselves, but you had to come up here!" The din of noise from the rain and hail forced him to yell even louder to be heard.

I kicked my feet, but Contreras held them fast. I reached on my belt and found the collapsible nightstick. I sprung it from its holder, threw out my arm to extend it, then sat up quickly and struck the big man on the head with it twice. He released me, and I scuffled backward toward the pistol. But Hunter flung himself onto me, grabbed my right arm, and pinned it against the ground. I raised my left forearm and pressed it against his chest, keeping him at bay. His weight was on my legs and I couldn't kick or knee him—only my left hand was free. I remembered Diane's hapkido instructions: *Always look for the weak point. There's always a weak point.* I plunged my left hand into Contreras's neck and clutched his jugular. I squeezed until I saw his face reddening, his eyes bulging. I dug my fingers hard into his throat. Hunter opened his mouth and roared. He pulled away from my grasp, and I twisted my right hand out of his grip, raised up, and struck him smartly on the temple with the nightstick. I wriggled my legs out from under his body as his head reeled backward from the blow. I turned onto my hands and knees and started to get up. But Contreras seized me around the waist from behind, picked me up, and rose to his feet. He moved toward the edge as I kicked and wriggled. He swung backward, ready to hurl me over the side, and I threw my arms behind his head and grabbed on tightly. Hunter roared again, and then suddenly released me onto the floor of the ruin. I dashed to the firepit and grabbed the gun. I turned it on him and he raised his palm as if to stop the bullet, the other hand clutching his chest.

We stood gasping, both of us, staring at each other, gulping air, the rain and hail pounding us. Hunter lowered his hand in resignation. "We never wanted to harm the boy, or the old man." He clutched his temples and shook his head. "We only wanted . . ." He looked toward the edge where Yellow Hawk had just flown. "They would have talked. We just wanted to keep them quiet, until we finished ceremony for this."

"We? Who? You and your old, senile shaman, Wolfskin?"

"That old grandfather knows the old medicine. We needed him when Yellow Hawk betrayed the tribe, just like his nephew did."

"Betrayed the tribe? How?"

"He was supposed to get that CD-ROM from his nephew after he gave him the truth medicine, bring it to the Scalp House for ceremony, so we could offer it to the war god. That is the old way when one of the People betrays the tribe. But when that old man took his nephew out to the buffalo for his judgment, you got involved. And the boy. And the old man never came with the disc. He was ready to ride up the mountain when we caught up with him. He told us he never found the CD, that his nephew didn't have it. But we needed it for the Scalp ceremony to appease Red Bear, to cleanse our spirits from the betrayal, to give us our power back."

"Who ordered Jerome Santana killed?"

Contreras winced. "It was voted that he be judged by the Bison People. It was the old one's duty to take him for that judgment. He was shamed by his nephew's actions. He wanted to do it. Now put the gun down, okay?"

"You poisoned my wolf!"

He held up both hands and shook them. "No, no, I didn't do that. We wanted to search your place, so Grandpa Wolfskin blew medicine in him, but he must have gotten too much. We didn't mean to hurt him."

I choked, my hands trembling with anger, the barrel of my automatic still aimed at his chest. "Well, you hurt him. You may even have killed him."

He shook his head. "Believe me, we didn't want to hurt him. We didn't want to hurt anyone."

"You put something in my water."

He nodded.

"Peyote?"

"We had to slow you down. We needed to take care of things."

"Take care of things? What things were you going to take care of? And why did you want to search my place? What did you hope to find?"

"What the one who just died was wearing around his neck. We knew someone from outside wanted the language. At first, I didn't believe it was you. But later, I tried to talk to you and you avoided me. All the while, you kept snooping, asking questions. We thought you found the disc."

"You thought I—"

Above us, a crash, and a blast of small rock, then the explosion of cliffs cracking and stones shrieking as they tore away from the side of the gorge. I jumped back to the overhang wall and stretched my arms over Sam Dreams Eagle just as a colossal boulder pounded to the ground, on top of Contreras. A river of water followed the stone, and a deluge poured in a newly formed waterfall. The once-silty floor of the space began to flood. Through the rain and hail, I saw part of a leg and a hand extending from beneath the massive rock. A dark red pool began to seep from under the stone and merge with the water spilling onto the ruin floor. I ran to the megalith and pushed with all my might, groaning as water splashed me. It was useless—the stone mass was too heavy. Another slide of shale fell, and I jumped back under the overhang. When I looked again, I could see no trace of Hunter Contreras's form, which was now buried beneath a mound of basalt.

"No! Oh, God, no!" I dropped my gun and my hands flew to my face as if to block out the sight I'd already witnessed. All the air seemed to have been pressed out of my chest, and I was unable to move. I started to sob, but no sound came, no tears. I watched the red stain swell into the pooling water. I stooped to pick up the pistol again and holster it, then retraced my steps toward the boy. *What can I do?* Across the ravine, I watched a half dozen other cataracts develop instantly, as the surge of rain rushed over the rim, carrying topsoil, stones, and small trees from the land above.

Another boom, and I heard more stone cracking, the scarp splitting nearby. I grabbed little Sam around the waist and tried to stir him to consciousness, but he whimpered and merely fluttered his eyes. I needed my arms to climb; I couldn't carry him. Pooling water in the floor rose toward the corners—I needed to get him up before he got any wetter than he already was. I lifted the child to a seated position and propped his back against the wall. His head bobbed against his chest. I took off my hat and slipped two of the three remaining ropes of prayer ties from around my neck, separated them, and used my knife to cut off the prayer bundles. I cut one rope into three sections. I turned Yellow

Hawk's jean jacket upside down and put the flannel shirt on the ground right side up above it, so that the shirttails overlapped just slightly where they met. I pressed a small stone under the two layers of cloth, gathered the fabric around the stone to hold it in, and tied sinew at the neck beneath this pebble head. I repeated this in the center and at the other side, effectively joining the bottom edges of the garments together—then tested to see if they would easily pull apart. My handiwork held. I had fashioned a makeshift sling. I threaded the other rope through the sleeves of the jacket alongside Sam's slight legs. I worked his arms into the sleeves of the shirt. *Climb on my back and ride,* I thought.

I spread Sam's legs open, sat down, and scooted my backside up against his chest, reaching around me for his arms in the flannel shirt. I pulled them around my neck. Then I reached behind me and lifted Sam's bottom, leaned forward, and pushed his weight onto my back. He groaned. I stood up, adjusted his legs so they came around my waist, and tied the ends of the rope emerging from the denim sleeves over my belt. I started to move, but I felt the child shift downward, his body slumping, his arms sliding back through the flannel shirtsleeves. I quickly grabbed Sam's wrists and pulled them back over my shoulders. *How can I keep him in place so I can climb with him?* Hail pelted my head and my arms. The rim of the canyon had split open in a dozen places, and water poured over rock slides and crumbled ledges. I had to move fast!

My handcuffs! I snapped them out of the holder on my belt and pulled on the boy's arms until I had them in position. His wrists were too small, so I cuffed each arm just above the elbow. I stooped to pick up the prayer bundles I'd cut off their strands. With no time for ceremony, I tossed them toward the boulder that now trapped Hunter Contreras's remains. I pulled the poncho on and worked to drape it over my passenger, as well as me, then donned my hat and tightened the chin cord.

I started around the megalith, feeling like a moving tent, with little Sam under wraps on my back.

◄ 38 ►

Guiding Spirit

Rain and hail battered us as I managed to drop down from the floor of
the space onto the thin shelf of stone. Ahead, where I normally de-
scended to bypass the large boulder and find the next ledge, the wall of
the ravine had been shattered. A river of cascading reddish water
gushed over a newly formed rock slide. We were trapped. I started to
edge backward. The ledge groaned and cracked, then belched a peal of
thunderous tearing. The outer stacked-rock wall, the floor of the ceremonial room, and the huge stone that had fallen there, all began to rip
away from the cliff and slide downward. I bent my knees for balance
and pressed my face and chest into a wall of flat rock, spreading my
hands out to feel for depressions to hold on to. I watched the sacred
ruin quake, crumble, and then plunge into the abyss. Water poured
from above in a vast, thundering falls past the place where I had just
stood.

Now my boots rested on a tiny escarpment, with nothing but slides on either side of me, mud and rock and surging water. I looked above me—only sheer granite. *How will we ever get out of here?*

There was nothing to do but to try to make my way down one of the slide areas and hope to find a better place beneath for a climb out. I reached behind me and readjusted Sam's weight, then stuck my good leg out into the rocks and silt to the side. I crouched, and then lowered myself on my good knee onto the slope, bending it deeply so that I would slide on my shins and elbows, protecting Sam's arms and legs, which met across my front. I let go—my swollen, injured knee only half bent and out to one side—and down we slid, bumping and ripping on rocks and roots. The poncho soon bunched up under my neck in front. My jeans and shirtsleeves tore, and my knees knocked into stones. The wet dirt worked its way under my pant legs and up my arms. My chin and cheeks grated against the ground. With a thud that made my afflicted knee ring with pain, my boots landed on a boulder. I flipped to one side, one foot caught on a root, I plowed face first into a slick of wet mud and pebbles, my back twisted and my legs toppled down to the side of me, and our downward slide came to a halt. My spine rebounded. My neck snapped back then forward again, and my forehead smashed into stone. My vision blurred and I felt myself slipping out of consciousness. I fought to stay alert. The ground started spinning, and I couldn't tell which way was up. I grabbed for a handhold and found the root. I clung to it and remained in my crouch while waves of dizziness and nausea threatened to make me black out, the weight of the boy on my back pulling me off balance. Finally I felt the spinning stop.

I assessed my new position: somehow I had managed to keep my weight off the boy, even as I tumbled and landed. His legs and arms had gotten scratched and scraped some, but that was the worst of it. I shook Sam's legs. "Are you okay, little guy?"

No answer. Not even a whimper. I looked around me. The rain continued to pound, new-formed water chutes thundered into the gorge, and now, a few hundred feet below me, a screaming river of whitewater swept through the floor of the gulch, ripping up trees and dislodging boulders. To my left, it looked like I could perhaps climb across a scarp and then take an upward path. But Sam's weight was more than I could manage and keep steady while climbing, especially with a wounded knee. I wasn't sure I could make the ascent with him. To the right, I saw a downward course leading farther into the ravine. Perhaps I could find some shelter from the rain, an overhang that was secure, someplace I could safely put Sam and then go for help. I had moved to climb downward when pebbles tumbled from above, striking the brim of my hat, my shoulders. I looked up.

Mountain stood on a perch above me, wagging his tail. I shook my head, disbelieving my senses.

"Mountain! How did you get here? Are you okay? Who's with you? Did Kerry bring you? Hello? Kerry? Hello! Anybody there?" The wolf yipped at me, and turned as if to lead me upward.

"I can't!" I cried. "We have to go down. We have to get down off this slide area."

Mountain locked eyes with me, something he had never done before. He lowered his nose and intensified his stare. Then he swung his head to one side, wagged his tail, and danced in place. He squeaked. *This way, come on!* he seemed to be saying.

"No, come here, buddy. You come with me! We've got to go down." I started to move downward.

The wolf yipped again.

"Oh, Mountain, I've been so worried about you. There's nothing I want more in this world than to be with you." I burst into tears. "But you have to listen to me. We've got to go down!"

My best friend dropped to his belly, lying on the slope. He lowered his muzzle onto his paws and continued to make eye contact.

"You've got to come with me. We've got to go down. Now come on."

I braced myself with my bad leg and tendered the other out for another foothold. A huge crack of thunder broke above us. A new burst of sleet and intensified rain pelted me, stinging my arms. Small hailstones drummed on my hat and the back of my poncho. Soon, I couldn't see more than a foot or two in any direction. Mountain was out of my range of sight. I clung in position, unable to do more. In a few minutes, the hail and sleet began to subside.

I looked up. The wolf was gone. A fist-sized chunk of basalt bounced past me and narrowly missed striking my head.

"Mountain! Mountain?" I had to find Mountain. I began to work slowly upward and to the left. I dug my hands into rock and silt, slammed the toes of my boots into red mud or tucked the tips of them onto shards of stone. I stopped every few feet to catch my breath, to readjust Sam's weight, to look above me for Mountain. I spied a rounded slice of rock that spanned the canyon wall horizontally. Through the rain, I thought I saw the flash of a tail wagging. I climbed to the shelf and pulled myself up, gasping for breath. A small ruin, a corn silo, rested beneath a deep rock overhang. I crawled inside and pulled off my hat, the poncho. I untied the sinew and released the boy's legs, then lifted his arms over my head. I pushed him farther back against the cliff wall to get him out of the weather. It was cold, the rain freezing on contact with the rock. There was just enough room for me to sit up in the cave. I huddled next to the child and draped the poncho over us to keep us both warm. Sam moaned once, softly.

Wild Indigo

A curtain of water poured over the overhang, nearly obscuring the view of anything beyond. It was as if all the moisture that had been denied the high desert for decades now gushed from the heavens.

"Mountain!" I called into the thundering downpour. "Mountain!"

◄ **39** ►

Getting Out

Rain and hail fell for nearly an hour. I continued to peer out through the sheeting water for signs of my beloved wolf. I saw glimpses of cascading chutes of whitewater on the opposite side of the gorge. I trembled with cold, my teeth chattering. Sam whimpered and stirred, but never woke.

When the downpour turned to drizzle, I slipped out from under the poncho and onto the slice of stone I'd crossed to the cave. I edged out as far as I dared and looked up toward the canyon rim, only about a hundred feet above me. At once, I heard a rifle shot. Diane shouted, "Over here! She's down here!"

Kerry held me up while members of the Mountain Search and Rescue Team loaded Sam Dreams Eagle onto the sled and into the helicopter.

"There are paramedics down below," Roy said, "but it's too muddy for 'em to get up the trail in a vehicle, even an ATV. We'll get the chopper to fly back for you as soon as they can."

"I'm all right," I said. "I just need to sit down, get my weight off this leg."

"You're beat all to hell," the Boss said, "and you'll get in that chopper just as soon as it gets back, and that's an order. We're lucky the storm finally broke so we could get that bird in here to get the boy. They're flying him to critical care in Albuquerque. Then they'll be back for you." He moved aside and spoke into his satellite radio.

Kerry gave me a squeeze and helped me to the tailgate of Roy's truck. "Whatever that guy put in my water," he said, "it sure messed me up."

"Me, too," I said. "It was peyote. He admitted it."

"Peyote? I don't know how you made it all the way up here, babe. And to navigate that canyon like you did, and get the boy to that cave . . ."

"I think I had some protection. Remember the tea Tecolote gave me?"

"Oh, yeah. I could have used some of that. I ended up backtracking for a while, heading down the mountain instead of up. I had the strangest visions. Then I remembered the prayer ties you gave me. I opened one of the little bundles and ate it. My head cleared right up."

"You ate the herbs in the prayer bundle?"

"Yeah, wasn't that what they were for?"

I smiled. "Maybe so. It never occurred to me to do that. How did Roy get up here? He said the trail was too muddy for the paramedics to come."

"I guess he had a hunch when you called him from the stable. He started up the back trail in his truck right about the time we came up from the pueblo on horseback. He got here before the main deluge started, and was going to hike over to the falls. He ran into Diane right after you'd gone down into the ravine, and he called for the search and rescue team. They came up on horseback because by then there was no other way in. I only got here an hour or so before them. Diane sent me after your buried cache."

"I thought this blanket smelled musty," I said, sniffing my woolen wrap.

"That was good thinking of you to tell her about that stuff. We've used almost everything you had buried in that old oil drum. Oh—and I found something of yours on the way here."

"What?"

He reached into the bed of the truck and produced the sunflower Tecolote had given me.

"Where'd you find it?"

"Just after we forded the wash, on the ground under a big tree."

I took the stem. The flower was smashed and muddied. "It looks like I feel."

A crowd of men stood near the horses, some of them packing rappelling gear. Two of them broke ranks and came toward Roy's truck. I saw that they were Tanoah men, wearing the apronlike black wraps, their hair tied at the back of their necks. One of them spoke to me. "Thank you for saving our nephew, Sam Dreams Eagle."

"You're his uncles?"

They smiled. "We are all his uncles, men our age. He is a child of our tribe. We are all family."

I sighed. "I hope he's going to be okay."

They nodded. "Thank you," they said in unison, and they walked away.

"How'd those guys get here?" I asked.

"My escorts." Kerry smiled. "I made the mistake of trying to go past the gate to Indigo Falls. I didn't get very far. After I explained what we were doing, and figured out where you'd gone, they rode up here with me to help look for the boy."

Diane strolled up to the pickup, grinning. "Hey, I guess the tribe has backed out of their claims about you starting the stampede. I don't know what's going to happen next, but I doubt you or I will be applying for unemployment. Sounds like there was a lot of kiss-and-make-up between agencies and nations when they found out you got the boy out alive. But if you ever get tired of resource protection, you could go into shoe making." She held up a vinyl-wrapped foot.

I smiled. "I'm tired of everything right now. I just want to go home." I suddenly remembered the spirit guide who'd led me to my stone sanctuary in the worst of the storm. "I want to see Mountain."

◄ 40 ►

The Journey

Wiley Mason answered the door himself this time. "Can my wolf come in," I asked, "or should we talk outside?" Mountain wagged his tail at the tall man.

Mason bent over to examine my companion. "So this is the famous wolf who practically rose from the dead, is it? They say they found the eye of an owl in the cup you left beside him. Is that true?"

"You heard about all that? Already?"

"Yes, well, I am the keeper of legends, my dear. The people bring me all their stories. Anyway, to answer your question: it seems I have no choice—unless, of course, I want to be rude to a local four-legged celebrity. And you're clearly unwilling to leave him, even for a moment. Besides, he's delightful. Bring him in."

Once inside, I eased my bum leg down slowly, and Mountain and I settled onto the tile floor of Mason's great room. The wolf laid his head in my lap. "We've been through a lot," I explained. "We just want to be close to each other."

"So I've heard," Mason said. "Tongues tired of well-worn lore have been wagging with this exciting new epic since dawn. I don't know how they managed before the invention of the telephone. When there's news, they can't wait to tell it. Especially about a white girl who lives with a wolf and performs heroic rescues. They are calling you La Loba. Did you know that?"

I rubbed Mountain's mane. "No, I hadn't heard. It's good, though. I like it."

A woman came with a tray of tea and left it. Mason poured us each a cup but remained standing, stopping to take a sip to test the flavor. He smacked his lips approvingly. "Now. Let's see. What can I do for you, Ms. Wild?"

"I wanted to tell you that the prize you were looking for is lost."

"The prize?"

"The CD-ROM."

He sobered, set his teacup down. "Ah. You know this for a fact?"

"I do. It went over the edge of the cliff around the neck of Yellow Hawk."

"Was it destroyed?"

"It was. Smashed into bits. As was the peyote chief."

The professor grimaced. His spine seemed to lose its strength and he collapsed into a nearby chair. He lowered his head and rubbed at his forehead—back and forth, over and over, as if wiping at a stain that refused to come out. I saw his Adam's apple quiver as he swallowed. Finally he found a little composure. "I'm sorry to hear that," he said, his voice shaking.

"And Hunter Contreras is gone, too. He was crushed by a landslide when the canyon rim began to disintegrate in the storm. He was after the CD to make some kind of offering to the war god. A scalp ceremony?"

He swallowed again. "Aha," he said softly. "Aha. To appease the gods for crimes of the People, no doubt. And count coup for defeating the enemy."

"The enemy?"

"Yes, the enemy." He took a wadded handkerchief from his pants pocket, removed his glasses from their case in his shirt, and began rubbing the lenses with the cloth, as if there were something important he wanted to examine and he needed his vision to be clean and clear. He didn't look up as he spoke. "Perhaps the enemy in this case was me, whether they knew it or not." After a few moments, Wiley Mason returned his handkerchief to his pocket, put his glasses low on his nose, and stood up and walked to the window of his great room.

"I think at least one of them thought it was me," I said.

He pursed his lips and nodded his head in agreement, then gazed out through the glass and didn't speak for a time. Finally, he said, "I wasn't going to publish it, at least not in this lifetime. I only wanted to preserve the Tiwa language. Santana was willing to help me do that, if I promised to keep it safe until such time as it was absolutely necessary, so that the language would not become extinct."

"And you were going to pay him for this?"

He turned to face me and nodded. "Yes, there was to be an exchange of some money. There was evidently a need for money in his family—a son by a previous marriage in trouble, and his wife . . . it sounded like there were problems there."

"And Gilbert Valdez? Was he the one who brokered the deal?"

Mason shook his head, frowning. "No, you have that wrong. I contacted him after I found out about Santana's death. I asked him to look for the CD-ROM among the dead man's things, because I knew Valdez was seeing the widow. I don't think he knew what he was looking for, what was on the disc. I told him it was some computer programs we were working on."

"It's interesting," I said, rising to my feet. "Madonna told me about a man her husband was working with. I didn't put it together until I saw the disc in Yellow Hawk's hand. It was the CD-ROM that Santana was making for you that he was working on, not a man he was working with. Santana must have been making a joke, inventing a character named Seedy Ron." I set my teacup on a side table. Mountain got up and stood beside me. He nuzzled my hand.

"Dear, dear. It's unfortunate," Mason said, taking his handkerchief out again and dabbing at his neck. "The whole thing's very unfortunate."

"Yes, it is. It's a sad story for Tanoah Pueblo." I waited, a long, awkward silence growing between me and the professor. Finally I said, "Well, I've got to be going . . . the pilgrimage is today. I promised to see some folks off on their journey."

"I'll show you to the door," Mason said. He gestured toward the front of the house. "And the little boy? Is he going to be all right?"

"Yes. He's going to be in the hospital for observation for a while. He was hypothermic, dehydrated, but he's coming along just fine."

"It's lamentable, I think," the scholar mused. "It seems like whenever we move to try to preserve these amazing cultures on the very edge of extinction, somehow we manage to do almost as much harm as good—if not more so."

I offered a gentle smile. "That's what my boss said about the ruins up above the falls. He said it was better just to leave them alone."

"Maybe it's already too late to save the past," Wiley Mason said. And he closed the door.

At the highest arc of the sun that day, the People set off on horseback for Indigo Falls. Mountain stood beside me as I bade my medicine teacher good-bye.

"It good you bring that wolf with you. You belong to him."

I smiled and stroked Mountain's head.

"You make good jerky," Momma Anna said, patting the square pouch tied to her saddle. "I have plenty meat."

"You taught me."

"You good learn. I only do. You learn you, not me."

"Momma Anna, would you permit me to ask a question. Just one?"

"You know we don't like question over here. We already got FBI everywhere over this."

"I know, but I have to ask. Do you know who left that nachi in my car?"

"That one, look like a scalp. Someone put prayers in that stick to have your scalp. That a bad spell. You put in water, like I told you?"

"Yes. I did just what you said."

"That make prayers happy. You keep yellow hair." She flattened her lips into a small smile.

I smiled back. "I was wondering if you would do something for me." I pulled the last rope of prayer ties from around my neck and handed them up to my mentor.

She turned her head to the side slightly, scrutinizing me. Her hair was tied in a tight pattern of intricate knots and red cloth at the nape of her neck—she had gotten up well before dawn this morning to have a woman in the village do the ceremonial hair tie for this special occasion.

"Could you put these in the water for me? For your brother?"

Wild Indigo

Momma Anna's lip trembled with grief. She took the strand of bundles from me and put them over her own head. "I am proud do this. I have many turkey feather, too. We need many prayers to heal. Many prayers. We cannot stay with him while he get ready for journey because they say mountain crumble when he . . . Now that way, way through sacred water, Eye of Great Spirit, under House of Dead, that way to where old ones live—it lost, no way through no more."

I thought about that. The connection—between the past and the present through Indian land, through the Indigo Falls—destroyed. I shook my head. My eyes filled with tears. Then I offered: "You can still get there, to what's left, anyway. There's a road, if you can call it that, on the other side."

"That road built by white man—that the new way. But we have no way back to time before. We must carry it with us. Here." She put a hand to her heart. "We have only today now," Momma Anna said, and she pressed her heels into the horse's flanks.

I watched her ride down the dirt lane and join the other members of the family, who waited on their mounts. Yohe wagged a hand at me. "Good-bye, White Girl," she said. Lupé waved and turned alongside Frank, who had Angel seated in front of him. Serena adjusted the white blanket shawl over her head, a sign of mourning. Anna's brothers Eddie and Pete solemnly fell in, each with a small child on board. The family of riders moved into the line of Indians on horses headed through the old walls of the pueblo and up the side of Sacred Mountain. I heard them singing as they rode away.

Across the fields and on the slopes of the foothills the grasses glistened, refreshed by the thirst-quenching rains of the previous day. The leaves of cottonwoods along the brook shimmered in the light. Even the run-down adobe houses along the dirt lane to Momma Anna's house looked washed clean. Father Sun sent golden warmth through a brilliant blue sky. Not a cloud in sight. A magpie scolded us, and came to light on the fence post at the end of Momma Anna's drive.

For an instant, I felt abandoned by my Tanoah family—left to stand here like an outcast, unable to partake in their journey, their celebration, even their grief for the ones I'd seen die.

But then, I looked down at my best friend—*my family*. His long mane shone in the sun, his tufted ears alert, his eyes watching, drinking in all of it—the riders, the magpie, the sky, the rippling leaves of the trees. He sniffed the air. His shoulder muscles trembled beneath his thick, handsome coat. It was a joy to behold his feral beauty, but I saw also that he could never again be truly wild. Or free. Time and circumstances had taken that from him—and given him to me for safekeeping. I smiled, and he looked up and gazed directly into my eyes. He wagged his tail at me. I dropped to one knee and hugged his neck. "We have today, buddy," I said. "We have today."

About the Author

Sandi Ault has employed her skills as a writer and story-teller while earning her living as a musician, bandleader, composer, journalist, editor, teacher, and novelist. She has toured and recorded with her own band, composed musical works for dance companies and other performances, and written a soundtrack for a short film.

For the past several years, she has taught writing workshops and classes while working on her own novels. While exploring the Southwest in her research for *Wild Indigo*, Ms. Ault taught writing classes at the University of New Mexico in Taos. In her home state of Colorado, Ms. Ault has taught workshops independently and through Front Range University in Estes Park.

Ms. Ault currently lives in a high mountain valley of the Rockies where—in addition to writing novels—she is a volunteer firefighter as well as a Fire Information Officer responding locally and nationally to wildfires.

She lives among the pines with her husband, Tracy, her wolf, Tiwa, and her horrible kitty, Wasichu.